PRAISE FOR M.

Tom Clancy fans open to a strong female lead will clamor for more.

— *Drone*, Publishers Weekly

Superb! Miranda is utterly compelling!

— *Booklist*, starred review

Miranda Chase continues to astound and charm.

— Barb M.

Escape Rating: A. Five Stars! OMG just start with *Drone* and be prepared for a fantastic binge-read!

— Reading Reality

The best military thriller I've read in a very long time. Love the female characters.

— *Drone*, Sheldon McArthur, founder of The Mystery Bookstore, LA

A fabulous soaring thriller.

— *Take Over at Midnight*, Midwest Book Review

Meticulously researched, hard-hitting, and suspenseful.

— *Pure Heat,* Publishers Weekly, starred review

Expert technical details abound, as do realistic military missions with superb imagery that will have readers feeling as if they are right there in the midst and on the edges of their seats.

— *Light Up the Night,* RT Reviews, 4 1/2 stars

Buchman has catapulted his way to the top tier of my favorite authors.

— Fresh Fiction

Nonstop action that will keep readers on the edge of their seats.

— *Take Over at Midnight,* Library Journal

M L. Buchman's ability to keep the reader right in the middle of the action is amazing.

— Long and Short Reviews

The only thing you'll ask yourself is, "When does the next one come out?"

— *Wait Until Midnight,* RT Reviews, 4 stars

The first...of (a) stellar, long-running (military) romantic suspense series.

I knew the books would be good, but I didn't realize how good.

Buchman mixes adrenalin-spiking battles and brusque military jargon with a sensitive approach.

13 times "Top Pick of the Month"

WHITE TOP

A MIRANDA CHASE POLITICAL
TECHNOTHRILLER

M. L. BUCHMAN

SIGN UP FOR M. L. BUCHMAN'S NEWSLETTER TODAY

and receive:
Release News
Free Short Stories
a Free Book

Get your free book today. Do it now.
free-book.mlbuchman.com

Other works by M. L. Buchman: *(* - also in audio)*

Other works by M. L. Buchman:

Short Story Series by M. L. Buchman:

ABOUT THIS BOOK

When a political conspiracy targets the White House's aircraft —only the nation's #1 air-crash investigators can save the country.

The White Top helicopters of HMX-1 are known by a much more familiar name: Marine One. The S-92A, the newest helicopter in the HMX fleet, enters service after years of testing.

When their perfect safety record lies shattered across a shopping mall, **Miranda Chase** and her team of NTSB air-crash investigators go in. They must discover if it was an accident, a declaration of war, or something even worse.

PROLOGUE

Naval Air Station Anacostia
Elevation: unlisted for security reasons
Washington, DC
Six days ago

MAJOR TAMATHA JONES FORCED HERSELF TO BREATHE CALMLY. Marine Corps helicopter pilots were not supposed to be nervous under any conditions, but today was proving to be the exception to the rule. Within the next thirty minutes, she'd be flying the President aboard his Marine One helicopter for her first time.

She worked her way through the preflight walkaround—a wholly redundant activity here at HMX-1. Their mechanics were the best in the world and the squadron's birds reflected it; they had to. And none more so than her helo. When the President of the United States stepped aboard and it became Marine One, everything had to be perfect.

But she still always did a full preflight inspection after the crew chiefs were done.

Then she took one more circle around her brand-new VH-92A Superhawk just...because. Sixty-eight feet and six inches of executive transport muscle. Marine green below, white top above, and, block-lettered in white down the sides, "United States of America." The only bright colors on the entire bird were also the ones that mattered most—the blue-and-yellow Presidential seals affixed below both pilots' side windows.

For her passengers' sake, the Superhawk offered luxury seating, including a pair of armchairs for the President and a guest, couches alongside, and more seating to the rear. Less obvious were the armor, attack evasion gear (both passive and active), a fully isolatable air system, and a communications suite that could run a war—at least a small one. This wasn't Air Force One after all.

During the last four years of testing and certification of the VH-92A, Tamatha had made the landing on the White House's South Lawn over a hundred times in the simulator. She'd also made it in the real world seven times—always when the President was *not* in residence so that he wouldn't be disturbed.

But today was the first transport of President Roy Cole aboard the Marine's newest bird. And unexpectedly, the first Presidential "lift" in a Superhawk had fallen to her—carrying him from the White House for the ten-mile flight to Air Force One waiting at Andrews Air Force Base.

Normally, HMX-1 commander Colonel McGrady was the President's pilot. But he was already prepositioned at Tel Nof Airbase in Israel, the first stop of the President's whirlwind global tour. The colonel would fly more than twenty-seven hours with the President aboard—and many more without him —during the next six days.

She'd be aloft for approximately six and a half minutes.

It didn't matter.

McGrady had tapped her for the Number Two slot, and she would be the first to fly the Commander-in-Chief aboard a Superhawk. Life just didn't get any damn better than being a Marine Corps pilot.

She trailed a hand over the shining paint job, after wiping her fingertips on the leg of her dress slacks to make sure she wouldn't leave any smudges. The dark green paint was mirror-bright enough for her to check the set of her short-sleeved Service C—or more commonly Service Charlie—tan uniform shirt. Even the hubs of the wheels shone. Not a spec of grease would dare blemish a Marine One helo, not when it was prepared by the Marines of HMX-1.

At the nose of the bird, Tamatha turned to face her helo directly and saluted sharply.

"Seriously, Major?" Her copilot strolled over from the ready room. Vance "Tex" Brown was from Texas rather than the great state of Colorado, so there was no accounting for him. They'd flown together back in the VMM-265 out of Okinawa, and he knew full well that she always saluted any aircraft she was about to fly. It was a connection to her grandfather, who had told her stories of doing the same.

Always thanked my birds for getting me home safe—before the flight. Musta worked. Then he'd laugh that glorious laugh of his. He'd flown three tours in Vietnam and come home to Boulder alive. As a little girl, she'd eaten up every story he'd tell. He was so proud, she was actually afraid he was going to die the day she told him she made HMX-1.

"Here be Dragons!" Vance practically shouted the VMM-265's motto.

"No longer a Dragon, Captain. You're a Nighthawk. Though I still don't know how you fit your Texan ego in the cockpit."

"I turn it down so it doesn't shame your mere Coloradoan past. Besides, once a Dragon, always a Dragon," Vance insisted. The emblem of the VMM-265 was *very* cool and she'd worn it with immense pride—a green dragon wound through the heart of the Japanese kanji *for* dragon. The dragons flew primarily out of Okinawa.

But now she wore the crossed rotor blades of HMX-1 and there was no prouder patch in the Corps except for the Presidential Pilot patch they'd both be cleared to wear after this flight.

She ignored Vance and circled to the right forward stair. Unlike the prior HMX-1 helos, the entry door was on the pilot's side. Whenever one of those landed on the White House lawn, the newsies were always photographing the copilot. Her big Superhawk would land facing the other way and she would be the one in the photographs.

Because of that, she double-checked that the Presidential Seal below her window was perfectly clean. Crew Chief Mathieson caught her at it and just grinned. Not a chance he would have missed that. There was an entire special protocol for cleaning and maintenance of the right front quadrant of the Superhawk. It, along with Sergeant Mathieson, would be the two most photographed Marine Corps assets for several years to come. Times ten today, as this was the first Superhawk flight.

It was only fitting that he was the one photographed while he waited to salute the President at the base of the stairs. It was really his bird; she simply was allowed to fly it.

They'd pre-staged at Joint Base Anacostia-Bolling at the juncture of the Anacostia and Potomac Rivers close by downtown DC early this morning. A sea fog was rolling in to their main base at Quantico near the mouth of the Potomac, and she hadn't wanted to risk being grounded.

At Anacostia, the Marines kept the HMX-1 hangar and the sixty-thousand square feet that made up the squadron's seven helipads as a forward operating base, so that a Marine helo would always be within three minutes of the White House. The rest of the old Flying Field had long since been consumed by office buildings, primarily the headquarters of the Defense Intelligence Agency.

Give her a helo cockpit over a desk any day of the week.

Once in and seated, she took that crucial moment to switch her brain over. The thousand worries from overseeing her section of the squadron—training new pilots and making sure every action or decision was properly updated in both the training and the logged procedures—all of it went away.

For the next hour or so, she was just a pilot and *nothing* else mattered.

She and Vance buckled in and started down the checklists. They could do it by rote, but they followed every step in the standard call-and-response that had kept pilots alive since the beginning of flight.

To her left and right, two identical birds were doing the same. HMX-1 always flew in flights of two or three—one designated primary and the others as decoy birds. In flight, the three of them would shuffle about the sky so that no one could guess which carried the President.

"Package ready?" she keyed the mic.

First, the two decoys acknowledged, then the two Night Stalkers' gunships that were already aloft in a high guard position. The black helos of the 160th SOAR typically flew overwatch of the official "lift package" as the Marine Corps flight was known.

Last of all, the White House Military Office confirmed. The WHMO was responsible for the scheduling of White House flights, and their call meant the mission was still a Go.

Tiny wisps of fog that had wandered this far up the Potomac were blasted aside as the three big VH-92As took to the sky for their first-ever Presidential lift.

Her world condensed even further. The key to flying at this level was to be completely present. And she was.

Two hundred feet above Anacostia, she sliced over the golf

course that divided the Anacostia and Potomac Rivers and turned upriver.

The route was the most highly guarded air route in the world. The P-56 Prohibited Areas surrounding the White House, the National Mall, and the Vice President's house were all tucked tight beside the incredibly restricted approach to Reagan National Airport. Except during an emergency evacuation, no one was allowed to fly the P-56 except the Marine Corps helicopters of HMX-1.

Just one more reason Tamatha was proud to be a Marine.

Hard right past the Jefferson Memorial.

Maintain altitude across the National Mall, well below the top of the Washington Monument.

That perfect instant when everything lined up. The Washington Monument and the Capitol building to the right; the World War II Memorial, the Reflecting Pool, and Lincoln to the left.

She always allowed herself a three-second glance to either side—to check that the airspace remained clear, of course. Unable to take her hands from the controls to salute the marble President, she always gave Lincoln a respectful nod.

No one except an HMX-1 pilot, not even the President, was privileged to have such a view of the nation's capital as she had through the wraparound windshield of her high-visibility cockpit. For now, she stayed focused. She could cheer later when she watched herself tonight; she'd been careful to set Record on CNN for the next two hours, plus the nightly news.

She and Vance did, however, trade grins.

Sergeant Mathieson had left his seat directly behind her own to stand between the seats and watch the city with them. It wasn't regulation, but no one deserved it more.

One of the decoy helos slid in front of her and headed for the South Lawn. At the fifty-foot treetop level, he peeled up and to the right, coming to a hover over the Treasury Building to the east. The other decoy was close on her tail until she began the final descent. He too peeled off to take up station above the Eisenhower Executive Office Building to the west. The two decoys and the two overwatch birds hung back far enough that rotor noise wouldn't disturb the President's departure.

First, she flattened the spray from the South Lawn fountain with her rotor downwash. Ducking down between the trees, the approach always looked impossibly small. But practice had taught her that the helo fit, as long as the pilot was perfect. A deep breath prepared her for the final move.

At twenty-five feet, she hovered directly facing the White House. A hundred cameras were focused on her, but the press corps was irrelevant and she ignored them.

She eyed the three six-foot aluminum disks, doing her best to fix their positions in her mind. As the White House ground crew had pre-placed them in the proper layout for her bird, all she had to do was hit the marks.

No ground crew, because HMX-1 Marine pilots didn't need them.

Instead, her guides were two six-inch-wide, twenty-foot-long strips of canvas tacked to the lawn.

The first step was to move directly over the disks. She wouldn't see them again until she was down.

"L marks the spot," Tamatha muttered to herself as she slowly twisted the helo to face to the left so that the entry door would be facing the West Wing and the President's route of arrival.

If she turned to look over her shoulder, she'd be able to see part of the disk that had to end up beneath her right wheel, but practice had taught her that was a distraction.

Head up, face front when flying. Colonel McGrady had made it clear what he expected of his Marine Corps pilots, and she'd given everything she had to getting it right by the McGrady Bible.

7

Must have worked; she was here.

She lined up the two canvas strips, one dead ahead of her nose and the other at ninety degrees to the tip of the nose, and eased down on the collective control with her left hand.

The wheels kissed down.

A nice tap onto a hard surface: no soft, missed-the-disk-and-hit-the-grass feel.

There was also no secondary jolt; she'd nailed the magic of putting down all three wheels exactly level. With a wheelbase that measured ten-six wide and twenty feet long, that was as much luck as skill, but she was glad Lady Luck was on her side this morning.

Set the parking brake. Engines to idle. Brake the rotors to a stop.

She was *here*.

Parked on the White House South Lawn. She glanced right as Sergeant Mathieson lowered the door, descended, and moved to guard the stair. Unlike the old Presidential helos, the Superhawk possessed only the one entrance—no back stair for everyone other than the President and his family.

Tamatha checked the clock, precisely five minutes early.

Exactly when she wanted to be.

Though she could do without the news-pool photographers who, for the next five minutes, would have nothing to photograph except her aircraft, her crew chief, and herself.

———

"You're both with me. Let's move."

"Are you sure it's not too late to resign, Mr. President?" General Drake Nason pushed back from the Situation Room table and rose to his feet.

An orderly somewhere blanked the display screen of the

recent clashes map of the Middle East they'd been studying along with the National Security Advisor.

President Roy Cole laughed, which had been the point. "If you resign, you have to give me notice so that I can quit first."

"I knew there was a catch."

"Between you and Sarah, I've got to find myself better help."

"Hey, I'm Jewish," NSA Sarah Feldman protested, "whining is part of the heritage. Just listen to my mother and her three sisters for five minutes and you'll know. I have no idea what *his* problem is, Mr. President."

The three of them had practically been in each other's pockets all week in preparation for this trip; few vestiges of formality beyond the President's title had survived such an effort.

Drake was actually looking forward to the trip. As a four-star general and the Chairman of the Joint Chiefs of Staff, he rarely left the circuit of the Pentagon and the White House anymore. Spending a week aloft aboard Air Force One was a welcome break—and even the *chance* to ease global political problems was exhilarating.

The Middle East was always a nightmare. Hopefully this trip would dial it back some...maybe...not likely. At each stop, while the President was meeting with a country's leaders, he and Sarah would be meeting with their counterparts in a three-pronged attack—executive, security, and military—which they'd agreed not to call an attack but definitely was.

The second part of the trip around the globe to Southeast Asia had much more potential for success. After two days of meetings in Singapore, then Hanoi, and brief stops in Australia and New Zealand, they'd fly to western Canada for the nightmare of the G-7 meeting.

It *was* going to be a brutally long week.

"How did this become my life?" He teased the President as he picked up the beautiful Berluti leather satchel that Lizzy had bought him for their one-year anniversary—which had probably cost as much as the pearl necklace he'd bought for her.

The President headed out the Situation Room door. "You both made the same damn mistake: you said 'Yes' when I asked you to serve."

"Damn it! I knew it was something," Sarah gathered the final files off the Situation Room table and slipped them into her own briefcase. She fussed with her pantsuit jacket.

"You look fine, Sarah…" Drake let the sentence drag like a tease.

"But what?" she glanced up at him as they followed the President up the stairs, then headed toward the Oval Office for the President to get his coat.

"But don't worry, all they're going to care about is him and his new helicopter."

Roy glanced back. "The new Marine One? About time. I was afraid they wouldn't be ready for the *next* President."

"The Marine Corps seems to think that being careful means four years of testing."

"Well," Sarah commented, "I for one am in favor of that. Helicopters make me crazy."

Through the Oval Office's bulletproof glass—so thick that everything outside looked like a watercolor that had been caught in the rain—Drake saw the VH-92A Superhawk shining in the South Lawn sun. He loved helos. As a 75th Army Ranger, he'd ridden in many of them. Even ones flown by Marines, God help him. He missed sitting on the cargo deck, kitted up with a band of door-kicking Ranger brothers, and watching the world zip by below his dangling feet. He was sure that the times weren't as romantic as he remembered them—definitely not the awful years of the Bosnian War—but the nostalgia still wrapped around him at times.

The VH-92A had been a long time coming.

It couldn't have any real relation to this trip, but it gave him hope anyway. Hope that maybe they could turn a few things around in the Middle East.

———

Major Tamatha Jones watched the President emerge from the Oval Office.

President Cole was a creature of habit, which wasn't always a good thing for security, but the Marine in her appreciated it.

His feet hit the South Lawn of the White House at precisely two minutes before scheduled departure. He took four questions from the gathered newsies. By his gestures, this time they were all about the new helicopter. She concentrated on looking busy, only watching with her peripheral vision.

At thirty seconds to go, he waved goodbye. When she glanced directly at him after he turned his back on the newsies, she could see the deep exhaustion he'd been hiding from them. Seven years in office had definitely taken their toll. Yet he saluted Mathieson neatly. Then he stopped to shake hands with him before boarding. A leader who treated his underlings as people was far too rare outside HMX-1 in her experience. Marine pilots were nonpartisan, but she knew in that moment that whether she flew one President or several, Roy Cole would always be the one she'd think of.

And that the President was ready to lift precisely on schedule was a surprise, though McGrady had forewarned her.

She bit her tongue when a fist thumped on her shoulder.

"Damn sharp helo you've got here," Roy Cole's voice was even deeper in person than on television.

"Brand-new just for you, Mr. President."

"I see that you finally shoved McGrady aside. Good to have a fellow Boulderite at the helm. Well done, Major Jones."

"Thank you, sir." She'd never actually met the President

before and was shocked that he knew her name *and* knew they shared a hometown. "He fought against it but it had to be done. I hope you won't miss him too much, sir."

To the President's left, Vance grinned. Her joke would definitely be getting back to the commander.

The President chuckled, "Not so's I'd notice. Going to get me to the airport in one piece?"

"That's the plan, sir. Unless you had something else in mind."

He squinted at her. "What? Like in two pieces, delivered separately for later reassembly?"

Vance rolled his eyes in mock panic.

She should have kept her damn mouth shut.

"I was thinking more along the lines of a sunny day on the Chincoteague shore. We can be there in under forty minutes, Mr. President."

"That suggestion, Major, just might get you made a colonel. You're on...next time."

"Yes sir."

"Go Marine," he held out a hand and she shook it. That he also shook Vance's was decent and would probably be the highlight of his mere Texan existence.

"*Semper Fi,* Mr. President. Now, if you'll sit down and buckle up, I'll see what I can do about the in-one-piece part of that deal."

He chuckled again as he turned for his seat, sounding lighter than he'd looked when he'd boarded her aircraft.

The rest of the flight went precisely to plan.

White House to Andrews, she departed twenty-eight seconds late but was careful to make up the time so that she landed exactly on schedule.

After the President had exited her helo and Air Force One was aloft, she lifted and turned for Quantico. The fog had burned off enough that she was able to land without needing her instruments. Once down, she and Vance headed for the mission debrief.

Sergeant Mathieson was already changing out of his dress blues. Even after so short a flight, the VH-92A would now undergo a full inspection that would take several hours.

"You're wackier than a horned toad at a frog-jumping competition, Jones."

"Gee, and I don't have being from Texas as an excuse."

"Offering to cut the President into pieces? Go Marine indeed."

They were both laughing as they entered the debrief room. Every step from the shift to Anacostia and the thirty-minute test flight that happened before every Presidential lift—called "burning off some fuel"—to the final touchdown would be reviewed in detail.

This was HMX-1 after all.

The squadron had a perfect record of never *once* since its 1947 founding, having an incident while delivering the President and other VIPs. That's all she ultimately cared about —their record was still intact on her watch.

1

Six days later
Boeing Field, Seattle
Elevation 17'

"CARAVAN 34Z, CLEARED FOR STRAIGHT-OUT DEPARTURE. RUNWAY
32 Right. Climb and maintain fifteen hundred."

Larry Block didn't answer the Boeing Field Tower. With five
hundred flights a day off their two runways, they didn't want a
radio call, they wanted you gone.

He eased the throttle lever forward, released the brakes,
and rolled down the morning-shadowed runway. Right on
schedule, they'd be climbing into the sunrise in moments.

"You're in for a sweet ride," he told the passenger in the
copilot's seat. The Cessna 208 Caravan was rated for nine
passengers but had ten seats because everyone except the FAA
had certified it for all ten. He never flew with a copilot, and
therefore one lucky passenger got the sweet seat rather than
being stuck in the middle of the cramped triple at the rear. He'd
considered ripping it out, but it was a bonus space for the rear
passengers. To keep it fair, he always let the passenger with the

closest birthday sit up front. It had already gotten him several extra tourists who came back on their birthday to get the seat.

"Awesome!" Stephen's thirtieth was only three days away. He was practically vibrating with excitement.

It was the first flight of the day, "The Sunrise Tulip Tour." Bless Marie. His wife was great at marketing.

No plane liked to fly the way a Caravan did. Sixteen hundred feet down the runway at seventy knots, Larry eased back on the wheel and the plane floated aloft. To the left was all Boeing: big hangars and a line of parked jets undergoing customization or awaiting repairs. To the right lay the two flight schools, the terminal building with its tower, and his own little tour operation.

Larry Block waggled his wings to wave at Marie, who always watched from the office window—no better woman anywhere. She'd stuck with him through the service years while he'd been flying as a crew chief on C-130 Hercules cargo lifters in and out of war zones. Now he'd done his twenty years, gotten his pension, and they were in the good times.

He and his daughter had earned their commercial licenses together just in time for the spring tours. If business kept building like this, they'd be able to afford a second plane. Then, instead of having to take turns, the two Blocks of "Around the Block Air Tours" could fly simultaneously, even offering personal aerial photos from the other plane—for a fee of course. Another one of Marie's great ideas.

"Wow!" Stephen gasped out.

As they climbed above South Seattle's light industrial area, the city came into view just as the first sunlight peeked over the Cascade Mountains to light the tops of the downtown towers. Seattle was a shadowed spread, climbing the steep hills, wrapped in a crescent around the most beautiful bay in the world.

It was one of those crystal blue spring days, the white-capped Olympic Mountains to the west shone as bright as torches, and the even more impressive Cascades still silhouetted to the east.

He could hear the camera shutters snapping from the passengers behind him.

So could Stephen in the right seat. He jolted in surprise, grabbed his bag from where he'd stuffed it at his feet, and dug out a big SLR camera with a forearm-long lens. Then he jammed the bag back down.

Larry glanced over to make sure Stephen had followed instructions to keep it well clear of the rudder pedals as he'd instructed. Stephen had. The knapsack was tucked against the sidewall and he'd planted a foot on it to keep it there. Good man.

They were at a thousand feet over the Seattle waterfront. Larry eased the nose down to level the plane for a moment so that Stephen could get the best shot of the Space Needle rising from Seattle Center at the north end of downtown. At the moment, only the top saucer shape was sunlit, so it really did look like a UFO hovering over downtown.

Stephen's camera made that zip-zip-zip rapid-fire photo sound. Oh God, he was one of those types. Larry made a bet with himself that the guy would shoot a thousand photos in the one-hour flight and never actually look at anything with his own eyes. He just hoped that Stephen didn't run out of memory before they reached the La Conner tulip fields—the main selling point of this flight.

Right now, hundreds of acres of tulips color-blocked the Skagit Valley in glorious swathes of color. They weren't quite peaked yet but they were close enough to wow the customers and ensure that he had four more full planeloads scheduled today. Each one, twenty minutes there, twenty minutes circling over the flowers and the San Juan Islands, twenty minutes back.

They were over Elliot Bay at the moment, and the curve of

the shoreline placed the Space Needle directly ahead—a perfect shot.

Larry eased back on the controls to continue his climb to fifteen hundred feet as Stephen's camera continued making its steady buzz of zip-zip-zip sounds.

Except the control wheel wouldn't move.

He could twist it a little side-to-side, but it definitely wouldn't pull back for a climb.

Had something broken?

He hadn't heard anything, not that he could have over the stuttering barrage of Stephen's cameras.

Airspeed was good. Engine RPM was fine. No imminent stall or engine failure.

He kicked the rudder a little to the right and left, he still had good control.

But the wheel wouldn't pull toward him.

"Something wrong?" Stephen stopped with the camera and looked over at him.

"Not a thing." Panicking a customer was never a good idea. But his voice must have given him away.

"What's wrong?" Stephen's voice was loud enough that Larry could hear it being picked up by the passengers behind them.

Larry shut out their escalating questions and focused on the problem.

The more he struggled to pull the wheel toward him, the more it moved in and angled the nose *down*.

Trim! He adjusted the trim to raise the nose.

No change.

From a high point of one thousand feet reached sixty-two seconds into the flight, the Cessna 208 Caravan began descending.

At seventy-three seconds, Larry Block gave up on trying to climb the plane as they descended toward seven hundred feet.

They were now exactly even with the top of the Space Needle, which towered six hundred and five feet above Seattle Center's hundred-and-fifteen-foot elevation. It seemed to be drawing them like a giant magnet and he couldn't get the plane to climb away.

If this was a C-130, he'd know exactly what had gone wrong. Every noise and shimmy of the four-engine Hercules was in his blood after twenty years.

He'd owned the Caravan for less than three months. It was a much simpler aircraft, yet he had no idea what had happened.

One mile—seventeen seconds—from the Space Needle, Larry knew this wasn't going to end well.

Crashing into the Space Needle wasn't an option.

He'd turn for the water and do his best there. The plane's fixed tricycle landing gear would catch the waves and probably destroy the aircraft, but it was better than ramming into a crowd of civilians.

Except now the plane wouldn't even turn.

The wheel was jammed and he couldn't move it.

At eighty-seven seconds into the flight and three hundred and seven feet above sea level, he was now aimed at the center of the Space Needle.

He kicked the right rudder and managed to steer the plane aside and miss the tower, carving a circular arc around the spindly tower legs that looked so impossibly substantial this close up. The flight, captured on video by an early morning jogger, would make national news, and win several photography competitions for its drama and beauty.

The arc continued.

At ninety-three seconds and an elevation of two hundred and thirty-two feet, he glanced over at the petrified Stephen braced in his seat. He wanted to apologize that he'd never get to see his birthday. That—

Then Larry Block spotted what had happened to the controls.

At ninety-four seconds, two hundred and thirteen feet above sea level, and traveling at one hundred and eighty-three knots—two hundred and eleven miles an hour— the Cessna 208 Caravan slammed into the stage tower of McCaw Hall, Seattle's opera house.

2

SIX THOUSAND, NINE HUNDRED AND SEVENTY-TWO POUNDS OF Cessna 208 Caravan impacted the west side of the hundred-and-ten-foot-high loft above McCaw Hall's stage.

The thin steel wall and its lightweight supports burst inward like a bullet tearing a hole through a playing card. The fifty-two-foot wingspan cleared the heavy structural beams at the corners of the tower. Had it failed to do so, the fuel-laden wings would have ripped open and a fireball would have consumed the plane, the tower, and destroyed eighty-five percent of the hall as well as the opera and ballet offices to either side.

Instead the high wing held strong, slicing a wide slot high on the wall. The single hundred-and-six-inch, three-bladed propellor mounted on the nose shredded a large hole directly in front of the fuselage.

The landing gear were sheared off by a lateral support beam. The three wheels would fall nine stories, impacting the roof over the three-thousand-seat house at fifty-four-point-six miles an hour. Their broken mechanical supports would each impact first, punching into the roof, leaving only the tires exposed to the sky.

Other than the missing landing gear, the plane entered the building largely intact.

The sole fatality until this moment was the pilot, Larry Block. One of the lightweight supports, rather than being shredded by the spinning McCauley propeller, was snipped off and heaved through the windscreen like a javelin that slammed into his heart. Little blood spilled as he died speared to his seat. Had he avoided the crash, he would have suffered a major heart attack over the tulip fields and died along with all of his passengers and two entire busloads of Japanese tourists who had flown to America specially to see the blooms.

But he died in the opera house instead.

The purpose of the fly loft tower was to allow for scenery, curtains, and lighting instruments to be lowered into view as needed yet stored out of sight above the stage when they weren't. To achieve this, a hundred feet above the stage and fifteen feet below the roof, a vast metal grid was hung. From this grid, one hundred and twelve pipes dangled horizontally above the stage, each spaced six inches apart.

Each of those pipes was supported from above by a series of ropes that ran from the pipe, up through the grid and over pulleys, then tracked sideways to the end wall. From there, the gathered ropes for each pipe turned once more to lay against the wall and descend into a vast system of counterweights: a centralized control area thirty feet above the stage.

The myriad array of ropes—some simply attached to an empty pipe but others from which hung hundreds, even thousands of pounds of lighting instruments and scenery— acted like an aircraft carrier's arresting wire to assist in a jet landing.

After the Cessna 208 Caravan punched through the wall, it had lost only twenty-seven knots of its speed at impact. The remaining one hundred and fifty-six knots were absorbed as the plane snagged more and more of the horizontal ropes.

Pipes jerked aloft as the plane was slowed by not just one-of-three arresting wires as on a carrier's deck, but by hundreds of heavy manila lines sharing the shock.

This is when the only other fatality occurred.

Stephen's side of the windshield had saved him from the debris, shattering in the process. At the moment of impact, the heavy camera and lens shot forward and tumbled onto the grid. The strap, which he'd placed around his neck out of habit, broke his neck before it slipped free.

As Stephen's body went lax due to his severed spinal column, his foot slid off the knapsack he'd been keeping pinned to the floor. The abrupt deceleration of the aircraft was accompanied by a sharp nose-down movement. The knapsack, floating independently in the chaos, flew free and followed the camera out the missing front windshield.

Though the Caravan was not destroyed, neither were the wings undamaged.

Highly volatile Jet A fuel spilled from a punctured tank and caught fire.

Because of the open nature of the steel grid on which the Caravan now rested, the fire spilled down over the set of tonight's opera.

To keep the audience safe—if there'd been one at this early hour—several events happened simultaneously.

Temperature sensors triggered the fire alarms.

The heat above the stage was sufficient to melt three thermocouples.

One released a massive deluge of water from the sprinkler system that showered the plane and the set.

A second opened the large louvers atop the fly loft roof and large fans engaged to suck the fire-heated air up and out.

The last thermocouple released the fire curtain. A metal-framed wall, covered on both sides in burn-resistant fiberglass, slid down across the proscenium. The sixty-foot-wide, thirty-five-foot-tall opening between the stage and the seating was now fully blocked.

The surviving eight passengers in the "Around the Block Air Tours" Cessna 208 Caravan—now parked atop the fly grid one hundred feet above the burning stage—began to scream.

3

MIRANDA CHASE ALWAYS ENJOYED A DAILY WALK TO MONITOR HER island. Spieden was one of the last of the San Juan Islands before the Haro Strait that divided Washington State from Canada. It had been her family's since before she was born and hers since her parents' deaths when she was thirteen.

Two-point-eight miles long and half-a-mile wide, it was her domain. Her kingdom. And her happy "subjects" were sufficiently exotic that walking among them always made her feel normal, or more normal than she knew she was. Spotted Asian sika deer, big-horned mouflon sheep, a hundred transplanted bird species—all left over from the island's brief period as a stocked game hunting park. It had been more like a shooting gallery, and she was glad that it was forty years gone. Good riddance.

For the last twenty-five years, she'd been the island's queen and sole occupant. Other than her National Transportation Safety Board's air-crash investigation team, visitors were rare as well.

Yesterday, the team's five other members had flown up to the island for a spring picnic. And though they'd stayed up late by the campfire, she'd woken with the sunrise and gone for her walk.

The island was divided in half the long way. To the west was a long strip of meadowlands. To the east, an equally narrow strip of cool conifer forest. In between, along the narrow crest, was her house, airplane hangar, and grass runway.

The perimeter trail ran six miles around it all and let her check in with her subjects. No throne room where they must come to vow allegiance. Instead they greeted her as she walked among them. Some special few had names, and often came to her looking for treats of an apple or a sugar cube, but most of them lived their own happy lives. Her favorites were the jesters —the myriad nameless Black-capped Chickadees who always perched on her fingertips whenever she dug a handful of black oil sunflower seeds out of her pocket.

Today, of course, none of them would come to greet her. She wasn't alone this morning.

As she'd left the house, Holly had asked if she could join in. And since her return from nearly dying in a plane crash, wherever Holly went, Mike was sure to be close behind.

Miranda liked them both, but would miss the company of her loyal subjects. They were so much less complicated than people. And usually happier.

The three of them had walked the first mile in silence. Was it companionable? Awkward? Were they waiting for her as hostess to speak first?

She did her best to set all that aside. She knew it was just her autism springing to the fore. Knowing that she couldn't easily read social situations made her worry about them much more than was justified. Worse, the more she worried about them, the more her fears of not fitting in, because she was on the autism spectrum, rose. And that acted like a heterodyne in a negative feedback loop without an overload regulator. Where was a good capacitor for her thoughts when she needed one? If only—

"This is such a beautiful place, Miranda." Mike spoke up. "Thanks so much for letting us come up here as often as you do."

"You're welcome." Miranda latched onto the rote phrase to dial down her own inner whirlwind.

"It's not half bad," Holly agreed. Her Australian accent was thick enough for Miranda to know that she was teasing. When her accent cleared, that's when she was dead serious.

"Not half bad at all," Miranda matched her and received a smile, meaning she'd read it right.

A few of the lambs popped their heads up out of the grass. The adults were tall enough to have seen them coming, but the newborns were hidden even in the lower grasses of spring. The herd favored the north end of the island where the growth was particularly lush.

The lambs watched the human intruders for several seconds before letting out sharp, panicked bleats. As soon as the adults answered, the offspring bounded to their sides. The mothers knew her and went back to eating.

"How long until they stop needing their moms?" Mike nodded back toward the lambs as they arced over the northern tip of the island and entered the cool woods.

"They'll stay close for two or three months. Then they're off on their own."

"So Jeremy must be a late bloomer."

Miranda looked to Holly, but her accent was gone. "What's he supposed to bloom into?"

Holly looked...uncomfortable? She was suddenly very interested in the surrounding trees, which was something Miranda knew she did herself to avoid having to look directly at others. She looked around herself but couldn't imagine what here would make a former Special Operations Forces soldier uncomfortable.

"Holly?"

It was Mike who answered. "We've been talking about it a bit between ourselves. It's time for you to let Jeremy run an investigation."

"But he's not an investigator-in-charge."

Holly took her arm and brought her to a stop. "No, but if he's ever going measure up—"

"He's five-foot-eight; that's four inches taller than I am."

Holly smiled, then started again without explaining her smile, "If he's ever going to be an IIC, he needs to fail a few times."

"Fail? Why would he fail?"

"Because he's not ready."

Miranda couldn't believe what she was hearing. Jeremy Trahn knew almost as much about aircraft as she did. His analyses were so detailed that she was often hard pressed to find suggestions for improvements. He—

"Can you just trust me that he isn't ready?"

She looked most of the way up to Holly's face. Finally stopped at her lips. Holly was six inches taller than her own five-four, so it was a comfortable angle—and she didn't have to try the difficult challenge of looking at her eyes.

Believe that Jeremy Trahn could be anything less than excellent?

She shook her head.

"I'm sorry, Holly. But he's nearly as good as I am. And you are always telling me I'm the best."

"No, Miranda. *Everyone,* from the President of your United States of America on down, tells you that you're the best— because it's true. But think back to the day we met. What was happening the moment before I arrived?"

"A one-star general was threatening to shoot me and appeared to be sincere in that declaration."

"What do you think would have happened if I hadn't shown up?"

Miranda thought back to the crashed C-130 Hercules cargo plane deep in the top-secret area of Groom Lake, Nevada. The heat had been oppressive and the general had been so angry that the gun barrel had actually been shaking less than a meter from her face.

Holly had done...something. Something she'd never understood. Standing barehanded, she'd threatened the general with severe bodily harm and, curiously, an immense amount of paperwork if he shot either of them. She'd somehow made it okay. At least okay enough to have him put away his sidearm rather than shooting her.

Mike had been there too. He'd taken the general aside and had even convinced him to cooperate—at least briefly.

Miranda never understood people, but she knew that, as her Human Factors expert, Mike understood them better than anyone she'd ever met.

"Mike?" Holly was a warrior, but he was the human factors specialist. He'd understand how skilled Jeremy was. "I can't believe that Jeremy would fail if he's put in charge of an investigation."

"He'd fail spectacularly!" Mike laughed aloud, eliciting more bleats from the lambs.

She hadn't meant it as a joke. They resumed their walk to get well clear of the herd.

"Told ya, mate," Holly's Australian heritage sounded more clearly. She too thought this was funny.

"But...why? He understands aircraft and crash-investigation methodologies very, very well."

"And, Miranda," Mike spoke more gently, "he's as clueless about people as you are."

"But..." Miranda actually looked up at his face for a moment, but he was serious. "But he's not an ASD like me."

"No. No autism, but he's an uber-nerd with as much understanding of people as... I can't think of a good analogy. Unlike you, he has the ability, but zero skill. In that, he's actually less skilled than you because you struggle so hard to learn it."

"That makes no sense. He has all of the skills needed to examine a crash."

"Because, gal-pal mine," Holly's Strine accent grew broader —a sure sign that she was very amused (an easily mapped correlative curve of accent thickness and humor), "because we don't want some general shooting him in the arse."

She never thought about that aspect of an investigation. Then she looked up at Holly and Mike. And...they were the reason that she didn't have to think about such things.

Holly might be her structural specialist, but she understood people's motivations—at least those who wanted to attack her. Mike's skills in human psychology let him keep everyone calm as well as digging out answers that people would prefer to keep hidden. She *was* safer for having both of them present at site investigations.

But there was one more thing.

"Why should I let him fail? We have a responsibility to investigate and solve every crash."

"We'll all be his safety net," Mike nodded to indicate the three of them. "He'll find the answer, because he is that good. But we need to open his eyes about the necessary skills to run a team: interpersonal skills, delegation skills, and project management to name a few."

"What about me?"

"Well, Miranda, you should play the slightly dumb assistant. Don't do anything unless he directly asks you to."

"No, I mean shouldn't I learn to run a team as well."

Mike opened his mouth, then closed it again, squinting at the ground.

Miranda pulled out her personal notebook and checked the emoticon page Mike had given her. Not angry—his cheeks weren't flushed. Maybe—

Holly pointed at "puzzled," which seemed to fit.

"Thank you," she tucked away her notebook.

"Miranda," Holly took both her shoulders and faced her directly.

Miranda shifted her focus to Holly's left ear just showing from under her long blonde hair.

"You do great!"

"But you said that General Harrington—"

"You make us *want* to work with you. I can't begin to tell you how rare a gift that is. We take care of managing strangers because you don't have any skill at doing that."

Miranda huffed out a breath. "Well, why didn't you say that's what you meant? I knew that."

Holly laughed. "All of us do, except Jeremy. He thinks that you and he can run a team just fine on your own. He needs to learn that isn't true."

Miranda understood now.

She turned away and pulled out a handful of sunflower seeds, cupping them in her hand. In moments, the birds she'd heard singing their question at her came to eat. They took turns perching on her upcurved fingertips long enough to grab a seed and go.

When she was alone, they'd often sit and eat several before spooking. But not with Holly and Mike so close by. Even briefly, their tiny claws gave such happy little squeezes on her fingertips as they dipped for seeds that she could do this for hours.

She supposed that being a team leader *was* a skill that Jeremy should learn.

It was hard to imagine that they shared an incompetence, but with the others' insistence, she was forced to believe them.

Maybe she'd watch and take notes, then she could try it herself.

One of the bravest of the airborne subjects took the mad risk of remaining perched with its tiny claws clamped about one of her fingers while it ate one seed. As it reached for another, her phone began to sound like a jet engine spinning up.

The chickadee didn't waste an instant, even to look panicked—it was simply gone so fast that it might as well have evaporated. She tossed the remaining seeds widely around her, hoping that the spooked bird would get at least his second seed.

Then she answered the phone. "This is Miranda Chase. This is actually her, not a recording of her."

At Jill's laugh of greeting, she knew there was a crash.

4

ANDI WU WAS HALF AWAKE, MAYBE EVEN THREE-QUARTERS.

If she faceplanted in the bowl of oatmeal on the table, perhaps she'd hit seven-eighths. As usual, she was the last one up. Miranda, Mike, and Holly were nowhere to be found, but their walking boots were missing from the mudroom. Taz and Jeremy had just been leaving for a morning run as she'd stumbled down the stairs.

What was wrong with morning people? For a decade as a helicopter pilot with the US Army's Night Stalkers helicopter regiment, she'd lived in a flipped-clock world. "Death waits in the dark," was one of their mottos for a reason; they lived and flew at night. Vampire jokes abounded inside the regiment. She could make up a rocking short-Chinese-woman-vampire story when she was in the mood.

Though she'd been out for most of a year, being on Miranda's team was still screwing with her circadian rhythm.

And Miranda was messing with her mind.

She finished her oatmeal, washed the bowl, and placed it precisely where Miranda liked bowls to be stacked. She was very particular about her kitchen layout and Andi did her best to accommodate that.

Pulling on her own shoes and shrugging into a jacket, she walked up to the island's midfield hangar. Circling around a pair of sheep that were almost as tall as her own five-two, she opened the people-sized door and went inside.

The early morning light shone through a high window and illuminated the aircraft inside as if she was in some shadowy fairy tale.

For months she'd been expecting to be shed from the team. Sure, she knew rotorcraft cold, but she wasn't a mechanic. Between Jeremy and Miranda, they knew more about how helicopters were built than she'd realized there was to know.

Only on the rare occasions when the team was investigating a helicopter crash did she feel as if she belonged. But most of their work was in fixed-wing aircraft. She knew almost nothing about those. Sure, she spoke "pilot" better than anyone else on the team, even Miranda, but it wasn't *that* significant a role.

Most of the time, she hung with Miranda, helping where she could—and waiting for the axe to fall.

But it kept aloft.

And now this!

There was a brand-new aircraft in the hanger.

Miranda's old four-seater Mooney M20V prop plane and the Cessna M2 bizjet that the manufacturer had *given* Miranda were parked at the Tacoma office.

This hangar currently held only two aircraft at the moment.

Miranda's Korean War era F-86 Sabrejet always drew the eye. Even with the guns and bombs removed, the silver jet still looked utterly lethal. Andi had always been a whirlybird gal, but to go winging around the country at almost the speed of sound in an antique solo jet did sound pretty freaking awesome.

It was the other aircraft that had her stumped.

It was an MD 902 Explorer helicopter.

Six seats including the pilot.

Seven million dollars of aircraft.

And Miranda had simply bought it. That she was hugely wealthy was a given, so that wasn't what was confusing Andi.

It was that Miranda couldn't fly it.

Miranda insisted that she'd bought it because she wanted to learn more about rotorcraft and it was very convenient for transporting the team locally.

She'd bought it the week after Andi had been recertified for flight—by FAA docs who obviously thought PTSD was some kind of...phase. She might test fine, but they weren't inside her head.

Miranda hadn't leased it either, she'd bought it outright.

And Andi was the team's only rotorcraft pilot.

Or so they'd thought until Holly had revealed she'd picked up a helo license when she was in the SASR—Australia's elite special operations team.

Miranda had bought it for *Andi* to use. As if Miranda expected her to have a long-term place on the team.

Or had it been some sort of twisted present? A bribe to make her...what?

Andi brushed a hand over its sleek silver-and-blue paint job.

Trying to pin a nefarious motive on Miranda simply didn't hold. Her concept of manipulation was very literal, like manipulating a wrench to loosen a bolt. Perhaps, just as she'd insisted, she hadn't even thought of the gift aspect of it. Miranda's autism kept her free from those kinds of games.

Andi rested her forehead against the acrylic panel of the pilot-side door and stared at the seat—her seat.

Miranda had given her back a piece of her soul and didn't even know it.

Was any woman ever that thoughtlessly kind? Certainly

none of her past lovers had been. But then none of them had been Miranda either.

She thumped her head against the acrylic.

Did she finally have a home? A place she belonged...on Miranda's team?

Andi closed her eyes and rolled her cheek onto the window. Maybe, just maybe she did.

Even if she didn't understand why or how...maybe she did.

The harsh rattle of the main hangar door sliding open startled her.

The team came streaming in.

"Let's go, mate. Got a launch and we're up." Holly walked up and dropped Andi's gear bag to the ground. Then she tugged a yellow Australian Matildas ball cap out of her back pocket and slapped it down onto Andi's head. "You forgot this." Then she strode around the bird to toss her own gear in the back, leaving Andi's bag resting on her toes.

Even when she'd been a decorated captain in the 160th Night Stalkers, she'd never exuded that kind of confidence.

"Why are you crying?" Miranda was standing so close that her toes were touching the other side of Andi's gear bag.

Andi reached up to touch her fingers to her cheeks, and they came away wet. Hopefully no one else had noticed—which was a stupid thought as Holly had just shoved her favorite women's soccer team's hat on Andi's head.

"I was crying because..." She searched for some way to tell Miranda how she'd made Andi feel and couldn't find the words.

Holly stepped up and shoved the preflight checklist into her hands. "Not at some lazy Sunday barbie, mate."

But Miranda was still waiting.

"They're happy tears, Miranda. Don't worry." And she turned her attention to the checklist.

At least she hoped that's what they were. Happy sounded far better that utter, desperate, insurmountable bewilderment.

5

Miranda sent Taz to ride up front with Andi, "There's a playing field behind McCaw Hall at Seattle Center called Memorial Stadium. Could you arrange for us to land there?"

"On it!" Taz yanked out her phone and was dialing before they'd even hovered out of the hangar.

Once they were clear of the island, Miranda switched the intercom to Cabin Only so that they wouldn't disturb Andi or Taz. The rear of the helicopter had the VIP configuration: two seats behind the pilots facing aft and two more at the rear facing forward. She sat in the back left with Mike beside her and Jeremy facing backward beside Holly.

"Jeremy, I'd like you to treat this as a training investigation. I want you to be the Investigator-in-Charge."

"Really, Miranda? Oh my gosh, that's so wonderful. Isn't that wonderful, Taz?" He turned to her but his seat was back-to-back with hers and she was still on the phone. Even if she had heard, he didn't give her time to answer before continuing. "I can't believe that you trust me to do that. But what are *you* going to do? I mean, you're the one who—"

Holly punched his arm hard enough to send him slamming into the closed door of the helo.

"Ow!"

Mike patted his knee consolingly. "Rule Number One of being an IIC, buddy: listen more—talk less."

"Got it. Right. Makes sense. Listen more, talk less. Listen more, talk less. I'll work on that. What else? Tell me more that I need to—"

Holly held up a finger.

"Uh-huh. Uh-huh. Listen more, talk less. Got it."

Miranda tried to think of what else to say, but Holly had told her that part of her role was to keep her mouth shut.

Holly was the one who answered him, apparently ignoring her own advice. "You're in charge now, Jeremy. Go on. Take the lead."

"Well, if I'm the IIC now..." he turned to face Holly, "...you can stop punching me."

"There's hope for him yet," Mike whispered in Miranda's ear as Holly patted him on the head hard enough to have him cringing.

39

6

"How did a plane that size cause such minimal damage?"

"That's part of what we're here to learn, Mike." Miranda thought that question was rather obvious for a seasoned National Transportation Safety Board investigator.

"I understand that. I simply never thought that a ten-person commuter plane could create less damage in a crash than a Cessna 152 two-seater might. At least when those tiny planes crash, you get a crumpled up ball of metal."

"It did crash into an opera house," Holly commented, her Strine accent easily indicated humor. "Tragic and ridiculous at the same time."

"Not a normal landing spot," Taz agreed over the helicopter's intercom headset as they circled above the downtown Seattle crash site.

Miranda had learned to recognize Taz's tone now as well. The point of Taz's jokes typically eluded her—yet another aspect of her autism—but she'd learned Taz's tone when she was using humor. Actually, over the last three months, Miranda had learned Taz's "being serious" tone. Treating everything else she said as a joke or a "wry commentary"—which also often eluded her—had vastly increased her comprehension statistics regarding the newest member of her crash investigation team.

Taz's primary specialty was as the team's liaison to the military and the defense contractors. It seemed that they were both terrified of the former Air Force colonel. She also offered many insights into how aircraft were manufactured, which had proved very useful.

Andi, the team's rotorcraft specialist and former Night Stalkers pilot, had flown them direct from the island to hovering above the McCaw Hall auditorium at Seattle Center in just thirty minutes.

Miranda decided that the brand-new MD 902 Explorer helicopter was a good investment. Her own understanding of helicopters was definitely lacking in first-hand experience. It also provided a degree of operational convenience in the Pacific Northwest region that she appreciated. For now, she was adapting to the passenger experience. Then she would shift forward and take lessons from Andi.

Andi was thoughtful enough to face the helo to offer Miranda's seat the best view of the opera house crash. Miranda didn't like crowds, so she never attended an opera performance, but she donated enough money that they allowed her to view the final dress rehearsal when the three-thousand-seat house was mostly empty.

That experience provided sufficient information to interpret the form of the interior from the shape of the roof: the lower roofs over the lobby to the west and the Seattle Opera offices to the east, the rising peak over the twenty-nine-hundred-seat house, and the twelve-story-high tower for the fly loft.

A fully loaded Cessna 208 Caravan had taken off from Boeing Field in south Seattle. Six miles after takeoff, in a direct line from the runway, it had flown into the top of the fly-loft tower just above the hundred-foot level. A large hole had been punched in the side of the tower but had not appeared out the other side, indicating that the aircraft had remained inside the building.

Only minor wisps of smoke still emerged from the building.

Mike was right; in surprising ways, it was a notably low damage profile for such an event. A hole in a wall ten stories above the ground and a thin streamer of smoke. Though the inside of the building could well be a different story.

The lines of emergency vehicles parked by the rear loading docks attested to that. Five fire trucks, hoses snaking all around them like a living mat of vines, and several ambulances were gathered there. Beyond them were a phalanx of police cars trying to keep the heavy traffic on Mercer Street moving along.

Even as she watched, two more ambulances rolled out and then raced away with their sirens going.

"Look! The landing gear," Miranda started laughing.

The others leaned over to where she pointed at the lower opera house roof, but no one seemed to get the joke.

"It looks like the plane landed on the inside of the ceiling but its wheels broke through. It landed in the sky."

Jeremy, who sat across from her, squinted. "I don't think they're in the right sequence. I think one of the side landing gear landed where the nose gear should be. And the dimensions are definitely off."

Mike and Taz merely looked puzzled. Holly didn't make any comment, but Miranda heard Andi's soft laugh over the intercom.

"Thank you, Andi." At least someone understood. "We can land now."

Andi landed close behind the opera house in the end zone of Memorial Field—the green grass white-lined with a confusing combination of a soccer field overlaid upon a football field. Or perhaps it was the other way around.

Miranda assumed that the players could make sense of the

two sets of lines, even in the heat of play; to her it was worse than an air-crash debris field.

She wondered if it would be possible to attend operas by helicopter. At present, she had to fly mere minutes from her private island in the San Juans to pick up her car in Anacortes twenty-four miles away—she didn't like the unfamiliarity of rental cars that might be available at some airport closer to Seattle. It was then a two-hour drive to the opera, and reverse the entire process afterward.

Though she suspected that they wouldn't clear her to land at Seattle Center for each performance. Besides, she hadn't learned to fly a helicopter.

"Do you like opera, Andi?" she asked as they both stepped onto the field and began walking up the stadium's rear ramp toward the damaged opera house.

"When there isn't a plane parked there, you mean? I don't know. I've never been to one."

"You could come to the next one with me. See if you like it. I get two tickets to the final rehearsals for being a significant donor."

"Who usually goes with you?"

"No one."

Andi studied her sideways for half the length of the thirty-meter ramp before replying. "Okay. But I don't think there will be any operas here for a while."

Miranda looked up at the wisps of smoke still curling out the hole in the stage tower and decided that was an astute assessment.

She led them to the west, toward the main entrance. It was the nearest access. The emergency crews were all around the far side of the block and she wouldn't enjoy the mayhem. The tall, glassed-in lobby looked quiet and showed no obvious signs of smoke damage.

They arrived at a yellow-tape barrier; "Police Line Do Not Cross" repeated endlessly down its length.

"I always felt that these need punctuation. Mike, who should I talk to about that?"

Now Mike laughed when she hadn't intended a joke at all. "How about we discuss that at a different time, Miranda? There *is* a plane crash." He lifted the tape for her to duck under.

"Okay." She stepped under the line and the others followed.

Now she was on-site and she hadn't checked her tools yet. She began tapping each of the tools in her multi-pocket NTSB vest to make sure everything was in place.

A policeman came over. "Hey, I need you people to stay on the other side of the line. It says, 'Do Not Cross' for a reason."

Miranda continued checking her vest until she was sure of the placement of everything. She then turned on her pocket recorder.

"Hey, lady. I'm talking to you."

She took out a fresh notebook, noted the location, date, and time, then tucked it away.

"You can't be here. Now please step back across that line pronto."

She spoke quickly when he left a brief gap to take a breath.

"I'm Miranda Chase. I'm the Investigator-in-Charge for the NTSB."

They were all wearing their yellow ball caps—probably looking like a group of fans—which could account for his confusion.

And that's when she realized what the real problem was. She pulled out her ID, turned it to face outward, and slipped the lanyard around her neck. Everyone else was already wearing theirs.

"What's the NTSB?"

"It's— We're—" She'd never been asked that at a crash site before and was unsure how to answer.

Mike spoke up. "National Transportation Safety Board, Officer. We're the folks in charge of investigating airplane crashes."

"No, Mike. You aren't all investigators-in-charge, so that constitutes an inaccurate statement. Don't mislead the officer. I'm the IIC, the rest of you are essential members of my team."

"Me? Essential? I like the sound of that." He looked terribly surprised.

"Why is he being so surprised?" she asked Andi. Andi and Mike often explained people's reactions for her, but since she was making an inquiry about Mike, he didn't seem to be the correct one to ask.

"He's being funny."

Mike was the one team member who could always deceive her that way.

"Airplane crash? Where?" the officer was looking in every direction except the right one—upward. "They just told me to run the tape and watch the line. Figured it was just a fire by all the trucks racing around to the loading dock."

Mike waved him over to stand just at the tape, turned him around, and pointed up.

The smoke seemed to have stopped, but the gaping hole remained.

"Shit! They never tell you anything."

Mike thumped his shoulder in what his easy nod indicated was sympathy.

Miranda didn't have to open the Team Attributes page of her personal notebook to recognize that. While his humor was elusive, Mike's kindness was always obvious. She wondered if that would surprise him for real.

She saw that Jeremy already had his handheld weather station out and was recording wind and temperature.

He had embraced his role and now it was her job to keep quiet.

"I'll catch up in a minute." Andi then turned to talk to the officer to make sure that he knew her helicopter had been cleared to land at Memorial Field.

Miranda nodded even though Andi was no longer facing her. Keeping her mouth shut, she followed Jeremy and the others into the building.

7

MIRANDA HAD SEEN AIRPLANE CRASHES, FROM TWO-SEATER training planes that had tangled into telephone wires to a shattered C-5M Super Galaxy, the US military's largest transport jet. Curiously, the two extremes had been her first and second solo investigations as a newly certified investigator.

She had traveled from frozen glaciers in the remote wilderness to a shattered apartment complex close by an airfield, and out to remote desert islands.

But the opera house was perhaps the strangest crash site yet.

There was a crash, except there was little sign of it.

They'd come in through the stage right door—the right-hand side as they stood on the stage and faced the seating. The offstage area was empty. A massive, multi-tiered set in the form of a stone castle dominated the stage. Through gaps in the set and side curtains she could see the numerous firemen and their hoses that had been strung into the opera house from the stage left side.

The stage was a hangar-sized space bigger than either of hers, on her island or down at the Tacoma office. What's more, unlike her hangars, it was a hundred feet high. It extended twenty feet to this side of the area visible from the house seating, and seventy feet to the other. Andi could park ten of their new helicopters in here without overlapping the rotors.

Today was their first local investigation since she'd purchased the MD 902. She'd wanted a chance to study rotorcraft flight dynamics personally, but was also pleased at how conveniently and quickly it had been able to transport them to a crash site. Two major advantages.

Looking abandoned in the middle of the stage, the elaborate set must be for the upcoming production of *Turandot*. It had never been one of her favorites; Puccini was so overdramatic and the set reflected that. The towering Chinese palace was, in turn, dominated by a great dragon hunched as if ready to attack.

He was now a tragic dragon, scorched and drooping as if burned by his own fire.

Miranda considered for a moment but was unsure if that would count as a joke or not.

Much of the set was scorched; holes burned through the facing material. The exposed innards were incongruously modern supports for an ancient Chinese palace. Everything was either drenched with water or spray foam. It all smelled curiously fresh, like a spring day right after a rain shower.

The proscenium opening that should reveal the house seating was blocked by a vast fire curtain. Its face was also scorched with a splash of fire, though in the wrong configuration to have issued from the dragon.

Jeremy and Taz were crisscrossing the stage to take photographs, hopping over firehoses and dodging rushing rescue workers. Mike and Holly were simply standing and watching them.

Miranda tapped the curtain material, fiberglass over a

metal frame. The only thing it allowed to escape into the house was the steady stream of water sheeting across the stage.

Even as she watched, a small group of stagehands rushed in and began laying sandbags along the base to stem the flow. They didn't have nearly enough and the water simply flowed between them.

The simple solution would be to lay one of the charged firehoses along the entire length. That would hold back up to three inches of water. Was that related to the crash or not related to the crash? She wasn't sure if she should speak or not.

Probably not.

Knowing that would bother her until she found a new topic to focus on, she pulled out her personal notebook and added an entry: "Research the design, operation, and fire resistance of theatrical fire curtains."

Then she tucked the notebook away and looked around once more.

Something was missing.

Which she'd always observed was much harder to notice than what was actually there.

It took her two full, slow turns to realize what it was amid the wounded grandeur of the emperor's palace.

"Where's the plane?" Then she slapped a hand over her mouth to keep it shut.

Holly pointed aloft as if the plane was still flying overhead.

And indeed, after a fashion, it was.

As her eyes tracked upward, she spotted several artificial trees high in the loft that were still badly scorched like the aftermath of a forest fire.

A hundred feet above the stage, on top of the vast gridwork of steel supports, lay the airplane, or at least the dim outline of one viewed between the gaps.

A plane flying over the charred remains of a fake forest.

How terribly operatic.

She was quite sure that was somehow a joke. But while she'd been looking, Mike and Holly had followed Jeremy and Taz on the long climb to the fly loft itself so she couldn't ask them.

That's when she realized that something else was missing.

"Where's Andi?"

8

PRESIDENT COLE ACTUALLY SLUMPED IN THE CHAIR IN HIS OFFICE aboard Air Force One. "Give me your opinions on the last week, and keep it short. We land in Canada in two hours and I need to get some sleep because I know for damn sure I won't get a wink during the G-7 meetings."

Drake glanced at Sarah but the National Security Advisor just shook her head, so Drake took the bit.

"Middle East first. I think you have only two choices, Mr. President."

"Am I going to like either one?"

"First, we could step in and provide area security, making ourselves primary targets for everyone."

"Old patterns."

"Exactly, Mr. President. If you do what you've always done..." Drake mused.

"You'll still be green—Kermit the Frog. I was a Green Beret, I know that particular truism well, Drake. So what's the *new* action?"

"First, if we no longer want to be the world's policemen, we have to stop the old. Have you seen Senator Ramson's latest?"

"I don't recall that in my morning briefing. When was morning, anyway, New Zealand?"

"That was ten hours ago and it's now past noon there, sir. This just showed up on Ramson's docket. He's pushing a foreign arms sales package through Congress. It would give the Saudis the F-35s, the MQ-9A Reaper drones, and the JASSM missile."

"That never crossed my goddamn desk."

"Sent to Congress by the Department of State. The Saudis are offering cash, and—"

"I've got a dirty Secretary of State?" The President's voice went cold.

"We don't know that sir," Sarah said carefully, "but I have people looking into exactly that."

"And the Chairman of the Senate Armed Services Committee is in the pocket of the defense contractors?"

"We haven't been able to prove that either but," Sarah sighed deeply, "yes. Even though Senator Ramson isn't chairman of the Foreign Relations Committee that has to approve the sale, he has the controlling vote there. His block controls seven of the twenty-two votes and we think there are another five he can swing on special votes."

"Christ! So he's got someone dirty in State who is feeding him sales to approve on Foreign Relations so that he can sit on Armed Services and order more high-end—" Cole cut himself off. "That man is a *major* problem. And the results speak for themselves. More goddamn Middle East and Southwest Asia wars. Please tell me there's another alternative?"

Drake nodded, "Vice President Clark Winston is an old Middle East hand and he also concurs. I think they're both right on this one. The Saudis have the second largest military budget by GDP in the world after Oman, fifth globally in raw dollars spent. Yes, they are enemies of several terrorist-spawning countries, but they combat that by pumping obscene amounts of funds *into* terrorism—billions. For years Clark has been saying in both classified and public reports that the US needs to rethink that relationship—*not* to the Saudis' advantage. We need to stop feeding them weapons, training, and support."

"God damn it, Drake. That does it. I'm voting for you as the next President. In fact, you can take over right now for all I care."

"Be better off with Sarah here."

"Why's that?" Sarah actually looked a bit alarmed, which was a first.

"First, you're smarter than either of us."

"Maybe than both of us put together," the President grumbled.

"Well, of course," she went for the joke but didn't quite carry it off.

"Second, we're both old warhorses who are ready to just stop. Time for the younger generation to take over."

"I'm about ten minutes younger than either of you." More like a ten years.

"See," Drake turned back to the President, "I told you she was smart when I recommended her."

President Cole was never one to take long making decisions. He stared at Sarah for about thirty seconds. Long enough that any lesser person would have been twitching. The only external sign he gave was a slow tapping of his left forefinger on the back of his other hand.

Then it stopped.

"Okay," he pushed to his feet.

He and Sarah both rose as well.

"I'm going to have the SecDef put a hold on the approval process for the Saudi arms sale. Then I *am* going to take a nap. Wake me ten minutes before we land with a plan of action that

I can sell at the meetings. And if there's a war, just deal with it for me, okay?"

He closed the door behind him, giving them use of his office.

"He was joking, right?" Sarah had only been on board as the NSA for the last seven weeks since Millard's heart attack had forced him to retire. Drake had served the President as the Chairman of the Joint Chiefs of Staff for the last six years.

"Are you asking about presenting a completely new model for world policy in under two hours or letting him sleep through a war?"

"Um," Sarah shrugged, "either?"

"The latter, yes. The former? We've got our work cut out for us. Don't worry. You'll get the hang of it."

Sarah didn't look convinced.

9

By the expedient of ninety-three wrong turns, Andi was standing in two feet of chilly water.

The officer had asked her to make sure the helo was locked to keep teens from rummaging around inside, which it hadn't been. Not the sort of thing she'd had to worry about in the military. By the time she'd jogged down and taken care of it, everyone else was gone.

The officer joined her as she tested the various lobby doors —all locked. He didn't look put out, enjoying the chance to flirt with her. He was very nice about it, so she let him.

As she circled behind the building looking for another way in, someone went hustling in through a steel security door. She'd managed to snag the handle before it latched, but her guide was long gone once she was inside.

That was the first of her ninety-three wrong turns trying to find her way through the labyrinthine pathways beneath the opera house.

The two feet of chilly water she'd plunged into was fast becoming three.

The logjam of chairs and music stands across the only other

exit was the giveaway to her location—in the orchestra pit. *Under* the stage when others were probably *on* the stage. At least she was close.

Large copper kettle drums bobbed on the surface of the water and the whole mess was papered over with floating sheets of music turned to mush.

And the water level was rising.

At five-two tall, this was going to get bad very soon.

Drowned at the opera, one tiny Chinese woman from San Francisco.

It was a headline she'd rather not be part of.

Through the swirling water, she couldn't see what was happening under the forward section of the pit. Was it a smooth floor that she could traverse out into the opera house seating, or a bottomless well of machinery where she'd be pinned and drown?

Better not to find out. She'd done enough pits of despair since Ken's grisly death. It was definitely time to look up rather than down.

When she did, she noticed that the underside of the stage floor had a trap door in it. It was at the front center of the pit. Over the orchestra conductor's podium? It would have helped if she'd come to an opera before this.

She sloshed over, testing the now thigh-deep underwater surface carefully with each step. Despite that, she rapped a shin hard on the sharp corner of the podium. Clambering up onto it, she was once again only calf deep in the rising water and could reach the trap. Andi hit the release and it swung down easily.

Too easily. The puddle of water that had accumulated over it dumped down onto her head, soaking her last remaining dry spots—like behind her right ear.

When it stopped and she dared to look again, she was shoulder-high to the stage floor.

The water had slowed to a trickle as she climbed up onto

the floorboards. At least it wasn't icy. Just damn cold. Water-main cold.

The thousands of seats watching her performance were unimpressed.

The stage was blocked by an ugly brown cloth drape.

There was no gap that she could see. No door to either side.

She looked back at the seating. The water was only ankle deep before the rows of seats angled upward to dry safety. But she didn't want to jump down into it to find another way backstage.

There were voices on the other side of the drape.

"Hey, how do I get in—"

Before she could finish her shout, the brown wall began sliding upward.

A low sandbag wall wasn't holding back more than a skim of water across the stage. *She* was wetter than the floor.

As it lifted further, she could see a strange shimmering reflection on the rippling water, like a fairy tale castle and—

She yelped!

A massive dragon was glaring at her as if it was ready to eat her alive.

"You're all wet," Miranda greeted Andi with that perfect logic of hers.

"I am. I was lost, but I looked up and now I'm found." Andi resisted the urge to begin singing "Amazing Grace." Besides, she hadn't been *that* lost, at least not in a while.

"Why did you yell?"

"I wasn't expecting to see Xuanlong the black dragon glaring at me."

"He's guarding the imperial palace," Miranda turned to the dragon.

"He shouldn't be, he only has three toes. That makes him Japanese or only fit for a Tang Dynasty nobleman's house. Imperial dragons have five toes. Though," she splashed a sopping boot in the thin sheen of water on the black stage floor, "he does dwell in the depth of mysterious waters, so maybe he is in the right place. Oh my God!"

"What?"

Andi grabbed her head. "How do I know that? I'm turning into my grandmother."

Miranda inspected her carefully. "You don't look like you're changing."

"I meant inside," and Andi decided she'd be better off with a different topic. "An imperial palace, huh? This opera about some nasty emperor? Maybe Xuanlong matches him." Andi wrung what she could out of the front of her t-shirt. "Is he fair or vengeful? Perhaps he excels at law or combat?"

Miranda studied the stage for a moment. "No, but he is overwhelmed and saddened by a strongheaded daughter."

"Like Wu Zetian—thirteen hundred years ago she became China's only female emperor. I can't believe everything Gram stuffed into my head without my realizing it. Does the daughter want to sit on the Dragon Throne herself?"

"No. She just likes killing princes who are courting her."

"Hard to argue with the logic." Despite her lack of interest in men, being a short, cute Asian, she'd certainly been a target. Andi did what she could to squeeze the water out of her shoulder-length hair, sending a fresh trickle of cold down her still-soaked front.

"Why— No. Let's not go there. What about the plane crash?"

Miranda pointed upward.

Andi looked up, *way* up. Ten stories above their heads was a massive gridwork of steel. Through the gaps, she could just make out the outline of an airplane.

Then she could see there were people moving around up there.

"Is that the team?"

"Yes."

"Why aren't you up there with them?"

"Holly and Mike suggested that it was time for Jeremy to fail. So, I'm doing nothing until he asks me. It's very..." she pulled out a notebook and flipped to her emoticon page.

"Frustrating?" Andi suggested.

"Yes, that's it. Thank you," Miranda tucked away the notebook without checking it on the page.

Time for Jeremy to fail?

That must mean that they were grooming him for a team leader role. She really had to start getting up earlier, she was missing too much.

She looked aloft again. A fully loaded Cessna 208 Caravan weighed eight thousand pounds.

"How much weight can that grid hold?"

"I'm not sure. I think each individual pipe can hold approximately four thousand pounds. There are several specific points that can manage ten-ton point loads."

There were perhaps a hundred pipes. The Caravan wouldn't have stressed the grid at all except for the impact of its arrival, though most of that shock would have been absorbed by it punching through the wall. A vast beam of sunshine through the hole lit the plane brilliantly now that she'd spotted it.

"It's amazing that it didn't blast out the other side."

"You can't see it from below but there are hundreds of ropes just above the grid. They must have acted like the arresting harness on an aircraft carrier, jerking it to a halt."

"Were there any survivors?"

Miranda nodded, "Apparently everyone except the pilot and a passenger seated in the copilot's seat. Several were suffering from heat stroke due to the fire but the sprinkler system kept them from being burned alive."

"And we're waiting for Jeremy to fail?"

Miranda nodded.

"And if he doesn't?"

Miranda actually looked at her in distress. Frustrating perhaps didn't begin to cover the depths of Miranda's feelings, even if she didn't know how to put words to them. Sidelined and unable to help on the investigation must be torture for an autistic.

"So—"

As he hurried by, a stagehand offered her a blanket that she gratefully wrapped around her shoulders and felt suddenly colder as all of her wet clothes were pressed against her skin.

She did her best to suppress a shiver. Then she looked again at the airplane overhead, and at the dragon glaring at them with its one unburned eye. She led Miranda off to the side.

"So, tell me about this opera that I'm not going to be seeing anytime soon." Andi hoped that would be enough to shift Miranda's one-track mind away from the crash and Jeremy to ease her worry.

"It begins with the Prince of Persia losing his head. Anyone who would court Turandot must answer three riddles and failure is a death sentence. Then a prince in hiding..."

10

————

Taz knew something strange was going on, but she had no idea what.

She stopped for a moment.

She and Jeremy were the only two inside the Caravan airplane.

No one else.

First, Miranda wasn't up here. Maybe she was afraid of heights. That she was both an air-crash genius *and* a nice person was awesome, but tracking her myriad quirks was something Taz could never wrap her head around.

In Taz's nineteen years as a general's aide at the Pentagon, she *had* learned that being both a genius and a nice-person was actually a common pairing—pity it occurred so rarely. It was as if the real geniuses, with nothing to prove, could afford to be pleasant. It was the wannabes who were utter egotistical assholes.

At least them she understood. Like knew like.

She'd survived Mexico and San Diego street gangs, and even the Pentagon officers, who were simply hall thugs in pretty uniforms, by being an A-1 certified bitch herself. It had worked for her...until she met Jeremy.

Taz looked at him again. Jeremy Trahn was mid-twenties to her mid-thirties and Vietnamese to her Mexican.

He had a family who had welcomed her easily. Their only shock was that Jeremy had brought home a woman at all, not that she was a nine-year-older, four-foot-eleven Latina.

Jeremy was studying the plane so intently, he'd probably forgotten she was close beside him.

No sign of Andi either.

Mike and Holly were just hanging back on the far end of a catwalk above the rope lines. Not doing anything. Not even talking.

They were both watching...Jeremy.

They were—

"Hey, Jeremy?"

"Uh-huh." He was now sitting in the pilot's seat, upside down. The two bodies were being removed from the cockpit as the NTSB team had arrived atop the grid—the passengers had already been debarked by medical personnel and were headed to the hospital with various breaks and bruises.

They'd been incredibly lucky. Any fuel that had leaked and ignited had all dribbled through the open steel gridwork and burned the curtains and sets below rather than destroying the airplane.

The windshields had been blown inward while breaking through the building's outer wall. Jeremy had cleared aside the smashed chunks of acrylic and now lay with his back on the seat and his feet on the headrest. His head was out of sight beneath the dashboard. One hand had reached up and was twisting the control wheel as he inspected the mechanism behind the console.

"Any idea why we're the only ones working on the crash?"

"Nope." He kept fooling with the controls.

"Well, it's damned peculiar."

"What is?"

She poked him in the ribs.

He flinched, banged his head under there, then squirmed and giggled. A grown man with a ticklish spot. He was like a space alien—one who was so familiar that she found herself wanting to stay on Miranda's team for him as much as for herself.

"That we're the only ones working on the crash."

"We are?" He scooched aside enough to look up at her from under the dash. "That's not right."

"Did anyone say anything to you?"

"Not a thing." He scooted out, dragging his t-shirt up to his armpits in the process.

She resisted the urge to blow a raspberry on his smooth chest. Over the years she'd had sex when it pleased her, but she'd never had a "lover" until Jeremy. It still made no sense, but she tabled that for later.

"Except Miranda telling me I was the IIC."

Taz blinked at him in surprise. "She did what?"

"On the flight down. She asked me to be the IIC. Like a training exercise."

He'd taken the lead on whole sections of an investigation before, but the others had kept working. Not now. This time was different.

So obvious now.

Of course Jeremy didn't get it. He was a nerd's nerd about aircraft. As compulsive as Miranda herself.

"Why aren't they at least helping?" Jeremy whispered as they both looked out the missing windshields at Mike and Holly.

"I'm not sure." Taz wasn't used to depending on others, except her general. And he was dead, almost taking her with

63

him in a final act of vengeance upon the world that had taken his wife.

"Should I ask them why?"

Taz grabbed Jeremy and dragged him into a kiss. And the boy could really kiss. When she broke free, she gave him a hand to his feet, then slapped his nice tight ass to get him moving toward the open door at the rear of the aircraft.

"What?"

"That's exactly what you should do, Jeremy. Go ask them to help you."

"But Miranda never does."

"She's Miranda. You're you. You're the IIC, you need to tell them what to do."

"Wouldn't it be better if I asked?"

"Right, yes. Ask for help. Go." Taz tried not to laugh as he picked his way over the rope lines to where Mike and Holly were smiling at him.

No, they were smiling at her.

They would know that Jeremy would never have thought to ask for help on his own. Was that her role on the team, helping Jeremy behave like a real investigator-in-charge?

Then she looked at Mike and Holly again as they laughed with Jeremy like friends before following him back toward the plane.

Taz had come to respect them immensely. Holly the Protector, who was still the only person to ever outdraw her in a knife fight. Mike the Peacemaker, who always found the common ground where everyone could get along and solve a problem.

Between them, they kept Miranda functioning and performing at the highest levels of the NTSB. Were they deluded enough to think that she'd take over that role for Jeremy?

She was going to...

Huh! She didn't have a good end to that thought. She no longer faced down people for her general. It had been decades since she'd had to defend herself and her mother against drug gangs. Now, she was...

Jeremy's lover and a member of Miranda's NTSB crash-investigation team.

And she was enjoying the challenges.

Enjoying herself?

That alone was a new concept.

Jeremy's liaison to the wider world around him?

Maybe that *wasn't* such a bad gig.

Taz could feel her competitive nature kicking in.

With reason, Miranda Chase was widely acknowledged as the best crash investigator living. Yet, unlike the Pentagon's warped mentality, in this field there was room for two at the top.

She yanked out her phone and dialed Miranda. There was a ring far below, down on the stage floor.

"This is Miranda Chase. This is actually her, not a recording of her."

"Hi, Miranda. I—" she smiled to herself. "Jeremy asked me to give you a call. Is Andi with you?"

"Yes."

"Could the two of you start interviewing the rescue workers and firefighters who are still here? Find out if they saw anything out of the ordinary."

"More unordinary than an airplane crashing into an opera house?"

"Yes, please, Miranda."

"Okay," and she was gone.

This could get to be fun.

She stuck her head out the door. "Hey Jeremy, don't forget to ask Mike to track down the survivors at the hospital and interview them before they're all released."

"Hey, that's a neat idea. Could you do that, Mike?"

"Sure, buddy," Mike rolled his eyes at her as soon as Jeremy's back was turned.

Taz shrugged in reply. She'd have to work on how to pass off ideas as Jeremy's and not her own. After nineteen years as a general's aide, she didn't need to lead—but she sure liked to win.

11

"Talk to me," President Roy Cole dropped into his chair and buckled up as Air Force One began its final descent into Victoria International Airport.

Drake considered the stack of notes he and Sarah had made.

As Chairman of the Joint Chiefs of Staff, it was his role to advise the President on military matters. Sarah's scope was wider. As National Security Advisor, her purview included all areas of national security. Neither of them had any direct power, unlike the Secretary of Defense.

Well, he'd done his years of service and had been granted dispensation despite passing mandatory retirement because of his job as the chairman. The worst the President could do was actually let him retire. Sarah still had years of service in the government ahead of her—perhaps decades. Politicians were like touring rock-and-roll bands, they were never too old, even if they were.

He took the bit first.

"Sir, we can come up with one reason to continue support

of Saudi Arabia ahead of others in the region, and dozens of reasons not to."

"How significant is the one?"

Drake smiled at Sarah before speaking it aloud, "Because we've always done it."

The President's glare was daunting enough for Drake to wonder if he was about to be retired on the spot. He began enumerating all of the "reasons" of the past and all of the reasons *not to* of the present and future.

"And?" The President was smart enough to know there was more.

There was a low grind and a loud thunk as the landing gear was deployed. They were on short final and had only a few minutes left.

Drake nodded to Sarah to take the positive.

"There's a second country in the region that it would be genuinely nice to have cooperation with. They're close to becoming nuclear. They were the ninth country in the world to pull off an orbital space launch on their own. Global top twenty in population. Despite sanctions and depending on how you count it, they're the second or third largest economy in all of southwest Asia. Definitely worth the trouble if we can figure out how to dial down the anti-Western rhetoric."

"You're talking about Iran."

"I'm talking about Iran," Sarah acknowledged.

"Who hates us."

"We've given them a lot of reasons to hate us. What if we considered giving them reasons to like us?"

He harrumphed.

"We also caught Vice President Winston before he went into his first meeting with the Southern governors. He concurred and gave us," Drake held up a sheaf of notes, "several possible strategies that he thinks could work. None of them are a short-play solution, but it could significantly shift regional alignments within a year or at least dial down the madness."

"Clark has a scheduled trip to Cairo and Jerusalem next month, doesn't he?"

"Yes sir."

"Well, let's see if we can get them to agree to add Tehran to his itinerary. Okay. What are your conclusions after our three days in South*east* Asia?"

The plane entered that giddy moment of floating. Seconds later there was a bright squeal of the wheels hitting the runway.

"Indonesia, Thailand, Vietnam, and the Philippines combined would make the eighth-largest economy in the world. Add in Australia and Taiwan and it's the fourth largest. All are US friendly, yet we've done our best to *not* set up advantageous trade and security agreements with them."

Drake slid two one-page summaries across the President's desk.

"Suggestions on both regions."

The President studied them in silence from the turn off onto a taxiway until the plane rocked to a halt. The only motion in the room was the light tapping of his left forefinger on the desk as if counting marching time. Then he dropped the page into the shredder over a burn bag.

Sarah looked at him in surprise, but Drake winked.

He knew that, whatever his decision, President Roy Cole wouldn't forget a single fact on either page.

"Time to fly." President Cole pushed to his feet and opened his office door just as the flight stairs were pushed up to the plane. "Hustle it up, you two. Don't want to keep Colonel McGrady waiting."

Drake and Sarah scrambled to pack their briefcases as he headed down the stairs. They both knew that if they weren't aboard the Marine Corps helos when the President was ready, they'd be marooned thirty kilometers from town. The motorcade was already in downtown Victoria waiting at the Camel Point waterfront heliport to deliver the President the one mile to the Empress Hotel—host to the G-7 meeting.

"Bloody Green Berets," Drake muttered as he reached the door, then had to double back for his coat and hat.

"Bloody 75th Rangers," Sarah told him as he nearly plowed her to the ground with his sudden change of direction.

"What's your excuse?"

"I don't need one, both of my parents were Marines."

They did their best to be dignified as they hustled down the airstairs together.

"Why didn't you follow in their footsteps?"

"I preferred being the UN ambassador until you snatched me away by dangling the NSA role."

"Politics," Drake shuddered as they reached the four steps up into the waiting VH-92A Superhawk. "I was never a political animal."

"Says the Chairman of the Joint Chiefs."

Which, sadly, was exclusively about politics.

Shit.

12

CLARISSA REESE RACED AHEAD, THE TREADMILL TILTING AS SHE pushed up the simulated grade of the first big climb in her 10K program. She could feel the sweat evaporating through her Victoria Beckham black-and-gold sportswear. Her TrailHeads headband kept her eyes clear and had a hole for her long ponytail as it whipped from shoulder to shoulder, helping her keep the rhythm. On the screen in front of her, the trail continued its climb up into the trees.

This afternoon, she was the only one in the small gym at Camp David. At least on her treadmill's screen it was a sunny day; Camp David was drenching wet. For now, it was just her and the array of machines.

Her phone buzzed—the Director of the CIA could *never* be out of touch. She punched Answer on the screen but kept running. Taylor Swift over her earbuds was cut off in the middle of her double-standards anthem, "The Man."

Clark's face showed. "Where are you— Oh, never mind. Good idea. I'll come join you. Bye."

Good. It saved her wasting breath on him.

Taylor slammed back in and Clarissa kept running.

Clark would come ready to do a workout...ish. He enjoyed watching her workout more than doing anything himself.

She sighed. It was all good. She liked keeping the Vice President on a short leash. But there were days she just wanted to run and be done. This wasn't one of those days.

Election campaigns would be kicking off in the next six months. She'd positioned her husband carefully to take over Roy Cole's legacy since she'd maneuvered him into replacing the scandal-ridden former VP a year ago. Clarissa still hadn't decided on her own best path to the Oval Office.

The treadmill notched up another few degrees: a breath-stealing push to take the peak at speed. She leaned into it, refusing to slacken her pace.

There were the two obvious strategies to land her in the Oval Office.

She could give up her power as the CIA Director and become that most useless of creatures, the Vice President—the first husband-and-wife team in history.

Or she could retain power *and* shine as the First Lady. Of course, then she'd be left to run against whoever had been his VP. Unless she helped the party choose someone who would *need* replacing. That's how she'd created the opening for Clark to be made Vice President so that she could take over his job at the CIA—finding the weakness of Roy Cole's first Vice President, then feeding it.

Now *that* was an interesting possibility.

"God you look awesome," Clark was grinning up at her as he shouted loud enough to be heard over the pounding rhythm of Imagine Dragons. Beckham's sleek and seamless gym clothes designs left no doubts about her level of fitness.

She hadn't noticed him or his Secret Service detail entering the gym.

"All for you, honey!" she managed to gasp it out as she crested the on-screen trail's peak and the treadmill flattened for the next stretch. She could see the next climb not that far ahead. She always chose programs that drove her to her limits.

Clark just grinned. "How far along are you?"

She glanced at the display, "Three of ten."

"Whoa! Go you!"

And there *were* things she appreciated about Clark. While she'd certainly leveraged his weakness for tall, built blondes—his cancer-dead wife and now her—he didn't hesitate about cheering her to excel.

Even after a year married, it was still a surprise.

He settled into his routine.

The Secret Service guys started their own workouts—much tougher than Clark's. Despite their isolation here inside the high-security perimeter of Camp David, she noticed that they took workout positions that let them keep their eyes on the doors and windows more than on her. The start of the next climb didn't leave her any excess energy to feel piqued about that.

Clark had done yeoman service for his own reputation this week. It had been overshadowed by Roy Cole's globe-trotting journey and his first day at the G-7 meeting, but she would make sure that people heard about it.

As Vice President, he'd spent the last three days mediating the resurrection of the Southern Governors' Association that had collapsed in 2016 after more than eighty years. He'd actually convinced them to behave more like humans than they normally did—which was an impressive feat.

Clark was always good with people. Just as he'd been good with her since she was a field agent bucking for a headquarters' directorship.

Her phone rang again, chopping off Hailee Steinfeld proving she wasn't "Most Girls."

The cyber twins, Harry and Heidi, showed up on her screen. Never a good sign.

"Go," was all she had breath for.

"We were monitoring overseas traffic and there was something odd. The British GCHQ picked up the signal off the Europe India Gateway undersea cable and processed it through—"

"Someone," Heidi cut off Harry before he could trace every electron for her, "is hiding encrypted traffic under a mask that makes the transmission look like it came out of India. Not only is this one new, but it's not in their style at all. We're thinking that it comes from another source on the same line, which includes Oman, UAE, Egypt, and the Saudis. We're seeing signs of a follow-on pulse in the trans-Atlantic cables that could possibly signal rogue activity. That's why we called."

Rogue meant terrorist. "Need any action from me yet?"

Clark looked over at her in surprise from the exercise bike he was presently spinning like he was on a bakery tour. Since becoming Vice President, he'd drifted so far out of the loop. The CIA had once been his mandate yet he'd let it completely go. She would *never* let that happen to her—not a chance. Even once she made President, she'd keep it close to hand. Knowledge was power.

As VP, she could easily outshine Clark; she could become such an obvious power behind the throne that she might be able to replace him after a single term. President before she was forty-five. That's what fast-track *should* look like. Then she could really clean up some of the messes that only people like the CIA Director could see.

She'd have to set up a dinner with the Ramsons—their normal first-Friday-of-the-month dinner was tonight and she'd had to cancel. Senator Hunter Ramson was the most powerful party member other than the majority leader. And his wife was the brains behind the man.

They'd have to sell the idea to the party leadership but, unlike Clark, she could rock the world from the Vice President's chair. Also, it was the best place to make sure that Clark didn't screw up her ride to the Oval Office.

"Sorry, what was that?" Heidi had said something.

"At this time, we just wanted to give you a heads-up. It has a fingerprint similar to the Saudis fomenting the civil wars in Iraq and Syria—though we can't prove it's them yet."

"NSA is on it?"

"As are we, but no one has cracked it yet. Whatever it is, it sparked a cloud of similarly encrypted chatter. The burst pattern mirrors a terrorist-attack scenario far more than a war scenario. US probable. Eastern seaboard possible. We thought you should know. The next twenty-four hours could be particularly interesting."

Heidi was always the queen of understatement. For the Head of CIA's Cyber Security, *a bit of a kerfuffle* translated to a concerted multi-country attack on the CIA's servers, which had only been fended off after fourteen hours of blazingly arduous work.

Interesting in Heidi's parlance meant that Clarissa should be headed back to the office right now.

She barely noticed the last of the climb as she crested the top of the trail and began the long descent through the alpine meadows.

There was a governors' dinner tonight before tomorrow morning's final meetings. Tomorrow would be all about self-congratulation for re-forming the Southern Governors' Association, but she didn't want to miss the dinner tonight. It was the main reason she'd agreed to come here on this trip. Tonight would be another chance to shine in front of the leadership.

She wouldn't float the idea of a husband-wife ticket yet, but she would ask the right questions to figure out who was open to it. Or where the weakest links were open to attack.

"Keep me posted. I'm an hour away if anything goes critical.

Twenty minutes if it's really bad." She'd co-opt one of the Marine Corps helos if it came to that.

"Okay." And they were gone.

"What's up?" Clark asked.

She pretended that she hadn't heard him as Steinfeld came back on, then faded out before her mix slipped into Lady Gaga's declaration that she was "Born This Way."

Sorry, Clark. I won't be in your bed tonight.

The instant the governors' dinner was over, she would be driving back into DC, even if the cyber twins hadn't discovered anything else. It was a relief to know she'd be sleeping alone tonight. She didn't mind Clark, but it was nice to have a break every now and then.

13

THE SAUNA IN CAMP DAVID'S GYM WAS JUST BIG ENOUGH TO DO what Clark wanted. It had become part of their routine when they were here, as the Vice President's house didn't have a sauna.

Clark was there first, of course.

He said it didn't matter, but she always took a quick shower to knock off the workout sweat. "Always smell clean for your man." The rule from whatever ridiculous preteen mag she'd read forever ago had served her well.

His workouts were never hard enough anymore to make him really sweat, so she didn't mind that he didn't shower. His few extra minutes in the heat sweated his body clean enough.

She entered the sauna and shook out her hair. Clark's guards wouldn't follow him in here. In fact, it was one of the few times she found them useful, making sure that they wouldn't be interrupted.

The heat scorched her; Clark liked it ridiculously hot. Probably all those years he was running undercover in the Middle East. And he definitely enjoyed the slickness of the salty sweat that was already springing to her skin.

She tossed two scoops of cold water onto the heater's hot rocks using the big wooden ladle. It flashed into a searing steam that left them both gasping for a moment. Once they could breathe normally, he pushed to his feet. She felt more sweat forming.

"How did I get so lucky as to marry you?" Clark tugged at the corner of the towel that she'd rolled tight above her breasts. A towel that barely reached past her crotch. The Secret Service agents' consistent indifference was getting annoying.

"Do you want me to tell you?" She kept an arm at her side, trapping the tucked-in end to tease him. Clark smiled as he slid a hand down to her hip.

"Yes," he nuzzled her breast just above the towel's line while his free hand slipped under the towel's lower edge.

"The truth?" she dug her fingers into his hair, knowing how much he liked that.

"Yes," he groaned into her cleavage as she guided him there.

She was half tempted to do precisely that.

Clarissa had *not* started sleeping with him to get promoted to being the youngest CIA department head and finally the youngest CIA director in history. That she was fully capable of doing on her own.

She'd done it to make sure that no one else took advantage of the possibility. He'd been far too vulnerable after his wife's death, so when the opportunity arose, she took him as a lover to block the bitch from the East Asia Desk. As if. Clark liked built, athletic blondes, not narrow-hipped, analyst brunettes—even cutthroat ones.

And she'd—

The hand from below and mouth from above finally freed the towel. She let it slide off one breast but not the other, forcing him to more effort to fully expose her.

—married him because he was the absolute best chance for her own path to the White House. If she was going to fix the world, she needed the Oval Office. She'd start by smearing the Russians and the Chinese right off the face of the planet. It wouldn't even take a war to do it. She had all the plans, just not the power to implement them.

"You got me..." she arched her chest against him because he was definitely a breast man, "...because I couldn't help myself, Clark. I wanted you from the first moment I saw you." At least the second part was true: he was obviously useful. That he'd eventually been trainable to being one of her better lovers was a surprising perk.

"Really?" That stopped him long enough to look her in the face.

She dumped another scoop of water onto the rocks. The flash of steam made the sweat slick on their skin. She knew Clark's weaknesses.

"Really. But you were still married then, so I had to wait."

"Yes. Poor—"

"Shh," she tugged his face back to her breast. "Don't think about her, think about this instead."

"You always take care of me, Clarissa."

"Always, honey." She dumped a final cup of water to steam on the rocks, then lay back on the wooden bench, knowing her body would glisten.

He knelt on the wooden floor and rested his cheek on her stomach. But she could tell he was hesitating. In the early days he'd only been interested in sex, but she'd slowly trained him that this was the time to talk about his day, especially what he'd heard from others.

"Is there a problem with the governors?"

She felt his slight headshake.

"What is it, honey?"

"I was just thinking about a phone call from Sarah."

It took her a moment to remember that Sarah was the new National Security Advisor, not some unknown lover. If she kept herself on a tight leash, then goddamn it, Clark would as well.

He began turning his attention to her body.

"What did she want?"

Clark traced a finger around and around her breast, slowly circling inward as if he was still a teenage boy testing the limits of what he could get away with. It was annoying, but she'd learned that preemptively moving his hand onto her breast broke the moment. She let him have his play.

"Anything interesting?"

"Yes, actually. Roy is considering a realignment of Middle East policy along the lines I've been suggesting."

"That's wonderful news."

He hummed happily, "I thought so, but I wanted your opinion on it. I gave them several basic scenarios, but I thought you and I could work those to make them more serviceable. It's time we stopped being so short-sighted in Southwest Asia."

"Anytime, honey." And if she didn't need the bastard to get her into the White House, she'd break his stupid neck right here!

As he moved his mouth to follow his hands to her chest, she fought to control her rage.

Now it all made sense—a terrible and awful type of sense.

When she'd become the D/CIA last year and studied asset allocation throughout the Middle East, it had no discernable pattern.

Clark had been shifting deep-cover assets for years, the kind that couldn't be replaced quickly, because he was so fucking naive. He only wanted to neutralize America's enemies —as if that was possible—not understanding that they needed to be destroyed!

A decade ago, the big three powers of the region had been in place, so ready to be aligned with the US until—

Had that been partly Clark's doing?

The Arab Spring had been botched in Egypt, breaking the US foothold there.

He latched his mouth on her like a suckling child trying to drain her life energy.

Turkey's "duly elected" dictator had slowly soured on the US to such an extent that the only easy solution at this point would be a nuke up his ass. Maybe not literally, but the asshole really did need that.

Clark slid his hand down between her legs to cup her hard.

The last superpower, at least by fucking lame Middle East standards, were the Saudis.

And Clark wanted to give them up, too!

Clarissa latched her hands on the edges of the wooden bench to keep from clawing at him.

She needed the power.

His desperate need to feed his ego by changing everything that worked.

She needed the Oval Office.

He ravaged her body with his mouth and hands as if he could control her too.

She drove against him to prove her power to defy him.

"God, Clarissa! You're incredible!" He gasped it out, then redoubled his efforts.

If her release could destroy him, let it!

It blasted through her as powerfully as the time she'd first understood that Clark Winston was her path to true power—to the White House—while she'd fucked him in the D/CIA's chair.

She had to remember that she needed him.

Clarissa curled up her body so that Clark would think he'd overwhelmed her and wouldn't try for intercourse as well. It wasn't hard to fake; he'd become an exceptionally fine lover.

Not today though. She didn't know if she could keep herself from harming him today.

Tomorrow she'd be calmer. By then she'd have a plan to fix this.

Because Vice President Clark Winston *was* her path to the White House.

But once she was in, his days were definitely numbered.

That completely clarified her path.

First Lady wasn't acceptable.

She had to be Vice President so that she could step in when he had...a brutal heart attack?

Twenty-one months to Inauguration Day.

And when Clark's heart failed, she would have the nation's and Congress' sympathy and could drive through her agenda before they had a clue what hit them.

"I like that smile," Clark kissed her and looked terribly pleased with himself for granting her such intense satiation.

Twenty-one months.

No, nineteen months until Election Day. Once they both won...

14

Taz woke before Jeremy, but the exhaustion still rippled through her as she stayed nestled in his arms. She'd never had a lover who was a cuddler, even in their sleep. It made her want to laugh at the strangeness and laugh again at how good it felt.

She risked opening one eye. The orange glow around the edges of the window curtains said that dawn was fast approaching.

The team house had become a home, of sorts. Ten minutes from the Tacoma office, it overlooked the waterfront at Gig Harbor in southern Puget Sound. Mike and Holly shared one room, she and Jeremy another. Andi had the one that used to be Holly's, and Miranda occasionally stayed on the spare bed.

Not last night. The very second that Andi had landed the helicopter outside the Tacoma hangar, Miranda had raced to the Mooney M20V prop plane and disappeared back to her island as if the Devil was after her ass. She'd been in such a rush that she hadn't even said goodnight to anyone.

Something must have been really pressuring her autism during the investigation at the opera house, though Taz had no idea what. Yet another thing she should have kept track of.

Taz had thought she was ready to lead an investigation team, even through Jeremy, but she wasn't. Never before had she really appreciated what happened on Miranda's team.

Having everyone acting only when asked had exposed just how complex an operation even a simple investigation was.

She'd been run ragged, both mentally and physically, trying to cover all the points that Miranda and the others did through instinct or ingrained practice.

Her boyo had neither of those and was a long, *long* way from running a team on his own. Especially at Miranda's level. The Cessna 208 Caravan in the opera house was trivial compared to her typical specialty in military crashes.

Her boyo?

They'd been lovers ever since her resurrection from the supposedly dead. For three months she'd let herself drift along with him. That's all she typically did in a relationship anyway.

The work *was* fascinating. She'd spent a career striving to get military aircraft built to spec—which she usually managed —and somewhere near budget—which never happened.

Now Miranda had given her a chance to see the million ways aircraft could break and to understand how they worked.

The problem was Taz had no idea how she *herself* worked. Browbeating a defense contractor or humiliating an avaricious flag officer were skills she understood.

But at the opera house crash site, she'd been on the hop all yesterday trying to create cooperation. Trying to build a team— rather than find its weakest link and break it, which had been her typical assignment for General Martinez.

And it nearly *had* broken the weakest link—Vicki Tasia Flores, the Taser, "Taz" Cortez. Changing back to her birth name had altered nothing.

She had no practice being the weakest link. Jeremy's skills were...breathtaking. In hours he'd ferreted out the cause of the Caravan's crash.

She kissed his shoulder and rested her head there without waking him.

The answer hadn't been aboard when he did his inspection, yet he'd found it.

There was nothing wrong with the plane.

The pilot had made no mistake.

Jeremy had found the answer in that nothing *was* wrong. Even while perched destroyed on the opera house grid.

Two of the passengers sitting in the cabin had recorded the crash on their smartphones. Everyone had studied the feed that showed the pilot's action in detail, playing it over and over, trying to interpret his actions.

The only words captured were, "Pull up! Pull up!"

But the pilot's profile showed it wasn't him doing the yelling. In the entire ninety-seven seconds of flight—from Boeing Field, then up and over downtown Seattle—he remained calm and controlled. No obvious problem until the last fifteen seconds.

And until the very last second, he'd been working the problem.

It was the second video that had revealed what that problem was.

The second passenger, seated on the opposite side of the rear cabin, had clearly been panicked. Their camera control was much poorer, swinging chaotically in ways that the plane's motion didn't warrant.

Most of it was a useless blur.

But Jeremy had found three frames, each several seconds apart that, when combined, had explained the crash.

The Cessna 208 Caravan was FAA-certified for one pilot and nine passengers. It had eleven seats. One passenger could either sit in the cabin or in the copilot's seat.

A passenger had sat in the forward seat.

They had carefully tucked their carry-on by their feet and

trapped it to the side with their knee. Just after takeoff, the passenger had pulled it out to retrieve his own camera and then tucked his carry-on back down. In doing so, he'd also snagged its slender strap over the steering column.

The pilot's and copilot's steering wheels were physically linked to move together—exactly the mechanism Jeremy had been inspecting while lying upside-down in the pilot's seat.

But with the strap trapped by the passenger's foot, it had pinned the steering wheel forward.

The frames showed in succession the increasing strain as the passenger became more and more panicked and braced his foot and leg harder and harder against the strap.

A blurred fourth frame revealed the knapsack, floating free, untangled, then flying out the missing windshield as the opera house grid's rope lines had abruptly arrested the airplane's flight after smashing through the tower's side wall.

The pilot's efforts to pull back on the wheel enough to climb safely had been fruitless.

Jeremy had explained, "Once I confirmed the elevators were still functional even after the crash, and I heard no failure of the engine in the two camera-phone recordings, I kept thinking about that crash in Jalalabad, Afghanistan."

"The C-130J Super Hercules on October 2nd, 2015," Miranda had nodded with an "of course" tone.

Mike and Holly had both looked as confused as she was, but Andi had nodded as well.

"I was there at the time. The pilot propped a night-vision goggle case behind the steering wheel to keep the tail section's big elevator flap raised to help the crew to offload his cargo. They departed at night and never saw that the case was still resting there on takeoff. They couldn't push in the wheel to descend."

"Exactly," Jeremy had declared. "The Caravan's pilot

couldn't pull the wheel *out* to level the flight. Yet he'd know that the plane had been fine a minute earlier as he'd just departed the airfield requiring exactly the same action. His front-seat passenger changed that in mid climb-out directly over downtown Seattle with the strap of his knapsack. He killed them both."

It seemed so simple in retrospect, lying here with Jeremy's arm curled around her waist as he snored quietly in her ear.

Yet in order to solve the Caravan crash yesterday, it had taken coordination with hospitals, taxi services who had taken several people home, and getting an airline to delay a departure until they were able to interview the passenger who'd had the raw nerve to want to fly home on a different carrier the same day.

The tasks had been endless. Evidence gathering and tagging. Interview coordination of the flight-line technicians at Boeing Field. Tracking down the plane's service log. The constant hectoring by the Opera House staff about the removal of the plane and granting structural engineers access to assess the damage.

And as much as she'd hated to do it to him, she'd made sure that Jeremy was at least aware of every single step that the team did.

After the day was all done and they'd crawled exhausted back to the team house, she'd been ready to curl up under the covers. But when she came out of the shower, Jeremy had been sitting cross-legged on their bed typing furiously on his laptop.

Together they'd gone over every step of the investigation, creating a spreadsheet guide to future investigations.

If Jeremy was anything, he was tenacious.

And he'd also been tenacious about keeping her at his side these last three months. Not just as lover, but as someone he trusted.

Maybe for now that was enough.

She rested her hand over his bare belly and let herself slide back to sleep.

15

THE NOT-QUITE-YET-AN-ASSOCIATION OF SOUTHERN GOVERNORS'
dinner had been encouraging, and had delayed her departure
until past eleven.

Clarissa had carefully tested the waters about female
candidates—which shouldn't be a goddamn question, but was.

She also led others into conversations about the roles of
couples in government. The governors had run with the topic,
saving her from directly asking about families split across two
offices. Kentucky's husband was a federal judge in the same
state. West Virginia's wife was launching a campaign for the
House of Representatives in two years.

There had also been two divorces over similar issues, one of
the women claiming it was because she'd made the state senate
while her husband had still been a struggling councilman. The
other because his state representative wife had fallen in love
with another woman.

The final tidbit that Clarissa had confirmed was that the
governors of both parties were very favorable to having a
woman on the ticket, if it was the right woman.

She'd ended up chatting with Arkansas' governor at length

about exactly who were the power players within the party. He did try to make himself sound more important than she knew he was, but she could write that off because he was also trying to get up the Second Lady's skirt. As if.

Mr. Arkansas didn't stand a chance. He'd never be repeating Bill Clinton's path into the White House. But while he might not be a power player, he certainly knew who was.

Clarissa had taken a car from Camp David, leaving Clark protesting on the stone walkway under the maples.

An hour later, at midnight, she'd entered the lowest subbasement of the New Headquarters Building on the CIA campus at Langley, Virginia, and spent the rest of the night with the cyber twins, Harry and Heidi.

The primary signal remained uncracked by the supercomputers over at the NSA.

"It feels like Saudi Arabia," Heidi had muttered while hunched over her console. "Why can't I prove that?" And that had *really* pissed her off.

But one thing Heidi had been right about.

The chatter around it was continuing to grow...rapidly.

16

Major Tamatha Jones watched as Vice President Clark Winston saw off the governors shortly after their last breakfast meeting. A green-top Marine Corps MV-22 Osprey would deliver them directly to Dulles International.

HMX-1 was divided into two sections: white side and green side. Both sides focused on executive transport, but no object passed between them. If the white side needed a spare part or a tool, it couldn't just go to green side and take one because security around the white-side Presidential aircraft was too high.

Governors could travel on the helos painted all green.

The President and Vice President exclusively traveled on a White Top helo like her VH-92A Superhawk.

Tamatha sat in her bird close by the Camp David hangar it had been parked for the last three days. The big green-side Osprey had returned to Quantico during the week and only just returned for the governors' departure, but the VIP lift didn't risk leaving the site as long as the Vice President might need emergency transport.

On this fine April morning, while the governors had their

final breakfast and meeting with the Vice President, Tamatha had already been aloft, doing a half-hour flight above Camp David to check all systems and pick up the other escort birds. Now she was once more on the helipad, engines idling at warm, and the rotor blades braked.

Trees towered all around her, towering being relative, of course. Oaks, maples, and ash rose six or seven stories tall here. Back home in Colorado, a Ponderosa pine was just stretching its limbs as it passed fifteen stories headed for twenty.

With the governors safely aboard their Osprey, the Vice President and several of his key advisors strolled over to her Superhawk. She could see that they were in a good mood; of course Vice President Winston usually was. It was one of the pleasures of flying with him. He didn't think much about the crew, not the way the President did, but she could feel the lightness of the mood whenever he was aboard.

Tamatha also noted that his wife wasn't with him, though she'd flown down with them. There was something about that woman that was always...off. She was too studied. Her clothes were always perfect as was her hair.

During her brief inattention, Mathieson had hauled up the stairs and closed the door, but she and Vance were ready by the time he took his seat behind them.

The heavy Osprey was waiting until she was clear and aloft, just another safety precaution. If anything went wrong with the takeoff of the governors' flight, it wouldn't do to have the Vice President in the area.

When Sergeant Mathieson took his seat, she released the rotor brake. Once the blades had begun to spin, she ran the engines up to full RPMs and lifted up and out of the trees. A glance down showed the MV-22 Osprey spinning up its own rotors. To either side, her two decoy Superhawks were even now sliding for a position change. From above, the overwatch gunships were also tracking her.

Just north of Lewiston, Maryland—five minutes into their twenty-minute flight—the much faster Osprey raced past her.

As she let her gaze track its passage, she saw it race above a rising smoke cloud across the route she had planned to follow between Walkersville and north Frederick. She began to veer aside but something about it bothered her.

"Vance?" Her copilot was on the radio to the Flight Center of the White House Military Office.

"They're saying..." he paused as he listened, "...farmer's field on fire."

Before she was even ten degrees into her turn, walls of smoke rose to the right and left of her flight path. "Big fire."

"Damn big."

Big enough that it would be hard to climb over.

Tamatha had been flying at five thousand feet, and the smoke was quickly climbing toward ten thousand. It would be a race to the Superhawk's operational ceiling of fourteen thousand.

She felt an uncomfortable itch between her shoulder blades.

Turning the Superhawk, she looked behind...to see yet another fire flashing to life. They were being boxed in.

17

"Thanks so much for letting me join you this morning, Rose. I hated missing our monthly dinner last night." It had become the one true fixture on Clarissa's social calendar.

Since she'd come back early from Camp David, they were making up for the missed dinner with a Saturday breakfast.

Senator Ramson had been called away, which was only a trivial inconvenience. It wasn't often she and Rose found time for just the two of them. In the luxury of the Presidential Suite's living room, with its fine view of the Lower Senate Park near the Capitol Building, it was definitely a pleasure.

"The Southern governors were not to be denied."

"Nor luxuriating at Camp David," Rose offered a wink.

"It's less fun than you'd think."

"Just try me. I could dine out for a month on the status alone." In addition to being the wife of the Chairman of the Senate Armed Services Committee, Rose was a former Miss Utah. She had matured from merely gorgeous into a great beauty.

She was also the real brains behind the Senator's lengthy career and had made herself one of DC's leading social power brokers. Often called "The First Lady of DC", she'd achieved nearly the status of Pamela Harriman, while staying true to one man. Of course, it was a different and in some ways more puritanical era now than when Harriman had ruled in the seventies after climbing over the backs of three husbands and a notoriously long list of lovers.

"I actually wanted to talk to you about Camp David in a way."

"An invitation?" Rose tapped the shell of her three-minute egg with the side of her spoon without looking up.

"I'm not in the position to offer one—at this time."

Rose smiled, as if to herself, carefully easing away the top of the shell. "Have you decided on a path?"

Clarissa might never have mentioned her plans for the White House directly, but that was part of the joy of speaking with Rose Ramson, she didn't need to. In answer, she simply cut a piece from her own Nova Scotia lox and egg-white omelet.

"You're going to run?"

Clarissa cut and ate a second bite before asking, "Possible?"

Rose hummed noncommittedly as she peppered her egg.

Without Rose's help, it wouldn't be, but Clarissa had an idea about how to guarantee Rose Ramson's support.

She waited until Rose glanced up to judge her pause.

Clarissa reached for her coffee. "Of course, every President needs a good Vice President."

Rose was sharp enough that she only had to blink once before a slow smile stated that *anything* was possible, including getting Clarissa elected on the same ticket as her husband. And once her husband was gone...

"How long?"

For Clark to be gone, opening the Presidency for herself and the Vice Presidency for Rose? Clarissa fiddled with her wedding ring as if impatiently.

"Bad?"

"Politically awkward," Clarissa decided was a better description. "Near-term awkward. There is support for certain policies that aren't..." Clarissa decided to splurge and selected an almond croissant as she searched for the right word, "...becoming."

"Or palatable?" Rose ducked a tiny spoon into the open eggshell.

"Not past election day," she placed a definitive timeline on it.

Rose eyed her speculatively, then offered a Miss Utah smile. She'd helped Clarissa remove the Vice President to put Clark in power. To offer similar assistance so that Rose herself could step in as Clarissa's future Vice President shouldn't bother her in the least.

They ate in a contented silence for a while as they each considered the implications.

"Any specific policy?" Rose asked as if it was mere curiosity.

"Saudi Arabia." Clarissa hadn't meant to lay that on the linen tablecloth like a piece of week-old toast but there it was.

There was the smallest bobble as Rose dipped into her egg once more. She broke off a piece of the shell, which fell into the center of the egg.

"Rose?" Clarissa felt a distinct chill, despite the morning sun now shining in the window.

She didn't look up.

"Rose."

At her continued silence, Clarissa looked around the room. Love seat, sofa, art, all the usual trappings.

Something was missing though.

"Where *is* Senator Hunter Ramson this morning?"

Rose cleared her throat and daubed at her lips with her napkin before finally looking up at her. "I'm not sure."

"Not sure?"

"He slips my leash on occasion. Every once in a great while, he insists on thinking for himself. When he saw this morning's recap on the news coming out of the G-7 meeting, he hurried away. That speech that the President gave last night about rethinking American support alignments in the region shook him up."

Clarissa could feel the blood drain from her face. "I, uh, missed that speech."

"No specifics. Instead he simply talked about putting past partners on notice of review and possibly seeking new partners in the region. I assumed it was simply a political tactic, but Hunter appeared...alarmed."

It was probably a good thing she'd missed the speech. If she'd stayed at Camp David and heard it with Clark, he'd have been immensely pleased at the President using his ideas. Then she'd have been much, much harder pressed to *not* damage his dumb ass.

"Then the President mentioned that he was placing a hold on all foreign arms sales throughout the region and had asked the other members of the G-7 to do the same. They agreed. Unfortunately, Hunter has been working on a particularly massive foreign arms sales package to the Saudis for some time, and it is coming to a Congressional vote soon."

Clarissa sat up, thinking of last night's untraceable chatter.

She swallowed hard to keep down her omelet and coffee.

"You're sure it was Saudi Arabia? Not Egypt or Turkey? Or even Israel?"

Rose merely shook her head.

Clarissa didn't waste time saying goodbye as she bolted from the room, pulling out her phone as she went to call for her car.

18

"SWITCH TO INTERNAL AIR," TAMATHA WASN'T GOING TO RISK THE health and safety of the Vice President.

At her order, Captain Vance Brown closed the external air feed and engaged the internal oxygen generator.

Most helicopters only operated below ten thousand feet and therefore could always use outside air without the pressurization an airliner needed. But this was a White Top and had to be secure against all types of attacks just like the Presidential limousine.

They could pass through the smoke wall in a few seconds, but the smell might bother the passengers.

And this definitely wasn't just a simple farmer's brush fire.

This might be a gas attack.

She slowed and circled once within the boundaries of the smoke-edged box to make sure none of the smoke entered their intake system.

"Anything on the threat detectors?"

"No unaccounted objects in the air. No launch flashes on the ground," Vance was right on it.

The Superhawk's emergency oxygen system was not like the tiny ones that were stowed above every seat section of an airliner, dropping masks in a crisis.

Their oxygen generator was the same kind used in submarines, and even in space, for catastrophic loss of life support systems. Each unit could deliver three thousand liters of safe, clean air sufficient for all twelve passengers and three crew for thirty minutes.

Under normal circumstances, the oxygen generators were loaded with a compound of sodium chlorate, barium peroxide, and potassium perchlorate. The thermal igniter would trigger a chemical reaction as it heated to five hundred degrees Fahrenheit, breaking down the mixture into inert elements and oxygen.

The primary emergency oxygen generator aboard the Vice President's VH-92A Superhawk had been replaced.

Because it was HMX-1, there was a second, fully redundant unit, but it would only be triggered if the first failed.

The first unit didn't fail.

The small percussive ignitor cap of tetrazene explosive to drive the reaction in the primary unit had been replaced by a much hotter thermite trigger. The generator's altered chemical core of methane and ammonia, wrapped in a platinum catalyst shell was ignited by the four-thousand-degree heat source. The chemical reaction produced a cloud of explosive hydrogen and hydrogen cyanide gas.

Major Tamatha Jones' ears popped so hard at the high-pressure injection of the gas into the helicopter's closed environment, that her vision briefly tunneled from the pain alone.

When she recovered, she was panting.

Too little air.

"Did you...start O2...generator?"

Vance's skin had gone pasty, as if his deep color was being leached out of him. He nodded once, but didn't speak.

Unknown to Major Jones, the farmer's smoky fire was simply a fire meant to elicit a response.

And she had responded.

19

THE TWO DECOY HELOS AND THE OVERWATCH BIRDS, WITH NO VIP passengers to worry about, merely cut the air intakes as they flew through the smoke wall, then reopened them in clear air.

Aboard Marine Two, the only bird to have remained at Camp David the whole time, the tampered oxygen generator flooded the cabin with colorless hydrogen cyanide gas. Major Jones was among the twenty percent of the population unable to detect its bitter almond odor.

Once absorbed by the body, HCN halted the helicopter occupants' cellular respiration by blocking their mitochondria's ability to create a key enzyme.

Twenty-eight seconds after Captain Vance Brown initiated the oxygen generator, Major Tamatha Jones' cells were already dying by the billions.

She managed to pull out the pilot's emergency oxygen mask.

It was linked to a compressed air bottle, uncontaminated with cyanide. The air inside the helicopter was no longer killing her. Deep gasps allowed her head to clear enough to become marginally aware of the helicopter again.

It would take time for the oxygen to purge the poison sufficiently for her to fully regain her cognitive function.

However, time was definitely lacking.

Her hands once more on the controls, she plowed through the smoke wall and into the clear.

This was good. She could fly straight and everything would be fine.

Somewhere, a voice was calling to her.

She turned to Vance.

Not him.

He was having spastic seizures.

His flailing batted their shared joystick cyclic control so hard that it slapped it out of her numbing fingers.

It took all of her concentration, blinking hard, to relocate the cyclic and then convince her hand to move to it and reengage.

"Marine Two! Marine Two!" The radio. Someone shouting into her ears.

She'd lost the cyclic again.

By the second time she'd found it, the horizon was all wrong—it sliced perpendicularly across her screen. That couldn't be right, could it?

She concentrated on her hands.

There was a microphone switch somewhere.

Her body knew it, even if she no longer did.

A distinctive click told a part of her failing brain that it was her turn to speak.

Right.

"Poison. Oxy. Generator."

She looked over at Vance as he slumped in his seat. His mouth hung open; his eyes wide.

Major Jones' instincts had managed to right the helo, but it was well past it's never-exceed speed and would begin breaking apart if it survived another fifteen seconds.

It wouldn't.

The buffeting of Major Tamatha Jones' debilitated attempts to pull out of the dive caused Captain Vance Brown to collapse forward, with his chest pinning the cyclic in place.

Major Jones could no longer move her joined control.

It didn't matter, she couldn't remember what to do with them.

"Dying," she said more to herself than the radio.

She looked out her windscreen and saw that she was about to do exactly that.

Or maybe she'd said, "Buying?" Which was also appropriate based on the sign across the front of the building they were about to impact.

It didn't matter.

She guessed that she was the last person alive on the Marine Two VH-92A Superhawk. Was Marine Two still the proper call sign if the Vice President was indeed already dead?

It was the last relevant thought she had—ever.

20

HMX-1'S PERFECT SEVENTY-FOUR-YEAR SAFETY RECORD ENDED seven seconds later.

Dead level and flying at two hundred and thirty-seven miles per hour, twenty-six-thousand pounds of helicopter flew into the Frederick, Maryland, Walmart Supercenter's front entrance.

If the helicopter had flown a single foot lower, it might have averted the disaster that unfolded.

By less than three inches, the Superhawk cleared the three-foot-high concrete bollards lined across the entrance to keep a truck from driving into the entrance as part of a burglary attempt.

The VH-92A Superhawk blew through the glass doors, its fifty-six-foot-diameter, four-blade rotor killing twenty-seven people at the checkout kiosks and another nine at the Subway sandwich deli to the side as the blades shattered.

It plowed through women's clothing first, then men's. It missed the toy section, but slammed through the paint section and gardening supplies.

By then the bulk of its momentum had been spent.

The last of it was sufficient for the Superhawk to breach the wall between the front and back of the store. Spinning end-for-end as it caromed off thirty-five pallets of canned soup, the VH-92A ultimately came to rest back-end first against fifty cases of Ben & Jerry's ice cream inside the store's largest walk-in freezer.

Captain Vance Brown had been atypically susceptible to cyanide gas poisoning and had been the only one to die before the Superhawk finally came to rest. The passengers in the helicopter had survived. If they were given emergency pure oxygen in the next three minutes, they would all recover—with varying degrees of debilitation.

The clean air that Major Tamatha Jones had been breathing had cleared enough of the poison from her system that she blearily opened her eyes and stared at a pallet of Marie Callender's frozen Cherry Crunch Pies.

Thanksgiving! Mom always bought those for the holiday. She looked around for her mom.

It was her final thought of any kind.

Her remaining lifespan was most accurately measured in milliseconds.

The superheated oxygen generator provided the ignition source for the excess hydrogen from the ammonia-methane reaction. For every molecule of hydrogen cyanide generated, there were also six molecules of hydrogen as a waste byproduct.

Much like the famous *Hindenburg* disaster, the hydrogen burned in a single fireball, expanding rapidly. The initial shockwave traveled through the length of the six-meter-long cabin in the first one-point-five milliseconds.

The up-armored Superhawk was stout enough that the pressure inside the cabin increased a hundredfold in the next fourteen-thousandths of a second. All of the occupants' lungs collapsed from the onslaught.

It didn't matter, as they were burned past saving in the same time span.

At twenty-three milliseconds, the windscreens in front of

the two pilots blew outward—fired like acrylic mortars back into the store along their damage path.

The fire shot out like twin dragons' flames, igniting everything in its path.

Jet-A fuel—that had been spilling out in a long trail since a pair of cash registers had punctured one of the tanks—fired off in a blast so near instantaneous that no one had time to shout in alarm.

Because of the Walmart Supercenter's lack of windows, the overpressure of this second-stage explosion was mostly contained within the building.

In the next eight-tenths of second, a third of the store's occupants had died and the remainder suffered burst eardrums. There was only one avenue of release for the expanding pressure wave. A stream of flame shot several hundred feet out the shattered front entrance like a flamethrower, incinerating most of the people and cars in its path.

That only released the overpressure of the secondary blast.

The thermite, burning forty-five hundred degrees hotter than a normal oxygen generator, finally melted free. Because of the angle at which the helicopter had come to rest, the still blazing thermite burned through the side of the hull and dribbled onto the second side sponson fuel tank, melting a large hole.

Because the fuel was still in a liquid state, it didn't burst into flame. Instead, the thermite, still burning, passed through the fuel, then spread and burned a larger hole in the bottom of the tank, releasing an additional three-hundred-and-eighty-three gallons of jet fuel into the store—enough to fill nine bathtubs ("Do It Yourself" section by Auto Care) to the rim.

This fresh supply of highly flammable kerosene-based Jet A fuel flowed back along the helicopter's damage path, flooding the garden center in a low tsunami.

It had just reached the store's supplies of fertilizer when it ignited.

The third—and final—shock wave, erupting from the improvised fuel-and-fertilizer bomb, was many times more powerful than both of the first two explosions combined.

The entire roof lifted several feet as the side walls were blown outward in a cloud of concrete-block shrapnel. The roof then collapsed to cover the whole store in twisted steel girders and metal roofing.

There were no survivors inside the store.

Outside, over eighty percent of the people in the parking lot were dead—*before* the wall of flame swept across the vast expanse of cars.

The closest survivors of the blast were in a car at the outdoor line of a Starbuck's takeout window five hundred and ten feet away. The rear of Hank and Margo Keller's car—the trunk filled with their crib, stroller, and boy-blue paint and rollers from Walmart—faced the explosion. The rear windshield had shattered but, as their seatback headrests had limited the shrapnel's carnage, they would live another six minutes. They died an hour and nine minutes before the search-and-rescue teams located them.

The nearest unscathed survivors were the crews of the two decoy VH-92A Superhawks, hovering at seven hundred feet over the crater where moments before there had been a sale on pot-bound begonias and bags of weedkiller for that truly beautiful lawn.

21

DRAKE HAD ALWAYS BEEN AMUSED THAT THE MOST IMPORTANT meetings took place in the most unlikely settings. All yesterday had been packed with large meeting venues able to accommodate the members of the Group of Seven along with their legions of advisors and support staff. His own, military leader-to-military leader meetings had seemed little smaller.

Canada was hosting them in the magnificent Empress hotel —deservedly rated top twenty-one iconic hotels by National Geographic—perched on the waterfront of Victoria Harbor. For over a century, in a city not yet two centuries old, it had dominated the waterfront with luxury and British-style high teas. Even with the G-7 in attendance, the vast three-story lobby had hummed along with a quiet dignity. He'd have to keep this in mind for his and Lizzy's second anniversary.

With France, Germany, Italy, Japan, the UK, the US, and the EU in attendance, sixty percent of the world's wealth sat around the room during the main meetings.

And as far as he could tell, despite all of those trappings, nothing of any real import had been achieved beyond the President's speech on the Middle East situation.

The crux meeting had started as a quiet moment at the back table in the Empress' library over a post-breakfast coffee. President Cole, he, and Sarah had gathered to talk strategy for the rest of the day's meetings. The UK Prime Minister and the German Chancellor had each dropped by for a word, joining them with suspiciously little coaxing.

They'd both waved off their entourages, but before President Cole could wave himself and Sarah off to the side, the questions had begun.

NATO strategies against aggressor nations like Russia and Turkey. The next trade agreements they were each considering. And most importantly, the security agreements that might come with those trade agreements.

Sarah was sharp enough to pick up on a tiny nod from President Cole. She broached the topic of Saudi Arabia as an aside. What had been treated as a mere "interesting idea" among world leaders until that moment became an intensely serious discussion.

Would the US actually be willing to withdraw support from the wild card kingdom? And what would be the side effects across the region? While the UK and Germany were still dependent on Saudi oil, and very aware of the kingdom's position along the Red Sea that could block the Suez trade route, they too had clearly thought hard about ending any favorable relations.

The consensus was that the kingdom was a tangled mess that everyone wanted out of—if the US could be counted on to lead a way.

Drake had been seated with his back to the corner—old 75th Rangers' habit. To his left, he'd had a view of the harbor with its seaplanes and sailboats, but mostly he was well positioned to admire the high-vaulted room. It barely had enough books to be called a library, but it had stately, comfortable seating and more than enough elegance to fully compensate for the lack.

It also let him see Agent Rick Danziger hurrying in their direction.

The head of the Presidential Protection Detail never hurried unless—

"Excuse me, Mr. President. We need to get you to a secure location immediately."

"More secure than this?"

Other members of the PPD, who had been discreetly in the background, now gathered and lined up as a blockade to the outside view. They weren't facing the President; they were searching through the glass for any possible threats.

"Yes sir. Right now."

Roy Cole rose to his feet and buttoned his jacket. "Any threat to my fellow leaders?" he nodded toward the prime minister and the chancellor.

"We...I'm sorry...we don't know. Vice President Clark Winston's helicopter went down between Camp David and Washington, DC. Foul play is suspected."

"How is Clark—"

At Danziger's grim look, he bit off the question.

"Morris. Helga." They'd both pushed to their feet as their own security teams moved closer. He shook each of their hands. "If you'll excuse me."

Drake grabbed Sarah's arm and got her moving.

"What?"

"When the Secret Service is on the move, two steps behind can get you left in Kansas."

"Sorry, I'm the *National* Security Advisor; it's my first *personal* security crisis."

"Wish I could say the same." He'd been in the White House for three separate "crashes" as they called a full security clampdown. Once it had included a trip to the PEOC bunker—

Presidential Emergency Operations Center—at closer to a run than a jog.

They were rushed at a brisk walk through a service door in the northeast corner of the library and down a narrow set of stairs. The agents moved as if they'd traveled this way many times before, which perhaps they had in practice.

At the bottom was a hallway several times warmer than the perfectly air-conditioned rooms above. It smelled of the moist heat of a laundry, the cooking of a variety of cuisines that didn't mesh terribly well in the thick air, and a lot of human sweat.

Halfway to the garage, Danziger signaled a halt and the Secret Service grouped so tightly around them that he couldn't help rubbing shoulders with the President.

"Shit," Danziger muttered, then called over his radio, "Confirm that." After a long pause he swore again.

"Not exactly what I want to be hearing from the head of your protection detail, Mr. President," Sarah was keeping her sense of humor, even if her voice cracked against a throat gone dry.

"Me either," the President's voice was grim. "What's the problem, Rick?"

Danziger held up a hand for silence, finally responding to his radio before turning to address them.

"We have a problem, Mr. President. The Marine Two pilot managed a brief transmission prior to going down. It seems that she—"

"Major Tamatha Jones. God *damn* it!" The President looked beyond pissed and well into soldier-furious.

Drake liked the President a great deal, but this side of him was something Drake appreciated down to the core of his being. The President cared about nothing more than his team —once a soldier, always a soldier.

Sarah looked puzzled. She might be smart as hell, but she'd

never served and wouldn't—couldn't—ever understand how important a team was to a soldier.

"She had to engage the emergency oxygen generation system due to smoke from a suspicious fire. It is possible that the system had been tampered with and released a poison that killed everyone aboard."

"You still haven't told me the problem." He spoke with a snap of command.

"The problem, Mr. President, is that particular emergency air system isn't just on the HMX-1 helos. We use the same systems aboard the Beast limousine and Air Force One. Marine Two's engagement of their system apparently killed them. I can't take the same risk with you until we've pulled and vetted all of the systems."

"Then don't use the emergency air systems."

"And if they attack with gas, we'll have to. Right now I don't have any vehicles I can trust. You're at a known location with a possible terrorist attack against our highest levels of government."

There was a grim silence broken only by the rattling wheel on a laundry cart that someone was hustling along the far end of the hallway.

Danziger held his wrist up to his mouth again and keyed his radio. "Come on people, work the problem. I need safe transport in sixty seconds."

All in all, Drake would much rather still be sitting upstairs in the library, enjoying the view out the window of—

He turned to Danziger and couldn't help smiling. "Is it okay if I find a solution before sixty seconds is up?"

Sarah gave an exasperated laugh of confusion.

Danziger's look said it had better be damned good.

President Cole only blinked once before he smiled.

Pretty quick for a former Green Beret.

22

"THIS IS YOUR GRAND PLAN?" SARAH TEASED HIM WHEN HE explained it.

Danziger had looked thoughtful for approximately five seconds, then he'd gotten them all on the move.

"In a small way."

They proceeded to the lobby gift shop and bought a variety of ball caps and jackets—the Empress was not the sort of place that sold hoodies. It was warm enough to go without jackets, but the Secret Service had to cover their shoulder harnesses. Their suit jackets were given to housekeeping to include in their respective luggage whenever it was able to catch up with them, and replaced with tweeds and woolens from the Empress.

The worst problem was the briefcase with the nuclear football. The colonel responsible for keeping it close to the President finally stuffed it in a plastic shopping bag that was suspiciously large and heavy, but that couldn't be helped.

Then Danziger led them out the front door of the Empress and straight down to the seaside quay. They gathered at the end of a floating pier where the next step would plunge them into Victoria Harbor.

"Small, but in a fun way," Drake joked.

"You have a strange idea of fun."

"All work and no play makes Sarah a dull girl. My Lizzy taught me that."

"That I'm dull?" Sarah shot right back.

"No, you're doing that on your own," he did his best to deliver that with a straight face. "It took the head of the National Reconnaissance Office to teach me how to have fun."

"Is that why you married her?"

"Only one of many reasons."

"Lucky bastard," Sarah muttered at him. He figured this wasn't the best time to point out that she had lousy taste in men. Her file spoke to two ex-husbands, both complete jerks.

At the end of the pier, a pocket-sized boat bobbed on the six-inch waves being kicked up by the spring breeze sweeping across the harbor. The boat looked like a miniature, double-ended tug. It was perhaps twenty feet long with U-shaped bench seats fore and aft under a low roof. In the middle, a taller glassed-in box had a steering wheel and a raised seat so that the pilot could look above everyone's heads in any direction.

There were twenty or so of these perky boats working the harbor waterfront. Some were painted in yellow with a black-and-white checkerboard stripe and a sign that declared "Water Taxi." The one in front of them was painted a bright green and said "Tour Boat" in equally friendly lettering.

"All aboard."

They clambered onto the boat.

"My aren't you a cheery lot! Welcome aboard my pickle boat." The driver sounded happily Canadian. "Where are you all from?"

"Colorado," the President spoke quickly, then looped a casual arm across Sarah's shoulders.

"Maryland," Drake spoke up, cutting off Sarah before she could react.

"That's a bit spread out. What brought you folks together?"

Danziger and the four others looked far too clearly military, even if they'd tucked away their earpieces. As he probably did too, Drake made a riff of it.

"We were in the Air Force together. The colonel here figured a reunion in Victoria sounded like fun. Ten years out and all. Good chance to meet his new lady while we were at it."

Sarah blushed. Or maybe flushed was the right word. Flushed with the heat of her I'm-going-to-kill-you-for-this look.

"Christ, are we that old?" Roy played along, squeezing an arm around Sarah's shoulders.

"You are, sir. Not the rest of us." Drake was actually a year older than he was. He threw in a teasing salute that made the boat's pilot laugh.

"And where would you folks like to go this afternoon?"

Drake smiled. "When's the next ballet?"

23

THERE WAS ONE RINGTONE ON MIRANDA'S PHONE THAT NEVER failed to wake her. She looked at the clock, ten a.m. She'd slept less than an hour of the last twenty-seven.

It was only as Jeremy and Taz continued to run the Caravan investigation without any significant help on her part that the problem struck home.

If Jeremy was ready to *lead* a team, then he'd no longer be on *her* team. The thought was almost too much to bear. Just when she thought everything was stable, it all changed again.

She *hated* change.

After she'd flown back to her island last night, she hadn't been able to rest. It had been maddening to do so little on the Caravan crash investigation. She'd barely avoided a meltdown by racing back to her island last evening.

She'd caught up with the garden, which had wanted a serious weeding, in the fading darkness—finally finishing by the light of a headlamp. Late April was not a convenient time to be so busy with crash investigations. It was as if all of the private pilots had forgotten how to fly over the winter and were going down faster than she'd ever seen before.

The automatic watering system hooked up to the rainwater catchment barrels had made the garden bountiful in the growth of winter vegetables, flowers—and weeds.

The vegetables that were past recovery she placed in feeders outside the garden fence for the island's wild sheep and deer. She'd taken several vases of tulips and rhododendron flowers into the house, which were very colorful.

When she was done with that, she'd cleaned the whole house but still been unable to settle.

Catching up on the NTSB crash reports had left her too wound up to sleep.

So she'd pulled out her current set of small notebooks.

Three of them were related to fully resolved crashes, and she filed them on the bookcase.

Her personal notebook had any number of questions, but she was on the island and had no one to discuss them with. Normally she was never happier than when she was alone in the grand house that her parents had left her, yet there *was* a... gap. She'd come to enjoy visitors. She could see Mike fussing in the kitchen. Holly teasing Jeremy and Taz teasing her right back on Jeremy's behalf. The quiet presence of Andi...

As much as she needed to be away from them all, she still missed them.

She made a note to think more about that.

Finally, still unable to relax even enough to go to bed, she pulled out her favorite. The leather was worn and battered with use. It was the tenth in a long-running series. The first had been started at the age of seven when her father brought home the quarter-sized version of a brand-new sculpture erected in the CIA Headquarters courtyard.

She could barely remember a time when the enigma of the bronze *Kryptos* hadn't stood in their garden.

Year after year, notebook after notebook had been filled with their shared attempts to crack the codes that the artist had embedded in the sculpture. Three of the four panels had been solved by NSA and CIA cryptanalysts, but the fourth remained a challenge.

She rubbed her fingers over the gold-embossed leather she'd ordered, then began flipping through the pages, hoping for a new insight among the old notes—something she'd missed from the last hundred times she'd done this.

Miranda had only reached page nine before she'd passed out.

And now her phone was winding up with the escalating sound of a C-5 Galaxy's massive turbine engine.

It was at well over eighty-percent rpm by the time she woke enough to fumble the phone out of her pocket.

"Miranda Chase. This is actually her, not a recording."

No laugh from Jill at NTSB headquarters. Miranda didn't need to consult her personal notebook to know that was unwelcome news.

"Jill?"

"I'm sorry, Miranda. We have a really bad one. The..." Jill cleared her throat several times.

"Are you okay, Jill? Do you have a cough? I suck on honey candy when I have that problem." Yes, that seemed like a helpful suggestion for someone who was sick.

"No. It's not that."

Miranda sighed. She thought she'd gotten that rule figured out, apparently not. She reached out to adjust the vase of pink rhodies next to her office chair. She'd fallen asleep with her head on her desk. Perhaps it was just as well that Jill had woken her after only an hour or she would have become very sore, especially after all of the garden work.

"The..." one more unexplained throat clearing, "...Vice President's helicopter has crashed."

"Was he aboard it at the time?"

"No, Miranda. He was on the fucking space shuttle at the time!"

"That seems unlikely. The last space shuttle was retired in—"

"Yes, of course he was aboard, Miranda. That's why it's called the Vice President's helicopter."

"Semantically, that still leaves an open question of—"

"Miranda!" Jill shouted. Jill never shouted. "The Vice President is dead. Along with several hundred civilians. He crashed into a Walmart store."

Miranda wanted to ask why he'd done that, but remembered in time that "why" was her job to solve, not Jill's.

"They're calling in all of the top investigators. You're needed in Frederick, Maryland, as fast as you can get here."

"Okay. Should I bring my team?"

Jill sputtered for several seconds before answering. "It's a crash investigation, Miranda."

"I understand that. But you only said that I needed to be there."

Jill took a deep breath, then let it out very slowly, which told Miranda nothing new.

"Miranda," Jill spoke very slowly and carefully, which Miranda always appreciated. "There has been a major crash. The Vice President of the United States died when his HMX-1 helicopter crashed into a Walmart in Frederick, Maryland. This is a team launch call."

"*Team* launch. Thank you, Jill. Thank you for being clear. We'll be there as soon as possible."

"O-kay. Bye." Jill called upon a divinity as she hung up. It was hard to be sure why.

24

CLARISSA IGNORED THE PHONE THREE TIMES, BUT THE SAME secure number kept calling back. She didn't have time for whatever their problem was.

She'd rushed from the George Hotel back to the CIA...for nothing.

Almost nothing.

Knowing that it involved Saudi Arabia hadn't helped them unravel where the attack might be targeted. The fact that it might include Senator Hunter Ramson and his connections with foreign arms sales had added no illumination whatsoever.

However, the cyber twins had picked apart one piece of the chatter.

Burn the fields. A text between cell phones twenty minutes ago allowed them to pin down a possible location a mere forty miles northwest of DC.

She'd wanted to dismiss it, as there was nothing on the ground there but the outermost edge of DC bedroom communities. But it had the earmarks of the chatter they'd been chasing all night and into the morning.

Maybe someone was going to fire off a nuke there.

But forty miles northwest of the city? No military bases, no intelligence groups, just suburbia.

Camp David was over sixty—

She grabbed the phone.

"Clarissa Reese here. What happened?"

"Ms. Reese," she didn't recognize the voice, "This is General William Hampton at the White House Military Office. I regret to inform you that there's been an accident."

"Where and how bad?"

Her ears started buzzing after his next two words...

"Vice President Clark Winston's helicopter went down at..."

After that, she only picked up a word here and there. In fact, she was staring at the disconnected phone and realized that the only other words she'd heard were, *No survivors.*

"Frederick, Maryland," she told the cyber twins. Apparently she *had* heard more. "Helicopter down."

There was a harsh rapid-fire blast of computer keys that made her twitch. Then they both froze, turning slowly to face her.

She could see *Breaking News* flashing on the screen behind Harry: *Maryland WalMrat Bombed.* First she saw the typo, then she felt the gut-blast of the words.

Over Heidi's shoulder, a shaky smartphone video was cycling—of a White Top helicopter falling out of the sky, then a massive fireball.

Harry looked grim.

Heidi looked surprisingly sympathetic, not her usual mode at all.

"Maybe he wasn't...?" Harry didn't finish the question.

Heidi looked down at the phone clenched in Clarissa's fingers, then back at her face. "He was," she said it softly.

He was.

Such simple words.

But they didn't make any sense.

"He can't be..." Clarissa whispered to herself.

"I'm so sorry, Clarissa," Heidi was solicitousness herself. As if she and the cyber twins didn't get along only because they had to—they both had career-ending information stashed away about each other.

"He *can't* be!" Clarissa shoved to her feet.

"Maybe there's been a mistake?" Harry turned back to his keyboard just as his screen changed from *Maryland WalMrat Bombed!* to *Presidential helicopter crashes at Wal-Rat.* She watched it for ten long seconds before the last was corrected to *Wal-tart,* then *Walt-art,* and finally *Walmart.*

Then they changed *Presidential* to *Vice Presidential.*

Why did their titler have all the panic when all she felt was numb?

It was still wrong.

President Cole was at the G-7 meeting in Victoria, BC. If he was the dead one, she'd be a shoo-in, helping Clark swear in this very morning. But Cole was still probably all hale and hearty in his cozy luxury hotel meetings.

Clark *couldn't* be dead.

She wanted to rage at the cyber twins for not solving the threat before it happened.

Wanted to tear them apart limb from limb.

Or Ramson. She could string him up by the balls if he'd had part of cutting off her shot at the—

But what if Clark hadn't died in vain?

Was this disaster...or opportunity?

"Find him for me."

"Your husband? But we already know—" Harry waved at the screen behind him.

"Not him. Get me—" then she became aware again of the

phone in her hand. As Director of the CIA, she had the President's direct number.

She dialed and then listened to the ring.

The President who needed a *new* Vice President.

It kept ringing.

25

"I DON'T HAVE TIME FOR THIS." THE PRESIDENT HANDED OVER HIS ringing phone.

Drake glanced at the screen, grimaced, then answered.

"Hello, Clarissa. Drake Nason here. I'm so sorry to hear about Clark." He kept his voice low enough that the boat driver wouldn't be able to hear.

"Is the President safe?"

"Yes, President Cole is fine and currently en route to a secure location."

"Good. Good. We, uh, had chatter about a threat. Regrettably, neither the NSA nor my people were able to decrypt it in time. Moments before the crash, there was a transmission about 'burning the fields' but that's all we have so far. Please let me know if the President needs anything."

"Will do. Again, my condolences."

"Uh, thanks."

He hung up the phone and handed it back to the President. "Christ, that is one cold woman."

The President tucked away his phone. "Too bad she's so damn good at her job. Not to speak ill of a dead man, but she's significantly better as director than Clark ever was. So, Drake, what's this secure location?"

"Well, this is pretty secure," he waved out at Victoria Harbor.

"Pretty, yes. Secure?"

"Last place they'd be looking for you, sir."

"I'll grant you that."

Their pickle boat was bobbing its way clockwise around the harbor at no better than a jog. The driver wore a headset with a microphone and was describing the sights over small speakers mounted in the overhead. They weren't too loud, just making him easy to hear—which was very un-American but charmingly Canadian.

"You folks are in for a real treat. Ex-American Air Force, you said. Then this will be like old home week. The Yanks' President has his whirly birds parked just around the corner here. They're quite the sight. I can get you close enough to shore for a photo, something you can't do on land because of security. They're right pretty, even if the colors you chaps picked are so drab."

President Cole grimaced.

It was strange to see the HMX-1 helicopters sitting there so close and not daring to use them. They watched in silence as the boat chugged past them.

"Selfie time, gentlemen and lady," the boat driver dropped them to idle, twisting the boat so that the helos were in the background. The pilot was finding something terribly funny about it as he herded them together and took a snapshot with Drake's phone.

Drake wasn't finding a lot to laugh about. But when the pilot handed back his phone, he had to admit it was a good shot despite the grim reason for them being here. The protection detail huddled close about the President and his "girlfriend", the Chairman of the Joint Chiefs, and the colonel who refused to be separated from his shopping-bag-encased nuclear football.

Beyond this point, the harbor opened out onto the rough Strait of Juan de Fuca, which opened onto the Pacific, so they circled once more toward the inner harbor.

Exactly as Drake had hoped, the ballet had begun. Eight of the fleet of tiny water taxis and tour boats had gathered in a group and begun an intricate dance on the water. First, they circled in one direction with a boat in the center spinning in the other. Then they broke into two spinning hoops.

This ballet of boats also attracted every eye around the harbor.

He stood up next to the driver, "Could you swing wide of them and run us over to the Harbour Air dock?"

"But we've only just started the tour," the man eyed him carefully.

"We need to catch a plane."

"It was just a three-minute stroll from the hotel to the dock," but he was already turning the boat.

"We prefer being unobtrusive."

Then the driver smiled and winked, "Thought you could pull one over on me, did you? Ex-Air Force not complaining when I called a Marine Corps helicopter one of your birds. Not likely. You chaps are up to something. No need to worry." He rubbed a finger alongside his nose like a cliché secret agent signal, "Mum's the word."

Drake squeezed his shoulder as they pulled up to the dock, and made sure to tip him well.

Harbour Air flew seaplanes from a waterfront dock. They were constantly buzzing across the surface, picking a new water runway each time between the water taxis and sailboats.

At the dock, Danziger did a lousy job of looking casual as he hurried to the flight-tour office.

"This is actually very slick, Drake," Sarah whispered to him as they waited on the floating pier.

Drake considered a teasing reply, but couldn't find the heart for it. He'd liked Clark. And until the President was secure, he'd rather be leading a squad of heavily armed Rangers than idly waiting on a Canadian dock. His ruse had worked so far, but for how much longer?

Danziger returned with a pilot in tow.

"I understand that we have a short tour. I have a flight in an hour," the pilot sounded cautious as he inspected them.

"A half hour should be plenty for what we want to see," Drake assured him.

"Are all you Yanks crazy? Sorry, shouldn't have said that," the pilot offered a smile of apology.

"Certifiable," Sarah assured him, earning her a half laugh.

It wasn't until they were aloft and Drake revealed where he wanted to land that the trouble began.

"I can't take you there. There's no bloody customs inspector."

Drake sighed. He'd been traveling military for so long that he'd forgotten about that wrinkle. He certainly didn't want to land at some customs dock and cool the President's heels for an hour out in public.

Thankfully Danziger knew how to handle that.

He was on the phone for less than sixty seconds before their flight was cleared from Canada into the US.

26

MIRANDA NEARLY BOBBLED THE CLIMB OUT IN HER F-86 SABREJET.

She'd called the team to prepare the Cessna M2 jet that she'd left in the Tacoma office's hangar. Then she'd been delayed by one of the island's sheep that had decided this morning was the perfect time to have a birth directly in front of her island's airplane hangar door. She'd managed to coax it to behind the hangar, but hadn't been able to stay for the actual birth.

As soon as she was aloft and about to light the afterburner, she spotted a de Havilland DHC-3 Otter seaplane idling up to her dock at the south end of the island.

She circled as she climbed and called over the Unicom frequency that all planes used around uncontrolled airports. "Calling DHC-3 Otter at Spieden Island."

"Otter here."

"You are not cleared to dock at Spieden Island. This property is privately held. There are clear No Docking signs at the dock."

"I'm told—" there was a painfully loud rattle of someone grabbing a headset with a live microphone.

"Just let me talk to her. Are you there, Miranda?"

"I will need to define 'there' before I can determine if that's where I am."

"You *are* there. Here. That's good."

"I'm also unclear about 'here' as well. If you are inferring that I'm still on my private island, I'm not." Below she saw the Otter continue up to her private dock.

"If you're not on your island, where are you?"

She checked her instruments and gasped. Untended, her circling climb had crossed her over ten thousand feet. She was breaking FAA regulations to be flying above ten thousand feet without supplemental oxygen.

Holding her breath, she dove the Sabrejet until she was once more below ten thousand.

"Where are you, Miranda?"

"Just crossing ten thousand feet."

"Good. I need to talk to you."

"I'm leaving, not arriving. I have a launch call."

"This is more important."

And that's when she recognized the voice. She would have done so sooner, but she hadn't expected General Drake Nason to be aboard an Otter seaplane. He'd certainly never been to the island before.

Perhaps she should have asked who it was earlier. She kept forgetting about such niceties that others seemed to find so effortless in conversations. She'd have to remember to create a special ringtone for him.

"I don't know," she radioed down to Drake. "It seemed that this call was quite important."

"Trust me."

Miranda did, so she circled back down to the long narrow strip of land at the western edge of the San Juan Islands.

As she did, she could see people climb out of the plane and step onto her dock. Seven, eight people. While she was lining up to land on the grass runway, hoping that the mother and newborn lamb wouldn't be overly disturbed by her return, the seaplane headed aloft.

Her grass runway had been right at the limits of what her F-86 could manage for a safe takeoff. To land, she needed just two-thirds the length, but she didn't land cleanly.

Just as she began the final flare, she remembered that she had no vehicle on the island capable of transporting eight people from the dock to the house. The island's golf cart could only manage six including herself.

She actually bounced several feet back into the air before sticking the landing.

27

THE PROBLEM WAS SOLVED BY THE TIME SHE HAD RETURNED HER plane to her midfield hangar, checked on the ewe and lamb (both were fine), and raced the golf cart down toward the dock.

She met Drake and his companions close by her house, which lay halfway in between. They'd used the simple expedient of walking.

"Hello, Drake. I'm sorry that I didn't think to suggest walking. I was worried about everyone not fitting comfortably in the golf cart. Perhaps it's because there are so many modes of transportation available now: Mooney prop plane, my Sabrejet and Cessna M2, this golf cart, the yard tractor, my backhoe, and a boat. I think purchasing the helicopter may have been what overwhelmed me; I'm not yet adapted to thinking about it as an island asset, though it's presently in Tacoma so perhaps it doesn't count as an island asset at the moment." She felt as if she was babbling, but she did like being accurate.

"You bought a helicopter?" The others had come up behind Drake. She led them toward the kitchen entrance, unsure if she had enough iced tea to offer so many unexpected guests.

"Yes. An MD 902 Explorer. It provides transportation

options that were not previously available to our team. We often spend a number of hours waiting for others to transport us to and from remote sites. That didn't seem efficient. And, as I seem to have more rotorcraft incidents of late, I thought it would be good to have better familiarity with the aircraft type."

Then she recognized one of the other people.

"Hello, Roy."

"Hello, Miranda," the President held the door for her and waved her inside.

The others, except for Drake, were looking at her a little wildly. She led them into the big kitchen and made sure to indicate where the ground floor guest bathroom was—which she'd learned was the first task of a hostess—before checking the refrigerator. She had just enough iced tea left over from the team picnic for a tall glass each. That would have to suffice.

She turned back to Roy, "Why are people always surprised when I call you by your first name?"

"It's...unusual."

"But you asked me to do that. I remember. I wrote it down." She pulled out her personal notebook to show him.

The woman at his side looked down at the entry she indicated and laughed.

Roy merely smiled. "Yes, I did. Please continue to do so. This is Sarah Feldman, my National Security Advisor. Agent Rick Danziger is the head of my security team."

She looked at each person in turn as they were introduced, cataloging their names as well as she could. But as they were all dressed the same, except for Sarah Feldman, she was finding it difficult. Faces of so many strangers at once were simply too hard to look at.

"Was I expecting you?" She turned back to Drake because he was the most familiar.

"No. We—"

"Oh," Miranda glanced west toward Victoria, BC, across the

Haro Strait—the departure direction of the de Havilland Otter. "You know something about Clark's crash that has convinced you that Marine One and Air Force One are potentially unsafe modes of transport."

"How did you know that?" Danziger spun to face her, yanking his weapon out from under his jacket.

That was a first. She'd never had a weapon pulled on her in her own home.

"Stand down, Rick," Roy snapped out.

"I'm the head of your protection detail. I'm not standing down until I find out how she knows that and can prove it wasn't her doing."

Drake's laugh seemed to upset the agent as much as her own conclusion. "Go ahead, Miranda. Tell him how you know."

"But I don't know; it is only a meta-sphere of likely conjecture. Though it fits."

"Tell us about your meta-whatever conjecture that fits then."

"Meta-*sphere*. It is a logical construct for anchoring assumptions to be compared against factual findings as part of a causal analysis during an air-crash investigation."

"Yes, explain that to him." Roy's smile was as big as Drake's.

Miranda looked for an out; Holly typically took care of situations like this. Agent Danziger still hadn't holstered his sidearm, though it was now pointed at her right foot. She very carefully slid her foot aside and was relieved when he didn't shift his aim to follow it.

"Clark's death was aboard Marine Two. HMX-1 has never had a service failure and it seems unlikely that it would occur in the VH-92's first week of usage after four years of certification testing. Their pilots are among the best trained rotorcraft pilots in the world, though Andi has made a few comments about them only being second best."

"Andi?" Roy asked.

"Captain Andrea Wu, formerly of the 160th SOAR, is now my rotorcraft specialist."

"Hard to argue with that kind of qualification for judging helicopter pilots," Roy nodded for her to continue.

"Precisely. But even estimating that the Marine Corps HMX-1 pilots are merely second best to a 160th SOAR Night Stalker, that argues strongly against pilot error."

"It does," Drake was still smiling.

"Roy," Miranda continued, "has arrived from his G-7 meeting in a particularly non-presidential aircraft with an entourage of seven, rather than the more typical five hundred personnel and thirty vehicles he would have in attendance during international travel. Making his lack of trust in his normal aircraft a direct conclusion."

"Right on track so far, Miranda, keep going."

"The fact that he doesn't trust any of his aircraft, and the fact that Marine Two crashed into a Walmart, which no pilot in any state of control would have allowed to happen simply because of civilian casualties, points to a shared hazard across two very distinct platforms, Marine One and Air Force One."

"Three actually," Drake wanted to give her one more clue and see what she did with it. "Also—"

"The limousine as well? Oh, I'm sorry, Drake, I didn't mean to interrupt."

"That's okay. Keep going."

"There are numerous systems in common across the two aircraft, but very few with the limousine as well. Anti-attack flare system, communications, and air supply are the only ones that come readily to mind. The two aircraft share many more features, including anti-missile lasers, both fly with General Electric engines—though from quite different series—and—"

"We have reason to suspect the air system, Miranda."

"Poison?"

"Shit," Danziger cursed, but still didn't re-aim his sidearm at her.

"I'm sorry. That's the best I can do until I've had a chance to begin my investigation, so, as I said, this is all conjecture, which I shouldn't have mentioned but you asked. Please excuse me."

Drake and Roy were smiling at her, but it was too much and she looked down at the still unholstered sidearm.

Agent Rick Danziger stared at her so hard that she had to turn so that he was glaring at the side of her head rather than her face. That wasn't enough, so she moved aside, only finding safety when she'd moved to stand directly between Drake and Roy. Though Danziger kept tracking her like she was a VOR beacon for navigation.

The woman...Sarah, was shaking her head.

"I'm sorry. What did I miss? I never should have spoken. It's just supposition."

"No, Ms. Chase. You are completely correct every step of the way. How did you just do that?"

"Do you actually want me to repeat it all?" She hated repeating herself.

"No," Sarah shook her head. "It's just... Mr. President, you seem to collect some very interesting people. Maybe when your term is done, she should take your place."

One of the agents handed a glass of iced tea to him. Miranda knew she was failing in her duties as hostess, but at least there had been enough to go around. But instead of sleeping for an hour this morning, she should have made cookies.

If only she'd known they were all coming.

"No," Roy continued, "I'd never wish the presidency on a nice savant like you."

"I'm *not* a savant!" Miranda slapped a hand over her mouth. Agent Danziger was again eying her suspiciously. "I shouldn't have yelled, sorry," she mumbled through her fingers.

"You *are* the world's leading genius about aircraft crashes," Drake spoke slowly.

Miranda nodded without removing her hand. To the best of her knowledge, she was. Except perhaps for Terence Graham who had trained her, but he was retired from fieldwork, so perhaps he didn't count any more. Even he had called her the best.

"So what's the problem, Miranda?"

She wished there was anyone else here to explain for her. Andi with her patience, Taz with a side jab of sharp wit, or Mike who would also get a laugh as he made it okay. Holly might just toss the President out the door even when surrounded by his Secret Service agents. Maybe it was a good thing she, at least, wasn't here.

A deep breath didn't help, but remembering to lower her hand before speaking did.

"If I say savant, you probably think of *Rain Man*. Being called a savant implies that I don't have any skill of my own, just some...weird ability. And while I'm autistic, I'm not challenged like those poor people."

"Point made, Miranda. I apologize," Roy bowed to her. "I'd never wish the presidency on a nice *lady* like you. Maybe I'll dump it on Sarah instead."

"Well, you do need a new Vice President, Roy."

Again, by everyone's reaction, she'd said something wrong.

Everyone except Roy. He shifted to that quietly thoughtful mode she'd seen him use several times in the Situation Room.

28

"FIRST THINGS FIRST," ROY ANNOUNCED. "DANZIGER HAS KEPT ME in touch with the White House Military Office, but I need to address the nation. CNN has probably learned that Clark was in that crash for over thirty minutes, poor man."

"We could place a satellite phone call to CNN?" Danziger suggested. "I don't want anything that can be traced to your present location."

"The island has a high-speed VPN capable of video over satellite from here that can offer end-to-end encryption. Would that do?" Miranda's gaze was focused on Danziger's left hand.

Drake hadn't noticed that he was keeping it near his weapon. Miranda had, of course. Even if she didn't want to be called a savant, she was beyond genius in remarkably interesting ways—one of which was observing details.

"Why would you have that?" Danziger snapped.

Drake was getting tired of this. "Miranda, please show Agent Danziger your ID card."

Miranda looked confused, but pulled out a wallet. "Which one?" She spread out her driver's license, FAA pilot's license, NTSB ID, concealed carry permit...

Drake plucked her NTSB card and handed it to Danziger. Danziger looked from the card to Miranda and back several times before speaking. "What the hell? Yankee White Category One?"

"Her entire team is cleared Top Secret or better. Miranda is cleared to be armed in the presence of the President."

"Should I be armed right now?" Miranda asked. "All of my weapons are in my gun safe at the moment."

"Hell no!" Then Danziger turned to the President and held up the card. "Is this for real, Mr. President?"

"I warned you that it was okay to stand down around her. You should have believed me."

Miranda spoke up. "Both of my parents were undercover CIA operatives, and it was easier if they were free to talk around me. I've only been Yankee White for a few years at President Cole's request after a series of missions I'm not at liberty to discuss with you as they were code-word classified. Oh," she covered her mouth again.

"What?" Drake could see Miranda was terribly upset.

"I'm not supposed to mention code-word classified missions to people who aren't also cleared for them, am I?"

"No, you aren't. I'll let you off the hook this time, but don't let me catch you again."

"You won't, Drake. I promise!" Then practically hit her own chin as she yanked out a notebook and started to make an entry.

Drake rested a hand on her arm, firmly as Holly had once advised him. "Don't worry about it, Miranda. I was teasing. That clearance says we trust you. Right, Agent Danziger?"

"Shit, ma'am. Uh, sorry about the language. Please also excuse my previous actions." He handed her ID back far more carefully than he'd taken it.

Drake noticed that Miranda was still holding all of her cards after she tucked away the notebook.

"It's okay to put them away now. Thank you, Miranda."

She did.

"Now, let's go see your rig."

She pulled a tablet computer out of the flight bag over her shoulder and tapped a few keys.

"Jeremy fixed it up for me to make it easy."

"Who's— Never mind," Danziger waved for her to proceed.

She tapped a final button. "Okay, who would you like to connect to?"

Danziger didn't say a word as he held out his own phone and turned it for her to read a number.

After this, she really had to call her team.

29

ANDI HUNG UP THE PHONE AND TURNED TO THE OTHERS WAITING
impatiently in the Tacoma Narrows Airport hangar office.

The Cessna Citation M2 jet was fully fueled and
already rolled out of the hangar, and still there'd been no
Miranda.

They'd all waited inside watching the news; not hard to
guess where they were headed.

There was nothing new on the Vice President's crash. News
helicopters were having to use long-range telephotos because
of the no-fly security perimeter. Two camera drones had
already been shot from the sky by the Secret Service using an
electro-magnetic anti-drone gun—which was making its own
news item.

She'd just been starting to worry that something might
have happened to Miranda when she called.

Now Andi was trying to make sense of the stream of
instructions. They sounded quite unlike Miranda, but she'd
refused to explain.

"Okay guys, Miranda won't be traveling with you all."

That certainly got their attention.

"Jeremy, you're to take the lead on the Marine Two investigation as soon as you get there."

"I'm *what?*" His voice squeaked with a crack that sounded silly on a twenty-six-year-old man.

"Miranda said to look for poisons in the air supply system. I have no idea where she—"

"Poison?" Jeremy stared at the ceiling. "Air supply system?" He stared at the floor. "Marine Two? Oh, crashing in a Walmart. That would mean—"

Andi tuned him out as he continued thinking out loud.

"Mike, you're to fly the team there in the M2 jet."

"I'm *what?*" His voice didn't quite crack, instead it sounded as if it would hurt less if it had. "But— I'm—"

"Miranda said that you're a good enough pilot to no longer be depending on her. You are type certified in the M2 after all."

"*Barely!*" This time his voice did crack and Holly sniggered.

"The weather is calm right across the northern part of the country. She said refueling in Minneapolis would keep you well north of tornado alley, which is apparently still hopping even though it's past the normal season."

"Holly and Taz, Miranda said it was probably a terrorist attack, so your jobs are to keep the boys safe."

"Aw shit! Terrorists?" Holly looked disgusted. "What about you?"

She shrugged. "I've got an errand." She was supposed to fly the helo up to the island, but Miranda had said not tell anyone on the team and not to leave until they were gone.

It would be just her and her unpredictable PTSD. At least if she went down, she wouldn't kill anyone else. Then she glanced at the TV screen still showing the devastation of the Marine Two helicopter crash at the Walmart. Or not.

Why did she have the nasty feeling that Miranda had forgotten she didn't dare fly solo anymore?

Except Miranda never forgot anything.

That meant Miranda thought she could do this.

Which seemed unlikely as hell.

The others headed out the door.

While she waited for them to take off, the *Breaking News* banner flashed again on the office's big TV, then dissolved into the President's face.

"This is President Roy Cole. I'm calling from a secure location to assure our citizens and our nation's friends that I am fit, healthy, and in full control of the government after the tragic event that has killed Vice President Clark Winston. I will say more to honor this fine public servant and my friend at another time. I have ordered the nation's top accident investigation teams to the site and will be continuing to monitor the situation closely. Again, be assured, there is no cause for wider concern. I will report further as soon as I have verifiable information. In the meantime, please send your good wishes to the civilians injured by this tragic crash and struggling to survive. My thoughts and hopes are definitely with them and their loved ones. My condolences to the families who have already lost people in this disaster. This is President Roy Cole signing off."

Andi could only stare at the screen.

It was all very reassuring, except for one small fact.

In the background, over the President's shoulder, had hung a glass-fronted display case filled with scores of tiny aircraft models.

Andi had seen it many times before—hanging on the wall of Miranda's living room.

30

"No, Miranda! I can't!" Andi kept her whisper low but it felt like a shout. She'd dragged Miranda outside, then slammed the door on General Drake Nason when he tried to follow. She hung on to Miranda's sleeve until they reached the wood pile.

"No one else here can fly a helicopter, Andi."

"That's not an answer."

"I thought that you were the calm one."

"Me? *Me?*" Andi thumped a fist against her chest hard enough to hurt. "What in the world gave you that whacked idea?"

"Because you are."

Andi could only look at her aghast. That was impossible. *This* was impossible.

"Consider it," Miranda instructed. "Holly is always ready for a battle. Jeremy gets rattled when—"

"What if I have a PTSD attack in midflight? I shouldn't be allowed to fly. The doctors who cleared me for flight are idiots. And you're asking me to fly the President of the United States —" she waved a hand up toward the sky because there was no way to finish that sentence.

"When was the last time you had a PTSD attack?"

"In about three minutes from now."

"I meant in the past." Miranda said matter-of-factly. How could *she* be calling anyone else the 'calm one'?

"Just— Just—" Andi tried to remember. A PTSD attack was not the sort of thing that she went out of her way to catalog.

"Several months ago, on Johnston Atoll," Miranda filled in for her. "And that was triggered by my own autistic... regression...triggered in turn by Major Jon Swift."

"Christ, Miranda. That was so awful. I'm so glad you're rid of him."

Miranda might not know her own feelings, but Andi found they were always clear on Miranda's face.

"Seriously, Miranda. Don't you dare have second thoughts about him. He said awful things about you—to your *face*. Trying to make you who you aren't."

"Trying to make me better."

"No! Goddamn it, *no!* He was trying to make you not be like who you are. Who you are is absolutely amazing. Anyone who tells you different is an idiot."

Miranda began rearranging the top layer of the firewood.

"What?" Andi knew that Miranda had to look completely away from people when something was bothering her.

"Roy... the President. He called me a savant."

"Did you rip him a new asshole?"

Miranda stopped with the wood and actually looked directly at her; she did that very rarely. Andi could see the worry in her eyes.

"You did, didn't you? Did you go and stand up for yourself, Miranda?"

She nodded, "I yelled at him. At the President."

Andi couldn't help herself and threw her arms around her. As they hugged, she whispered in Miranda's ear, "I'm so proud of you."

Miranda hesitated only a moment before she nodded and whispered back. "If you say so, I'll have to trust you on that." Miranda briefly hugged her back, which was new. Miranda tolerated the occasional hug, but never returned one.

Andi stepped back before she herself could read anything more into it but kept her hands on Miranda's shoulders. "I do say so."

"Okay."

"So, trust me when I say that I can't fly the President, General Nason, or the National Security Advisor. It's too much strain, I just can't do it yet."

"I suppose I can understand that."

"The helicopter isn't big enough to carry everyone anyway."

The head Secret Service agent had been very worried about the logistics. There were three VIPs here at the house, but Andi didn't dare fly any of them. And then there were the four Secret Service agents of the Presidential Protection Detail, and the colonel toting the scary briefcase.

"That's true," Miranda nodded. "See? You are the calm one. I do have an idea though."

"That's good. Your ideas are always good." Except the one about Miranda trusting her to be the calm one.

31

Colonel Blake McGrady had been put on alert the moment the Marine Two aircraft crashed. For thirty-seven minutes, they'd sat in the VH-92A at Victoria Harbour Heliport with the engines spinning at idle without ever being called. Thirty-seven minutes without a goddamn thing to do but watch the tour boats come to gawk at his aircraft and take selfies.

He finally called the White House Military Office only to be told that the President wasn't in Canada anymore! And they weren't telling him shit else.

After three tries, he managed to reach Captain Helen Ames, HMX-1's liaison to the WHMO.

"His location is classified Top Secret."

"I'm the fucking commander of HMX-1."

"Honestly, sir, I'm not supposed to say this, but we don't know either. He just addressed the nation about the Vice President, but did so from an unknown location. He's way out of pocket, wherever he is. His team isn't going to make a peep until they get him back under wraps. As to Marine Two," she knew his second priority after the President's safety, "poison in the emergency air generator. At least that's what Major Tamatha Jones' final transmission implied."

He'd closed his eyes against the pain. It had been an easy guess that Tamatha had gone down with the Vice President— he'd drawn up the flight schedules himself—but that didn't diminish the impact of having it confirmed. And that she'd gone down knowing what was happening to her was simply too awful. He'd been planning to recommend her as the future first female commander of HMX-1. She was—had been—an exceptional Marine.

For half an hour, right there at the Victoria Harbour Heliport, he and Crew Chief Warren had torn apart the VH-92A's emergency air system. And they'd found nothing.

Unlike a Black Hawk, they couldn't fly with the door wide open for air circulation. So he'd lowered the rear ramp to the small cargo area, opened the rear access door and the pilots' windows, then flown to Victoria International Airport.

Still nothing.

The team had broken down the birds for transport and rolled them aboard the waiting C-17 Globemaster III in record time. Thankfully, with the new VH-92A, the breakdown only included folding the rotor blades along the fuselage and dropping the tail rotor blades. Despite being longer and having more load capacity than a Black Hawk, it was also seventeen inches shorter to the top of the rear rotor mast, making the load that much easier.

For the entire flight across the country, the Air Force wouldn't let them touch the helo, just in case it triggered a poisonous gas release.

All he could do was sit and feel his hands itch to get around the throat of whoever had tinkered with one of his helicopters.

That.

And wonder where in the hell the President had gotten to.

32

"ARE YOU SURE THAT DANZIGER'S HEART IS GOING TO SURVIVE this?" Drake chuckled as he looked over at the MD helicopter flying just off the wing of their plane.

"He is the best at his job or he wouldn't have it." Roy commented from the back seat where he was squeezed in beside Sarah.

Danziger had insisted that the person in the back of a small plane would be a lesser target to a sniper, therefore the President had to sit in the rear. Even if he fit, Drake would feel foolish squeezing in the back and placing Sarah in the danger seat.

Which had left Drake himself to sit up front beside Miranda as the target. Not that they were all that far apart; Miranda's Mooney M20V four-seater airplane was smaller than the MH-6M Little Bird that he'd often ridden the side benches of when headed to battle as a Ranger. He just hoped that, if it came down to it, his separation from the President would be enough to make a difference.

The helicopter flew fifty meters to their starboard side with its side doors slid open. The four Secret Service agents sat to either side, watching out the doors with the rifles they'd borrowed from Miranda's gun safe at the ready, though out of sight. Danziger flew up front with Andi. Danziger's arguments had been trumped by Andi's CAC card as well, which listed her as a Captain of the 160th SOAR, and also possessing Top Secret clearance.

It didn't help that both Miranda and Andi were slender, short, dressed in working clothes, and wearing yellow ball caps for an Australian soccer team. They *were* surprisingly hard to take seriously unless you knew them. Drake always enjoyed watching others stumble on Miranda's "stealth" mode—which had certainly tripped him up in the past. She and Andi standing together were at least stealth squared.

Miranda's plane could have covered the distance in half the time by itself, but Danziger had refused to have the President out of his sight. Miranda kept even with the helo's top speed.

She also insisted on teaching him the basics of flight to land the plane. When he'd asked why, her reply had been both matter-of-fact and simple, "In case I'm the one who is shot."

So, for the length of the forty-minute flight down Puget Sound and past Seattle, he'd practiced flying the plane.

"I've never been at the controls of a plane before. Nor flown in a plane so small."

"But you're the Chairman of the Joint Chiefs."

"Don't be so shocked, Miranda."

"But aren't you supposed to know everything about every service?"

He laughed right in her face. Drake knew she didn't take well to that, but he couldn't stop himself, everything about flying was foreign to him. That a single gun shot could place the President's life in his hands was...a damn good reason to focus.

"Sorry, Miranda. My job is to advise the President. I know

what the world's various military forces can *do,* especially our own. It doesn't mean I know *how* to do it myself."

"The truth is out," the President called out from the back seat.

"With all do respect, Mr. President, go to hell."

"Then shut up and fly the damned plane." The President had the decency to laugh along with his order.

"Yes sir, Mr. President, sir." Drake didn't salute because it would mean taking a hand off the controls and he didn't dare to unclamp either from the small steering wheel.

Enough minutes later for Drake to be convinced that he'd never get it, Miranda waved him off the controls. His palms were slick and he was glad to let go.

"It's time. We'll be in their airspace in two minutes."

Drake pulled out his phone and dialed Joint Base Lewis-McChord. One of the largest military bases in the world, it lay just a hundred miles south of Miranda's island.

"I have an encrypted priority call for your base commander," he informed the operator who answered.

"Encrypting now," the operator was efficiency itself. The phone squealed sharply in his ear. Drake yanked it away and set encryption on his own phone.

"I need a clearance code," the operator responded.

Drake gave his.

"Verified. Hold please."

"Colonel Williams here," the base commander answered seconds later.

"Colonel, this is General Drake Nason, Chairman of the Joint Chiefs of Staff. You have an E-4B Nightwatch on station. This is a klaxon launch warning. I'm currently inbound in a flight of a private aircraft and helicopter. We need immediate clearance direct to the E-4B's hangar. This is a high-security event."

33

Andi stayed just off her wing as Miranda landed at JBLM. It was funny seeing the Mooney land on the ten-thousand-foot runway designed to handle the biggest and heaviest jets in the world.

She hadn't been privy to the plan, just told to stay on the President's wing, even if it was actually Miranda's plane. Danziger had the humor of a rock and apparently trusted nobody. Of course, if her job was protecting the President and he was out in the wind like this, she'd probably feel much the same.

However Miranda had arranged it, they were given top priority on the runway, and several big aircraft were left to cool their jets on the taxiway. That the Mooney was just twenty-six feet long made it look comical. Of course her helo was all of thirty-two feet from tip-of-nose to end-of-tail-boom, so she wasn't exactly in a position to brag.

The Mooney needed so little of the pavement, Miranda could have turned off at the first taxiway, except it was blocked by a hundred-and-seventy-foot, four-engine C-17 Globemaster III jet, waiting for departure clearance.

She wished she could hear what the plane's pilots were saying about their two tiny aircraft.

So, she and Miranda hurried side by side down the massive slab of concrete to the next taxiway.

Andi held station a hundred feet off Miranda's right wing and two feet above the grassy verge.

She hadn't flown into a military base since she'd been forced to leave the Army. To once more be back inside prohibited airspace had sent waves of prickles over her skin as if she'd been irradiated or something. Actually landing at a base? That was pumping her heart rate toward catastrophic.

She was a former Night Stalker, goddamn it. She could do anything.

Her nerves were less than convinced by her pep talk as they turned toward the third hangar in the long row.

On their side-by-side approach to the hangar, the massive door split down the middle and began rolling open.

No one had told her what to expect and she nearly screwed up her hover. The bulbous nose of a shining white 747 with a thin blue stripe down the side loomed in the shadows. The tip of the nose itself, where the primary radar was installed, was unpainted. And it had the most obvious giveaway of all: a second lobe on top of the bulge of the 747's upper deck for the super-high-frequency antenna.

An E-4B Nightwatch.

There were just four of them ever built and, despite being forty-five years old, they were among the most sophisticated planes in the sky. They were like the VC-25s used for Air Force One, with all of the pretty bits replaced by specialty equipment. A Nightwatch had no seating for the press, nor a squad of Secret Service, nor luxury spaces for guests. It wasn't a flying symbol with a Situation Room; it was a flying NORAD control-and-command center.

They were hardened against electromagnetic-pulse attacks,

could trail a five-mile-long antenna specifically for communicating directly with deep-submerged missile submarines anywhere in the world, or use that rooftop antenna to steer a satellite. No other aircraft anywhere carried as much electronics—or could oversee a war so effectively.

Instead of nearly four hundred passengers that a typical 747 could carry, it was operated by a crew of a hundred elite technicians. With in-flight refueling, it could stay aloft for a week or more with no other resupply.

"Set us here," Danziger pointed down, "then get the hell out of the way."

Andi thudded the skids down onto the tarmac with all the grace of her first training flight in a TH-67 Creek helo.

The five Secret Service agents dumped out of her helicopter without so much as a "Thanks," then raced over to Miranda's plane that was still taxiing toward the built-in stairs extended from the 747's right belly.

Unsure where to go, Andi hesitated.

Apparently that was a moment too long.

A security team, with their rifles in hand—still pointed at the ground, but for how long?—lined up between her and the 747 now fully exposed by the big doors. Then an aircraft marshal stepped directly in front of her. He waved his palms upward. Rather than giving her a depart signal, he waved her into a clear space in the now wide-open hangar.

She eased forward...slowly. She could have crawled faster on her hands and knees. The air marshal clearly wanted her to, but she didn't dare.

Finally, she settled beneath the end of the E-4B's high wing. He crossed his arms low for her to land.

Once she was down inside the hangar—a tiny bit more gracefully this time—he gave the cross-throat signal that either he wanted her engines cut or he was going to cut her throat to keep this all secret. Because the latter seemed unlikely, she ran through her engine shutdown procedure checklist in record time.

As she climbed out, Miranda taxied over to park beside her.

The Mooney's shutdown only took seconds. An airman had the plane's wheels chocked before she was out of the seat.

"What now?" Andi sidled up. She had to shout, because the 747's engines, over their heads, were spinning up fast.

Miranda shrugged.

They both turned to look at the airstairs. Drake was signaling them urgently from the head of them.

Even hesitating to grab her NTSB vest and go bag caused frantic gesticulations.

They started at a trot, but were at a dead run by the time they were racing up the stairs.

The stairs began retracting into the underbelly of the jet close on their heels.

"Here," Drake pointed at a line of seats mounted sideways along the aisle beside the door.

By the time the three of them had sat down and kicked their gear under the seats, the plane was in motion.

"Jesus," Andi twisted to glance out the window as the big jet drove forward. "It's going to make a mess of the hangar."

"It's a klaxon launch, that's the least of our worries."

Andi looked at him, but he was serious.

She looked at Miranda, who sat as calmly as if it was a Sunday stroll.

"Hang on," Andi whispered.

"Why? What's a klaxon launch?"

"In an alert fighter, like the interceptors in place to protect the White House, they're able to be airborne in three minutes from the need-to-launch warning, and on-site over the White House thirty seconds later if they go supersonic from Andrews. In a 747, I have no idea what it means."

What it meant was that they didn't taxi to the far end of the runway. They ignored all of the waiting jets. From the hangar, they rolled directly to the runway, then firewalled the engines.

She'd always heard that the VC-25s of Air Force One and the E-4B Nightwatches were massively overpowered for just such moments, and now she had proof. The gigantic jet *slammed* aloft; there was no other word for it. It continued to climb hard at a far steeper angle than any commercial airliner would ever attempt. Thirty-five tons less people and no cargo certainly enhanced the performance as well.

Andi checked her watch, then looked out the window. It didn't take long until they were above the height of the fourteen-thousand-foot peak of the dormant volcano Mount Rainier. It was so massive that it always seemed to hover over Tacoma though it lay forty miles away.

"Eighty-two seconds," Miranda observed quietly.

Andi hadn't seen her look at her watch.

They'd been climbing at ten thousand feet per minute, triple what most airliners would do during maximum climb.

More than anything else, that brought home to Andi just how different a world they had stepped into.

34

"WHAT ARE THEY DOING ABOARD?" DANZIGER GLARED AT THEM. He'd come down the stairs from the main deck above just as they were standing.

"Don't you ever trust anyone, Danziger?" Drake asked him.

"Not part of the job description." Danziger spoke as if it pained him.

Miranda thought that was an interesting, though advisable, requirement to place in a Secret Service job description. "Was it also part of the job application as well as in the description?"

"What?"

"Was there a question when you joined the Secret Service about whether or not you trusted anybody?"

Danziger looked at her for a long moment, then barked out a laugh. "Damn well should be. Drake, you and the President clearly trust them. As long as neither of them is armed, we're fine."

In their race to the airplane, she and Andi had both shrugged into their NTSB vests. Miranda looked down and considered her own.

"Well, there are a number of tools in my work vest that

could be used as weapons," Miranda held out a heavy-duty pair of metal shears as an example. They could remove a finger as neatly as they could slice through an airplane's sheet metal skin.

When she looked back up, Danziger was once again clutching his holstered sidearm. She was glad he hadn't brandished it inside a pressurized airplane.

But he wasn't looking at her.

Miranda turned to look at Andi; she was his target.

Andi held out her left palm like she was stopping traffic, then flicked her right wrist downward. A black swing-blade knife dropped into her palm, which she then held out unopened.

Danziger kept his distance, so Drake took the offered blade without blocking Danziger's line of fire, and opened it himself.

"A Cold Steel Recon Tanto blade," Drake twisted it in the light. "I always liked this knife. I carried an early version of this as a utility blade back in the day. I had to be careful in the field because it wasn't black-anodized to be nonreflective like this one."

Andi looked over at her and shrugged.

Miranda had forgotten about how quickly Andi had pulled that knife to stop an incipient bar fight after a Chinook helicopter crash last fall. It had appeared in her hand magically. Now she knew how.

Drake snapped it closed and waved it at the Secret Service agent but didn't hand it over.

"It's a good reminder to not underestimate anyone on Miranda's team. Andi may be five-two of American-born Chinese. But she's also Captain Andrea Wu formerly of the 160th SOAR, one of the most elite helicopter pilots in the world. I wouldn't try messing with her, Danziger."

"She's not cleared Yankee White One. She should not be armed in the presence of the President."

Drake made a point of handing it back to Andi despite Danziger's valid point.

"I'd wager that the President is safer if you have this blade than if you don't. I'm also betting that you're lethal with that weapon, Captain Wu?"

Andi slowly tucked it back into her sleeve. "I'm good. But not a patch on Taz or Holly."

"Who are they?" Danziger removed his hand from his weapon, much to Miranda's relief, then rubbed at his eyes as if exhausted.

Drake nodded for Miranda to answer.

"A former Pentagon Air Force colonel and an Australian SASR operator, both members of my team," Miranda answered, then remembered to tuck her shears back in their pocket so that it wouldn't be perceived as a threat. "Mike used to work with the FBI, and Jeremy is..." Curiously, he was the only one on the team other than herself without any governmental association beyond the NTSB.

"He's Jeremy!" Andi finished for her.

"Yes, that's an accurate statement. And more than its obvious tautological completeness implies."

"Christ," Danziger rubbed at his face, "I think I'm losing my mind. This way," he led them up the stairs from the cargo deck, largely filled with banks of electronics, to the main deck.

At the head of the stairs, he waved aft.

"You two can go sit at the conference table or in the briefing area, neither one is in use. Just make it somewhere I can't see you. General Nason, the President has asked you to join him and NSA Sarah Feldman in the office."

And as suddenly as that, she and Andi were standing alone. She could see the President at his desk in the forward compartment. The room and desk were as utilitarian as Jeremy's workbench in the aircraft hangar, though the few seats grouped around the desk were business-class comfortable by the look of them.

She and Andi turned toward the rear of the plane.

The first room was a conference room with all the charm of an air freighter's cargo hold. White metal walls and a metal table big enough for nine seats and a narrow passage down either side. There was a large plasma flat-screen and four world clocks above.

"Movie night?" Andi whispered.

They peeked into the next room. Three rows of economy-class seats could accommodate about twenty people facing a podium and two more display screens. In the last row sat the three Secret Service agents of the President's detail and the colonel with his case on the seat beside him.

"Briefing room," Miranda whispered back.

Through the window beyond, she could see scores of technicians in Air Force uniforms seated at console after console.

"What's all that?"

"Communications," Andi squinted through the glass. "Anything we don't recognize on this plane is probably to do with communications. If there's a nuclear event, they get the President or Secretary of Defense aloft in one of these birds. These Nightwatch 747s are what the SecDef flies in when he goes overseas. There's also always one at a standoff airport whenever the President travels, just as this one was at JBLM. This plane is in addition to the Navy's smaller E-6Bs that are always aloft with a general aboard in case we lose all ground-based command capability at once due to an overwhelming enemy attack. I have no idea about the security, so we'd better not go back there."

Miranda decided there were things she'd rather not know about how the world worked and returned to the conference room.

They sat in adjacent chairs at the corner of the table.

"Now what?" Miranda could usually lose herself in the work, but because of all her insomnia last night, the only work presently outstanding was the report of the Cessna 208 Caravan crashing into the Seattle Opera House. And she couldn't work on that because it was supposed to be Jeremy's investigation. Except Jeremy was on *her* plane, somewhere in the middle of the country by now.

"I have a stupid suggestion." Andi reached into her vest pocket, but didn't pull out whatever was in there.

"Anything would be welcome at this point." Miranda felt tired in ways she'd never been before. She still hadn't been able to shake the possibility of losing Jeremy. And she had taken a liking to Taz even if Miranda still didn't know how to interpret her actions.

And the thought of *replacing* them was beyond burdensome and into—she pulled out her notebook and found the correct emoticon far too easily with its droopy eyes and downturned mouth—depressing. With an addition of wide-eyed, open-mouthed fear.

"What?"

"Anything," Miranda took the risk of repeating herself and tucked the notebook away again.

"Well, Jeremy—"

Miranda cringed inside.

"—wants us to test the latest version of his game." Andi pulled a small box out of her pocket. The whole team had worked on this game on and off over the last six months, though no one as hard as Jeremy.

Andi opened the box and turned over the first set of cards labeled *Character ID*. And there was—

"I'm supposed to play myself?"

"Who better?" Andi asked.

Which was true, she did know herself.

Jeremy had made fake NTSB IDs for each of them.

"Why does it say I can't solve Diplomatic Emergencies?"

"Because, Miranda," Andi rested a hand over hers, "you suck at diplomacy, remember?"

"Oh, right." She did. "What about you?"

Andi shuffled through the character IDs to find her own. "Um, I get to jump to wherever a rotorcraft card lands. I'm guessing that's an advantage."

"You're a helicopter pilot, so that makes sense." Miranda was glad something did.

Andi began laying out the world map gameboard across the E-4B's conference table as they flew high over Idaho.

35

"ARE YOU OKAY, MIKE? YOU'RE LOOKING LIKE YOU ATE A BUG. Maybe a lot of them."

Taz actually had to catch his arm. At the end of the four steps descending from the Citation M2 jet, he stumbled as if he expected the stairway to continue straight down into the pavement at the Frederick Municipal Airport. The place was quiet: private planes only, no commercial flights.

"It's a small-town airport, Mike. Not the sort of place with a stairway straight down to the flaming pits of hell."

"Says you. I just flew across the country. Solo. In a jet. For the first time ever! Give me a break."

"Okay, any special requests? Tibia? Femur? Right arm or left? Maybe just a finger or two?"

"What, Taz? Not going to offer to snap my neck? Pity, it's about the only thing that would help right now."

But Taz also noted that having to dig for sarcasm had steadied him. She wished she could have somehow helped on the flight, but for all of her nineteen years in the Air Force, she'd never been a pilot.

"Next step," she offered. "Let's get a car. The crash is just three miles north of here."

"Yeah, I saw it coming in. It looks ugly. We've been in transit for six hours and there are still whole fleets of fire trucks and ambulances there with their lights going."

Taz wondered if her life would ever be done with death and destruction. She'd seen plenty during her career, even more when her Air Force career had ended. But now, on Miranda's team, it was their job.

"C'mon, Mike. You can ease off now; you did good." She handed him his gear from the rear baggage compartment since he'd made no move to fetch it himself.

Jeremy was already donning his vest and checking his gear much the way Miranda did each time. He was so cute when he was trying to be Mini-Miranda. Would she still think that twenty years from now?

That froze her in her tracks.

She very slowly looked away from Jeremy, not comfortable with what she was seeing. She'd be even less comfortable if Jeremy saw it on her face.

Taz also didn't spot any stairways to the underworld, which was a good thing at the moment or she might race down them for sanctuary.

They'd been together less than six months. The fact that it was a record for either of them should not have her thinking thoughts like that.

They were good together, but that's all it was.

"Sucks, doesn't it?" Mike was now the one grinning at her.

"What?"

He nodded toward Jeremy.

"What?" She was sounding like a slick-sleeve raw recruit without even an airman stripe.

Mike's expression turned serious, which was a bad sign.

"Your face. I've seen that look in the mirror lately about—" he tipped his head toward Holly as if he still couldn't say it aloud.

"But..." She *was* still a brainless slick-sleeve.

"You want to know the scary step?"

"No!" She definitely didn't want to if it was scarier than this.

"Well, I'll tell you anyway. It's the day you have one of those thoughts and it feels normal instead of freaking you out."

"Not gonna happen to this—"

Mike's smile said otherwise, then he stepped over to Holly and gently nudged her shoulder with his.

Rather than throttling him, as Taz had seen her do in the past, she simply nudged him back without turning.

Mike grinned back at her.

Holly and Mike were good together, and that was all it was for them.

Wasn't it?

Taz couldn't help but admire her. A woman who'd been an Australian SASR operator and was the only person to ever outdraw Taz in a knife fight were both compelling arguments in her favor—especially in favor of staying on her good side.

Yet something had been different about Holly and Mike since she'd nearly died in the plane crash on her way to Australia. They'd been together before that, but they'd become *close* ever since.

Holly was...looking up at the sky.

Taz followed the line of her gaze. It was the first aircraft flying above the airport since their arrival.

An ancient UH-1N Huey helicopter was on final approach. She knew its colors even though it was silhouetted against the afternoon sky—dark blue with a gold stripe and a white top. The only military units flying these Vietnam-era birds were, of course, her own former branch, the US Air Force. Out of the sixteen thousand ever built, sixty were still in military service and fifteen of those were part of the USAF 1st Helicopter Squadron out at Andrews.

"What's an Andrews' bird doing here?"

"Two guesses," Holly must have overheard her.

Taz gave it a moment's thought. "I wish it was Miranda, but it's probably Major Pain-in-the-ass Jon Swift."

"Bingo." Holly had made the same two guesses.

Taz slapped her hip to make sure that she still had her Taser. She didn't. She took a moment to dig it out of her go bag and strap it to her hip.

When Holly looked at her, she explained, "Shot him with it once. Glad to offer a repeat performance for the fans."

Holly's affirming nod felt good. It said Taz belonged—she liked that.

So what did it say for her future that they were training Jeremy to lead a team? That meant he'd eventually form his own investigation team. She was barely used to being part of Miranda's and now they were getting rid of Jeremy? Or *her* and Jeremy? That suddenly seemed particularly important to know. Would her future depend on Jeremy's path? That was too bizarre to think about right now.

The old helicopter thudded down out of the sky with its distinctive heavy two-bladed beat and heavy downdraft, drowning out any ability to ask. It landed lightly near the Cessna M2.

"Yes!" Holly offered a fist pump when Andi and then Miranda stepped off the helo and ducked as they scuttled out from under the spinning blades. "You slippery bitches!" She met them at the edge of the Huey's rotor sweep and swept them both into a hard hug.

Taz's hand clamped hard around the butt of the Taser when Miranda's ex, Major Jon Swift of the USAF Accident Investigation Board, was next off the helo. To his credit, when he was halfway clear of the rotors and spotted her, he flinched —hard. Good!

And then a pair of Gianvito Rossi black suede boots preceding long legs and a sleek red skirt, which stopped notably above the knees, emerged from the passenger door.

"Shit, Holly. We needed three guesses."

Holly turned and swore, "Oh, fuck me dead."

CIA Director Clarissa Reese ducked out from under the rotor blades to join them.

36

"MA'AM, YOU CAN'T COME IN HERE."

"Talk to them," Holly waved the policeman toward Jon and Clarissa.

As soon as his back was turned, Holly walked around the barrier that had been set at the head of the driveway into the Walmart off Monocacy Boulevard as if it wasn't even there.

Miranda could only watch in surprise.

Andi took her arm and tugged her forward around the barrier.

She didn't like to ignore authority, but Holly seemed so certain. The others walked ahead, so she let Andi lead her after them.

Once they had woven through the layers of police cars, ambulances, and fire trucks—dodging emergency workers and sheet-draped stretchers every step of the way—the whole team stumbled to a halt at the edge of the debris field.

It didn't extend beyond the parking lot, but the devastation there was the worst she'd ever seen in an air crash.

Most of the building had collapsed.

Great swaths of scorch marks indicated that fire had swept

across the parking lot, destroying vehicles that had burned and become their own centers of fire. Shopping carts were jumbled with car tires and cans of groceries with the labels burned off. It was by far the most complex debris field she'd ever seen.

"Are you okay with him being here?" Andi asked.

"Who? Jeremy or Mike?"

Andi laughed at her. "I meant Jon."

Miranda had still never fully settled her feelings about Jon. After most of a year as occasional lovers, she hadn't seen him since the Johnston Atoll crash. It had been an abrupt breakup and she didn't remember any of it due to the autistic meltdown he had triggered in her—before Taz had tasered him and Holly had dumped him on the next plane out.

Now, months later, he had simply joined the helicopter flight from Andrews Air Force Base where the E-4B had landed as if it was the most natural thing.

However, Drake had given her an update as they'd deplaned from the E-4B, and she'd spent the short flight to Frederick focusing on that. Its core conclusion was that they knew little more than she'd already been told.

The words of the pilot's final transmission: *Poison. Oxy. Generator. Dying.*—with a question mark on the last—was still classified as Top Secret. Videos from the escorting helicopters had been collected. She and Andi had studied them on the flight from Andrews. Even to her non-rotorcraft-trained eye, the final flight was in keeping with decreasing pilot function. Andi had concurred.

So far, there were seventeen smart phone videos shot by civilians. Only two covered the flight from its first appearance above the Walmart. One captured the back of her husband's head rather than the final crash, but two more tracked the final moments of the Marine Two helicopter flying into the store's front entrance. The remaining videos were worth future study, but were all of the fireball and the subsequent explosion and building collapse.

"Hell of a way to go shopping," Andi had remarked as they'd watched the video during the flight from Andrews. "Most people make do with just a shopping cart."

Miranda never got jokes, but as they walked into the devastation of the parking lot, she finally got this one.

"Can you imagine motoring up and down the aisles of Walmart in a helicopter?" she whispered to Andi.

"There would be teddy bears and toiletries flying every which way in the rotor's downwash."

"Home electronics on the starboard side. Discount shoes on the port."

"At the turn, find special bargains for all your home-improvement needs. Oops, never mind, the tail rotor just destroyed them all."

They bumped shoulders and shared a laugh as they picked their way down one of the long lanes of pavement blown clear of all vehicles.

She appreciated Andi's humor, it mitigated facing such devastating destruction and death. The crews would still be removing bodies from the parking lot for hours.

The two store entries looked as if they'd been engine exhaust ports, two great paths washed clear of all but the smallest debris.

"What is wrong with you two?" Jon came up behind them.

"Jon! You are the—" Andi stopped when Miranda rested a hand on her arm but Andi's anger was obvious, even to her.

"Major Jon Swift," Miranda greeted him. "I—"

"This is a disaster site. The Vice President has died and we don't know why. Show some goddamn respect, if you know what that is."

Miranda started again, "I—"

"You are wasting my time; we're no longer together so I

don't have to do that anymore. I'm in charge of this site pending the arrival of General Jack Macy. Until then—"

It had become clear that she wasn't going to get a word in edgewise.

Andi had dropped her knife into her palm, but Miranda decided it would be better if Andi, a retired captain, didn't stab a superior officer.

"Taz," she called out. Taz was much better at dealing with these kinds of problems than she was.

Jon's gaze jumped over Miranda's shoulder. "Not ag—"

He was cut off by a sharp crack from behind her.

Twin electrode leads flew past her right shoulder and plunged into Jon's left one.

He twitched once, then collapsed to the pavement. His body spasmed as he rolled in the debris. All he managed was a pained grunt through a locked jaw.

Taz stepped up from behind her to look down at Jon as he continued to shake uncontrollably. She held her Taser, letting the weapon run its full five-second discharge. It made a horrific, Dr. Frankenstein kind of crackling noise as it did.

"I was only going to ask you to talk to him. You're better at dealing with military people than I am."

Taz simply smiled. "This is the best way to deal with them."

"You. Fucking. Bitch!" Jon grunted out.

She pressed the Arc Switch on the Taser and a fresh five-second charge slammed into Jon over the electrodes embedded in his shoulder. He grunted loudly and spasmed again.

"I didn't know that," Miranda answered once the second round of loud crackling had ended.

"Trust me," Taz smiled, then turned to Clarissa looking down at Jon in horror. "Isn't that so, Director Reese?"

Clarissa's face was unusually pale as she replied slowly. "If you say so, Colonel Cortez."

"It Flores now." Taz turned and smiled at Miranda. "Aw, she remembers me. I'm so touched."

Miranda began pulling out her notebook to check Clarissa's expression.

"Fear, Miranda," Taz whispered loudly enough for anyone to hear. "Director Reese may have just peed her silk panties."

Andi snorted out a laugh from Miranda's other side.

Clarissa's cheeks went red and her frown definitely matched Anger. She started to speak but Taz cut her off.

"I haven't deleted that picture, Clarissa. Don't *ever* forget that," Taz suddenly sounded as dangerous as an Air Force colonel.

Clarissa's jaw clenched even more tightly.

"What picture?" Miranda wondered what it could be.

"Doesn't matter. As long as *she* remembers." Taz ejected the spent Taser cartridge and tossed it onto Jon's chest. Then she snapped in a fresh one and reholstered the weapon.

"Don't you forget either," Taz stabbed a finger at Jon.

Jon had recovered enough that he had no control of his body, but his look said he wouldn't forget any time soon. Miranda could see that even without her emoticon guide.

Taz hooked her arm through Miranda's and turned her around. "Come on, Jeremy's waiting for you to get started."

Out of nowhere, Andi's elbow caught her in the ribs before Miranda could agree.

"What?"

Andi raised her eyebrows a couple of times quickly.

Miranda tried it herself. It was awkward at first, but then she got the feel for it. If she were to do that to someone else, it would mean...

"Oh, you're reminding me of something."

Andi laughed. It was a very friendly laugh and made her feel better about laughing with her earlier despite the situation.

It only took a moment longer to connect that Andi had been trying to remind *her* of something...

Oh!

"You can tell Jeremy to stop waiting. I said it would be his investigation, and it is."

"Jesus, Miranda." Taz waved toward the massive wreckage. "The Vice President died in there. You think Jeremy's up to that?"

Miranda nodded.

"As long as," Andi looked around Miranda at Taz, "you're helping him."

"Yes, that, too," Miranda agreed.

Miranda glanced at Andi when she couldn't interpret Taz's grimace.

Andi just shrugged. She must not know what it meant either.

Whatever it was, it looked very uncomfortable, like she'd just bitten into a lemon.

37

CLARISSA OFFERED JON A HAND UP WHEN IT BECAME CLEAR THAT he wouldn't reach his feet any other way.

"Thank you," his voice was rough.

She didn't answer, her throat was so dry that she probably couldn't.

Today was not a day she needed to be reminded of the various threats to her career. Colonel Taz Flores' photo of her when she was much younger and running a torture center at a CIA Black Site would not play well with today's mild-mannered, politically correct rhetoric. Being reminded of her powerlessness, her vulnerability—so close on the heels of Clark's and her plans' deaths—was such gut-wrenching agony that she couldn't even puke though she felt the need to.

She'd stayed at the CIA, trying to back-trace to the origins of the chatter that the cyber twins had uncovered—until the President had suddenly returned to Andrews Air Force Base without any warning.

Neither he, nor anyone else aboard the E-4B Nightwatch had contacted her once during the six-hour gap. She was the head of the CIA and was working the problem of the attack on the Vice President, yet nothing!

Well, she'd fix that.

A report that an NTSB team was departing Andrews aboard an Air Force helo gave her an idea. She'd had them reroute to pick her up, and rushed up to her office to change.

Neither the comfortable pantsuit she'd been wearing, and wrinkling through the long night, nor a funereal black would do. She'd dressed in a red power suit with a black silk blouse that made her pale complexion and white-blonde hair particularly stand-out.

The suit shouted *I'm important and I am busy at the business of the country.* With her long legs, it was also short enough to make sure that it grabbed any man's attention.

Now it was time to be front and center at Clark's death site. There was more than one way to get the goddamn President's attention.

And to start?

She was wasting her time helping a lowly Air Force major to his feet.

She hadn't counted on the NTSB team being Miranda Chase and her Chinese sidekick. Ready to pull a knife on her? Clarissa would destroy the puny woman for that. Though she'd forgotten about Colonel Taz Cortez-Flores-Pain-in-the-ass recently joining Miranda's team. The reminder of that incriminating photo had been a rude shock.

Wait!

Clarissa spun to look for Miranda, but she'd already disappeared into the clutter of a fresh round of ambulances.

Most of Miranda's team had already been here when their helicopter arrived. Yet Miranda and Andi had been on the helicopter from Andrews despite normally being stationed out of Seattle.

Why Andrews?

Goddamn the bitch to hell!

Clarissa had been shut off from the President for the last six hours.

And, in order to arrive at Andrews, Miranda must have been on the President's plane traveling from the G-7 meetings in Victoria, BC. How did that lame excuse for a woman do it?

There'd been another important fact mentioned, too...

What was it?

Not by Miranda or Taz. No, it had come from—

She spun to face the Major who'd been on their helicopter flight and then tasered.

"You were screwing Miranda Chase?" That was it.

What was his name? Swift!

Jon Swift looked at her like she'd lost her mind. Then he shuddered. So he had been fucking Miranda. How bizarre that anyone could want to.

"Lousy?"

"No," Jon began the impossible task of setting his clothes to order. There was dirt on his uniform, soot all down his back from where the parking lot pavement had been scorched by fire, even black stains from sun-softened tar. "She was great."

"So, what happened?"

"She's kinda broken but I was okay with that. However, every time I tried to help Miranda to be even halfway normal, Taz was all over my ass. That woman is a damned psycho."

Clarissa knew for a fact that she wasn't; the woman was lethally sane.

Jon winced as he bent over to retrieve his briefcase. "Christ I hope the news services didn't see that."

Clarissa asked why, not that she cared about this little man anymore.

"If Drake saw that, it'll be the center of every family reunion for as long as I live."

"Drake?" It wasn't a common name.

"Chairman of the Joint Chiefs, General Drake Nason." He made another attempt to dust off his pants. "He's my uncle. Has a real penchant for telling stories at family events."

"Um, your hair." She hadn't been planning to bother telling him that his hair was in total disarray, looking exactly as if he'd just been electrocuted.

Imagining Drake Nason being anything other than a dictatorial, tin-soldier stiff was hard to imagine.

But if Jon Swift was his nephew, he was about to be her new best friend—at least until she'd see if he could achieve the near impossible and get her on Drake's good side. Drake and President Cole were tight and, if Drake recommended her as the next Vice President, maybe she could still get there.

She knew she was flailing if she was betting on such a long shot but it was the best she had at the moment.

"Come with me." She turned and began to walk away.

"But the crash is that way."

"You dear, naive boy." He looked to be about her own age. She hooked an arm through his and guided him away from the crash. "The news cameras are this way. And they're just dying to hear from the Second Lady."

38

HMX-1 WAS THE LARGEST AVIATION SQUADRON IN THE ENTIRE Corps, and McGrady had called them all in. They were ready at HMX-1's Quantico hangar by the time the C-17 had delivered him and his helos back across the country.

"The President will not be flying in a Marine Corps helicopter until we can certify them safe. We will be going over every system in every bird until we find out what happened during the Vice President's flight."

The silence in the big hangar was deafening. There were usually tool noises, chatter, systems checks, and the like.

Now there was only silence among the hundreds of Marines crowded into the center of the hangar.

"If it was mechanical, then something got through our White Side security." And if it wasn't, that meant he had a traitor in the house. "I'm ordering both white and green sides to fully inspect every aircraft, every supply on every shelf, every part. As soon as this meeting is over, we'll be notifying our teams at Anacostia and Andrews as well as those stationed at every single supplier."

The men and women lined up inside the hangar remained dead silent at Parade Rest. Not a single movement in the ranks.

"Our sum total of information includes three words: poison, air, generator. You will not assume the source was in the emergency air system. You will start there, but you will not assume it was a poison. You will not assume *anything*. I don't care if we have to take every single one of these birds down to scrap metal. We will find the problem that killed the Vice President, Major Jones, and her crew. We will trace back everything and verify *everything* right down to the metal grade on the bolts on the lavatory seat cover."

McGrady stared at the gap where the VH-92A should be. At the empty spot where Major Tamatha Jones would normally stand. None of her fellow pilots had shifted to fill in that space.

"You will only work in teams of two or more. I want double eyes on everything."

Which didn't fool anyone; they weren't idiots, they were Marines. They knew it meant to trust no one.

"Your families will be notified. All three bases are now on full lockdown until this is solved. Cots and food will be provided. I want cause, source, and fix within forty-eight hours. Master Sergeant Whalen and I will be proceeding to the crash site. We'll keep you posted. Make me proud, Marines. Dismissed."

"Oorah!" echoed off the hangar's hard metal.

Then everyone scrambled to get to work.

Whalen stepped up and snapped a salute.

"What is it, sergeant?"

"Just wondering what transport I should arrange?"

"A goddamn helo."

"One of ours?"

McGrady felt the knife plunge square into his gut as he looked at the lines of helos arranged in the big hangar.

He wanted to rage in the poor man's face. But it wasn't

Whalen's fault that he was the unit's top mechanic on the day HMX-1 failed its mandate. However, while it was definitely his *own* fault that he himself had been the commander when it happened, he wasn't going to take it out on his crew. He took a deep breath and held it until he felt he could talk normally.

"No. Borrow a bird somewhere."

"Yes sir." he saluted and turned to go.

"Whalen, do me a goddamn favor and at least make it a Marine Corps bird."

"Never crossed my mind not to," he smiled. He actually *smiled* amidst all the disaster. There was a reason he liked having Whalen as his crew chief.

"Carry on, Marine." It was the highest compliment he knew how to pay.

39

"WE HAVE A PROBLEM," SENATOR HUNTER RAMSON KEPT HIS voice down even though he was the only one in his office and the door was closed. The burner cell phone felt slick in his palm.

"Isn't that why we pay you? To solve problems."

"No. You don't pay me—"

"Would you like to preview the notice we could issue to the Securities Exchange Commission for insider trading, based on the pre-announcement information we have provided to you in the past?"

Hunter tried again. "You don't pay me to *solve* problems. You, ah, assist me with my investment strategy in exchange for early knowledge of legislative issues that may impact your future sales. Would you like me to paint a picture for the press of precisely what you do to obtain Congressional approval of foreign arms sales contracts for your weapons?"

There was a glum silence on the line.

"Good. We understand each other."

He received a reluctant grunt of agreement over the phone.

"This time your people crossed *way* over the line. I'm in a position to kill the type of legislation that concerns changes to arms sales strategies. Did you think I couldn't do it this time as well?"

"No. You've proven you can do that."

"Good. So what the hell were you thinking?"

His contact sighed deeply before continuing. "It wasn't us. At least not directly."

"Then who—" And Hunter knew.

And if *they* decided that he wasn't serving them well enough?

He swallowed hard but couldn't seem to clear his throat.

"Yes," his contact continued. "Now we have the *same* problem. What are *you* going to do to *solve* that?"

Holy Christ! He had no idea.

40

"TERENCE!"

Andi jumped at Miranda's shout. Miranda never shouted. It was loud enough to be heard over the roar of a departing air ambulance.

"Mirrie!" The Director of the NTSB Training Center cried just as loudly.

She rushed away from the team. The director wrapped her in a bear hug. For the first time in Andi's experience, Miranda returned the hug without any hesitation.

Andi had only met him once, as he'd dragged her from class and shipped her out to Groom Lake to join Miranda's team on no notice. On that occasion he'd been the stiffly polite and slightly terrifying head of the training center—an elegant African American with hair gone past gray to white. As much of a legend at the NTSB as Miranda herself.

"I'm so glad they called you! Now that the absolute best is in charge here, this old man can go home and put his feet up again," Director Terence Graham declared.

Andi was close enough to hear him whisper to Miranda. "Don't take that seriously. I'm here to help for the duration."

Andi breathed a sigh of relief. The director clearly knew how to handle the literal aspect of Miranda's autism.

"I'm not in charge," Miranda explained once the director released her.

"Really?" he was smiling as if it was a joke. "Who then? You, Captain Wu?"

"Jeremy Trahn is, sir." Andi held out her hands palm out while shaking her head fast. No way was she an investigator-in-charge. She was impressed, though, that he'd remembered her name and title.

That sobered him up. "Really? Is that boy ready for his own team?"

"That's what we're finding out, sir," Andi explained. "We're backstopping him on an opportunity to fail—not that Taz would let him."

"I'm not a sir, Captain."

"I'm not a captain either. I'm an Andi."

"Terence." They shook on it. "Jeremy and who?"

"Retired USAF Colonel Vicki 'Taz' Flores."

Terence looked aghast, "You unleashed the notorious Taser on young Jeremy."

"What do you mean? Shouldn't I have allowed that?" Miranda sounded suddenly worried.

Andi rested a hand firmly on Miranda's shoulder. "It's okay, Miranda. You know how good they are for each other."

"That's true. She's right, Terence. They were both efficient and effective on yesterday's crash in Seattle."

He inspected them both carefully. He stared at Andi's hand on Miranda's shoulder until she yanked it away. Terence would know how few people's touch Miranda could tolerate and she didn't want him reading anything into it.

"I never thought Jeremy would be the one to tame the beast."

"Beast? What beast?" Taz had preternaturally sharp hearing

and stepped over from where Mike and Holly were still with Jeremy.

"He was referring to you," Miranda didn't have a clue about playing it coy.

"Sweet, innocent, little," she patted a hand on top of her head, "me? A beast? Who are you to call me that?" Her voice, thin and pouty, made Andi laugh.

Terence must have caught her expression because he held out a hand to Taz and offered a smile, "Terence Graham, Director of the NTSB Training Center at your service."

Taz looked down at his hand. "Don't know as we need a schoolteacher."

"He's also been my mentor for the last eighteen years," Miranda spoke up.

"Well, aren't you the cagey bitch, Miranda? Welcome then," she grabbed Terence's hand and shook it once hard.

"I don't mean to be," Miranda whispered.

Andi placed a soothing hand on her back and whispered, "Joke."

"Oh. I'm never good at those."

Andi rubbed a soothing hand on Miranda's back until she realized what she was doing and stuffed it into her pants pocket.

Then an evil smile creased Taz's face. "Beast, huh? Yeah. Damn straight, people. Now let's get a move on. I already had Jeremy remind the incident commander to get us every floodlight he could. Sun is setting soon and it's gonna be a long night, so let's get our asses moving. The cranes are setting up to start clearing the debris."

"Black Hawk and...a Viper." Miranda said before anyone could move.

Andi listened and could just barely make out the sounds of two approaching helicopters over the hubbub of the emergency crews. The beat frequencies were hard to separate but she ultimately decided that Miranda was right.

"Wow! How could you hear that over everything?"

Miranda tugged her sleeve, pulling her over tight against Miranda's side, then she pointed to the east.

A parked fire truck had blocked her own view, but not Miranda's. The two helos were approaching fast, not settling for landing at the nearby airport.

"Taz is right. You can be sneaky."

"I don't mean to be," Miranda said again.

"Joke," Andi whispered once more.

"Again," Miranda sighed.

The team watched as they circled in, then landed side-by-side on the grassy field that separated the parking lot from the highway. Few of the rescue workers spared them a glance.

The narrow Marine Corps AH-1Z Viper gunship landed first. Two men in combat utility uniforms clambered out and came over to their group as the big transport landed beside the Viper. An older man, wearing Air Force combat fatigues that didn't actually look all that different, came from that transport.

"Who's in charge of the investigation here?" The Marine Corps colonel, she could see his insignia now that he was close, snapped out. "I'm Colonel Blake McGrady of Marine Corps HMX-1. I'll be taking over this investigation."

"Actually, Colonel, you're outranked on that—by me. General Jack Macy of the US Air Force Accident Investigation Board. At least I thought I'd be in the lead," the Air Force general said in a much calmer voice, "until I saw this man. How you doing, Terence? Can't believe they dragged your old carcass back into the field once more, even if you are the best investigator ever."

"Actually, not anymore. With Miranda Chase here, I'm not the one you want in charge."

They all turned to face Miranda.

"Hmm, might have heard some about you."

"I'm not the one in charge this time, General. The IIC for this investigation is—"

"No, Miranda," Terence cut her off. "Apologies to Jeremy, but this one is too important. You're on deck."

Andi could see that the change was upsetting her. "It's okay, Miranda."

"No prob." Taz agreed very quickly.

Andi didn't mind seeing that Taz even *could* be cowed, however briefly.

Miranda looked at them both for a long moment before nodding her acceptance and turning back to the others.

"I'm Miranda Chase. Investigator-in-Charge for the NTSB." She stated her rote line, drawing strange looks from the new arrivals.

Andi saw that Terence gave Miranda a smile and a satisfied nod. So he knew about her strange ways.

"You sure about this, Terence?" General Macy didn't look happy.

"Why wouldn't I be?"

"Well," the general tipped his head toward Miranda, "some of the reports I've heard—"

Before he could continue, Jon rushed over and saluted sharply. "There you are, General. Now we can get this moving."

" 'Some of the reports I've heard'," Taz stepped in front of Jon, who stumbled back. "What the fuck lies have you been spreading behind Miranda's back?"

"They aren't lies. They're—"

Andi didn't wait for Taz to shoot him with her Taser again.

She shifted from Miranda's side and, putting every bit of training she had into it, she punched Major Jon Swift square in the nose.

He swore loudly as he stumbled back, tripped over a

twisted shopping cart, and landed on a pile of fire hose. He clutched his bleeding nose. She could only hope she broke it!

Andi tugged down on her t-shirt to straighten it and turned to the general.

"Captain Andrea Wu, formerly of the 160th Special Aviation Operation Regiment—1st Battalion. Don't believe everything an idiot neurotypical says about someone he never understood, sir."

"Neurotypical?" But he didn't sound as if he was asking what it was. Instead, he glanced at Terence for confirmation before turning to Miranda. "You have staunch defenders, Ms. Chase."

"I do, General Macy. I find that..." she pulled out her notebook and flipped to her page of emoticons.

Andi pointed at "comforted" but Miranda shook her head. She tried pointing at "happy."

"Almost... Oh, this one. And that one. Pleased...*and* surprised. Can I be both at once?"

Andi nodded, "Except there's no need to feel surprised. You earn it, Miranda."

"If you say so," she turned back to the general. "I feel pleased, General." He'd been watching her carefully as she tucked away the notebook.

She must have noticed his attention.

"I find emotions difficult to understand, General. I do not have the same issues with aircraft incident investigations."

He finally nodded. "Then let's see you do your stuff."

Miranda pulled out a different notebook, turned to a clean page, and carefully wrote "VH-92A" across the top then the date and place.

Next, she tugged a weather gauge out one of her vest pockets and held it aloft.

She had to wait as another air ambulance, racing by low overhead, blasted them with the downdraft.

41

Drake sat at the PEOC conference table with the President and Sarah. The new Presidential Emergency Operations Center was five stories under the West Wing entrance driveway. The old PEOC under the East Wing was far too distant and outdated for use in a true emergency. And Roosevelt's original hardened bunker under the North Portico had been such a small and uncomfortable space that even Roosevelt himself hadn't used it.

The only thing that had happened out of the ordinary since landing was the eight-minute flight from Andrews Air Force Base. A small fleet of helicopters from the 160th SOAR Night Stalkers—far more than the usual overwatch protection for Marine One—had whisked them to the White House. Each of the three of them had worn full HazMat suits complete with isolated air bottles from the E-4B's lower hold until they were secure in the PEOC. SOAR's pilots had worn the same.

The press hadn't been notified of the President's return and the phalanx of Secret Service agents had immediately hidden the HazMat suits from view.

The President and Sarah had spent much of the flight on

the E-4B Nightwatch putting the shambles of the G-7 meeting back together—videoconferencing from the sky.

After another brief announcement to reassure the nation, they were seated at the big conference table finishing the last cobbled-together sessions of the meeting remotely.

Drake had listened in for a while, but found nothing to add. It was out of his hands now and up to the politicians. So he'd taken a seat at the far end of the table, out of sight of the conference, and set one of the side screens to CNN.

His aide was feeding him all of the moderate-priority items that he'd been holding in abeyance during the week-long trip. Drake began working his way down the list as he kept one eye on the news.

Even though Clark had been dead for less than seven hours, speculation ran hot and heavy on his replacement—a question the President hadn't said a single word on. Even when they were reporting on the stock market, the "money shot" of the stark scene at the Walmart where Clark had died remained behind the anchors.

Their long telephotos were following all the worst aspects of such a massive rescue. As the parking lot casualties were cleared, tow trucks had swept in, clearing swaths of broiled cars. That allowed the arrival and setup of heavy equipment for lifting away sections of the collapsed building. The cranes were up and big dump trucks began arriving to cart away the wreckage.

But they were still a long way from reaching the obvious epicenter of the disaster near the center of the structure.

He caught a brief glimpse of Miranda's team, their vests with the large NTSB letters across their shoulders making them easy to pick out when the news camera focused there. Then it swooped back to the carnage, seeking anything new to show after so many hours on site.

"Well, that's done," President Cole dropped into a chair beside him.

"Is the G-7 still up and running?"

"Maybe we should crash an executive helicopter more often," Sarah slid into a chair across the table. She scrubbed two hands over her face. "Christ! Please pretend I didn't just say that. What time zone are we in anyway?"

"It *was* how they were behaving though," the President sighed. "Ridiculously pandering lip service. For whatever reason, I did get them to sign off on several of our key priorities with impressively little quibbling—at least until the next meeting. Anything new in the world?"

"Bookies are going to make a fortune on who replaces the Vice President. Even the news anchors are laying down bets," Drake pointed at the screen. "Nobody's pulled my name out of the hat, so I'm feeling pretty okay about the whole game. Looks like you're in the clear too, Sarah."

She offered a sigh of relief.

President Cole simply grunted in exasperation.

They'd finally gone to a new story—for about ten seconds —then they flashed the *Breaking* banner for about the tenth time since he'd started watching. Behind it was an image of Clarissa Reese.

"This should be good," Drake turned up the volume.

An anchor spoke over the banner, "We're switching to the crash site in Frederick, Maryland, where the Vice President's helicopter crashed this morning and killed over seven hundred people—mostly shoppers and employees of a Walmart. The following happened just a few minutes ago."

"Grieving widow?" Cole asked.

"No. That red power suit definitely belongs to the Director of the CIA," was Sarah's guess.

Whatever it was, Drake supposed that she'd chosen her background carefully. The disaster of her husband's crash was clear behind her, accented by the long shadows of the evening sun.

Then the camera pulled back enough to show the man standing close beside her.

"Isn't that—"

"My nephew," Drake groaned. He'd been getting reports of Jon's treatment of Miranda through his wife, and he wasn't happy with the boy. Now Jon was in the shark's clutches and who knew what could happen next.

"He looks like he slept in a gutter."

Indeed, his uniform was badly stained and his hair was a mess. His eyes were unnaturally wide. "Bambi in the headlights now."

The on-site reporter took over. "We're here at the crash site with CIA Director Clarissa Reese, the wife—" the reporter blanched for a moment before continuing awkwardly "—the widow of Vice President Clark Winston, whose body still lies in the wreckage behind us. Director Reese..."

Something had the reporter looking up—then ducking abruptly.

A loud roar came out of the television's speakers as a pair of helos swooped by close overhead: an Air Force Black Hawk and a Marine Corps Viper, both in their landing flare as if they'd tied in a race to be first on site. A camera made a dizzying, and unsuccessful, attempt to follow their flight.

The picture blurred and was blanked as the cameramen were battered aside by the wind, but they recovered quickly.

The screen split, one image tracking the helicopters as they came in to land, and the other—

"First time I've seen her looking less than perfect," the President observed.

Indeed, Clarissa Reese looked disheveled. Her jacket was askew, her leather portfolio clutched rather desperately, and her hair was out of its permanent ponytail and looking distinctly windblown. For half an instant, she looked pissed as hell.

Someone had stolen her spotlight.

Then she glanced to her side and looked truly livid for just an instant before regaining control.

"Where did your nephew go?" Sarah was the first to notice.

"There," President Cole pointed at the other side of the split-view screen. "Showing the good sense to get away from Reese and rejoin the crash investigation team. That is his job after all."

The reporter attempted to recover from his bumbled introduction, Clarissa's face shifted back, not to sad, but at least to businesslike.

"Director Reese, please let me add my condolences to the nation's; we're all grieving tonight. Your husband was a great public servant. Can you tell us how you're holding up?"

"I'm...okay."

"And what will you miss most?"

"Other than having my husband beside me? I think that I'll most miss the close collaboration we shared as we strove together to preserve and protect our great nation."

"That doesn't sound like any version of Clarissa I know," Drake studied her face to see what she was up to.

"Not the grieving widow," President Cole watched the screen closely.

"I bet she's running for office." The moment he said it, Drake knew it was true.

"I will miss him," Clarissa managed to look sad. "And I will keep the memory of him alive as I strive to fulfill our shared dreams for the safety of America and Americans everywhere."

"You each owe me five bucks," Drake would like to be wrong about Reese, even just once.

Sarah laughed at his chances of collecting on that. Cole just grimaced.

"I will grieve for him later. But as the Director of the CIA, I will not rest until—"

"Yipes! That had to hurt!" a voice shouted over hers.

The other half of the split screen zoomed in to fill the entire screen, pushing Clarissa out of view.

They replayed the segment.

The group of inspectors were gathered near the helicopters. Three small women and one older man with NTSB emblazoned across the back of their vests were facing mostly away from the camera. Three military men had approached them from the newly arrived helos.

And Jon.

"That's General Jack Macy," one of the commentators noted as a pointer circled his face. "He is the lead investigator for the Air Force's Accident Investigation Board. The man next to him is believed to be the commander of HMX-1, responsible for the Vice President's helicopter that crashed here today. And we're not sure who this is. He left Director Reese's side, apparently feeling that he had to be part of that discussion. There, we can see him gesticulating..."

And then one of the NTSB women half a foot shorter than Jon hauled off and punched him in the face. He tumbled over backward, adding a massively bloody nose to his dishevelment. Even at the distance they were being kept back, the news team had picked up his yelp of pain.

"Nice one, Andi!" President Cole practically cheered. "Um, I'm assuming your nephew deserved that, Drake. Either way, it was a beautiful punch."

Everyone else on the investigation team continued talking as if nothing had happened.

Drake sighed. "Sadly, I'm sure he did. The boy lacks tact."

But he couldn't let the President get away with besmirching the family honor even more than Jon already had.

Drake turned to him and asked in his nicest voice, "So, Clarissa Reese is your choice for VP."

"I'll let the party leaders know," Sarah chimed in.

Roy Cole glared at them both as Sarah laughed in the President's face.

Drake tried to, but it struck him that just might be her plan.

42

By the time the cameras actually came back to her, Clarissa was past rage and into depression.

Clark was dead, cutting off her path to the White House.

She was out of the loop with the President.

And now she was going to have to suck up to Miranda Chase of all people.

When Major Jon Swift tried to return to her side, she considered punching his nose herself—as if he'd be an asset now that he'd made an idiot of himself on national television. She would have flattened him simply for the satisfaction of it— if she hadn't been standing in the middle of the news pool.

She'd been so angry at Clark for dying and Jon for walking away that she'd come close to declaring on national news that Clark's death was an act of foreign terrorism. That would be beyond a *faux pas* and right over into disclosure of classified intelligence—an actionable offense. She'd been stopped only by Jon getting his face mashed in by one of Miranda's little women.

An act of terrorism...

Of domestic terrorism?

If so, the FBI and the Secret Service were all over the site already and had it covered. As the CIA Director, she had no role here except the pitiful widow—which was so beneath her.

Her job was overseas security and intelligence.

Like all that chatter last night and this morning.

That chatter...hadn't been domestic.

She hadn't slowed down enough to think about it.

This *wasn't* domestic terrorism. She needed to verify only one fact to be completely certain of that.

"We're back again with CIA Director Clarissa Reese and the widow of Vice President Clark Winston. The first thing I'd like to ask you..."

Clarissa tuned the reporter out.

All of that chatter had to mean that it *was* a foreign attack on US soil.

That information should go to...who?

Jon Swift had been a mistake, useless. But the lead on the investigation would be—

Miranda!

Figured. The woman might be irritating, but she was on a first-name basis with the Chairman of the Joint Chiefs, the President, even her late husband.

"Where's Miranda?"

"Who?" The reporter looked at her like she'd lost her mind.

"Never mind."

She'd partner with Miranda and find out exactly who had murdered her path to the White House.

And if that didn't work, she'd drag Senator Hunter Ramson into a CIA interrogation site and see what she could learn that way.

43

"WHAT ARE YOU DOING?"

Miranda ignored the Marine Corps colonel while she recorded the weather readings.

"*Musica universalis.* Music of the spheres," Terence saved her from taking the time to explain to the colonel. "You're still using that investigation model, Miranda?"

His question meant she *did* have to take the time. She forced her attention from the readings and noted that she also had General Macy's attention.

"It's a method of logical approach to a crash investigation site that Director Terence Graham and I developed to form a methodology for me. Outer sphere of environmental conditions such as terrain and weather. Next, the edge of the debris field followed by inspection of the debris itself. Then the aircraft, and finally the human factors." She turned back to Terence. "At my team's suggestion, I've also added an outer causal meta-sphere to which we may attach conjecture and compare those to the facts discovered in the successive inner spheres."

"Now I'm lost," Colonel McGrady complained.

Miranda ignored him.

"And you never skip a sphere?" the general asked.

"I find it very confusing to do so, therefore I don't do it often." Then she considered. The nested spheres of an investigation had been a model that Terence had developed to help her during her academy training. It hadn't been needed by other students.

Did the other members of her team need it? Perhaps not.

"That's a fascinating thought, General."

"What is?"

Miranda turned to Taz. "Take Jeremy and Holly. The three of you should proceed toward the center of the crash as fast as is safe. Based on the final words of the pilot, it's a reasonable conjecture that she was accurate about that aspect of what was happening. Assume there was a poison, I think we can assume that the air has cleared, but don't touch anything without gloves. Send Mike back to me."

Taz nodded once and sprinted away.

"Colonel McGrady, as the commander of HMX-1, I assume you are a good enough pilot to assist Andi."

"To *assist*? I'm the President's pilot. I'm—"

"Andi," she decided that ignoring him had been a good initial choice. "Please review every image you can find of the final flight from Camp David including the crash event itself. I expect there are now a wide variety of them posted online. I want you to particularly study any control issues. Also look for why the pilot engaged the emergency air system. That's a very unusual action."

"Hold it," the colonel spoke softly.

She prepared herself to ignore him some more. It was exceedingly difficult as he kept pulling her attention from the task at hand.

"You're right. Why the hell would Tamatha have done that?"

"That's why I suggested it as a line of research."

"I'll take care of that," the colonel insisted.

"No. Andi knows what I'm looking for."

"Who is she that—"

Andi squared off in front of him. "Captain Andrea Wu of the 160th SOAR, Colonel. I've flown overwatch protection on your HMX-1 flights. And as I'm discharged from the armed forces, allow me to point out that I'm not above offering you the same inducement to cooperate that I just delivered to Major Swift. Every one of your interruptions is causing Miranda a great mental hardship."

The general smiled at her before turning to the colonel. "Yes, McGrady. Now would be a fine time to shut up. And if you doubt her, according to her commander, Captain Wu was SOAR's absolute best pilot. A pleasure to meet you at last, Andrea."

"Andi."

He nodded. "Not another word, Colonel. Just go."

"Excuse me for disagreeing with you, General," Mike hurried up to join the group, slightly out of breath.

Miranda gasped out her own relief. Mike would take care of the troublesome colonel *without* hitting him in the nose.

"I need to speak with the pilots of all of the related flights: the decoy aircraft, the overwatch, and the governors' flight."

The colonel responded easily to Mike. "Except for the 160th's overwatch team, you can find them all at the HMX-1 hangar in Quantico. But it's on full security lockdown until we solve this."

Mike groaned.

Miranda for once understood why. Quantico was over eighty miles away.

Then she noticed that Andi was on the phone and listened in. "Hello, Colonel Stimson. This is Andi Wu and we're at the site of the Vice President's crash. ... Yes sir. A great tragedy. Could you please have the overwatch pilots meet me at the site and bring any data and imaging from that flight? ... Yes, thank you, sir. And I can't believe that you told the tall tale to General Macy about my being your top— Thank you, sir. Please let me just say with all due respect that I think you're full of it, sir."

Then she laughed and hung up.

"They'll be here in under twenty minutes." Then she turned to glare at the colonel. "Do you have any other dumbass ideas on how to stonewall this investigation, Colonel McGrady? Or are you going to get your pilots airborne right *now?*"

McGrady stared down at Andi as if she might be a live grenade with the pin already pulled.

"Wait!" Miranda took Andi's arm. "Is that a metaphor? Thinking that you're like a live grenade with the pin already pulled?"

"Yes it is!" Andi smiled at her, then held up a hand. "Well done, you. High five, girlfriend."

Miranda slapped it.

"What the hell?" Colonel McGrady muttered, but pulled out his cell phone and began arranging for his pilots to join them here.

Terence also held up a hand.

Miranda slapped that one as well. Maybe she finally was getting metaphors figured out.

44

CLARISSA DID HER BEST TO ASSESS WHAT THE HELL WAS GOING ON. The colonel on the phone looked pissed. Some general she didn't recognize looked amused. And the others were all high fiving each other like they'd just won at Bingo.

Thankfully there was no sign of Holly or Taz.

"Miranda," Clarissa dragged her aside a few steps. "I have information for you. I don't know what it means yet, my people are working on that, but I have reason to believe that it is relevant to this situation."

"Okay."

"We intercepted a cell phone message that said, *Burn the fields.* It was sent approximately ten minutes before Clark's crash. We pinpointed the location to an area just northwest of here—that's the direction of Camp David." It wasn't until she said it that she understood exactly how neatly it fit the crash scenario.

Miranda just looked at her blankly. Or perhaps at her hair.

Clarissa reached back to check her ponytail and discovered that her hair was loose and spread over her shoulders. Her clip was gone and she didn't have another with her. No one except

Clark ever saw her hair loose. And yet she'd just been on camera—

Yet another piece of herself she'd lost today.

Miranda still waited.

"That's all that I can tell someone at your level about. But I thought it might be useful."

Miranda simply held up her ID with her finger pointing to her security clearance.

"Yankee White Category One? You can be *armed* in his presence? Why the hell are you cleared to that level? Even I don't have that."

"Roy felt it was advisable. Feel free to tell me what other information you have."

It took Clarissa a moment to connect that Miranda meant the President. Roy?

"Not with your goddamn shadow here," she scowled at Andi.

Andi reached for her own ID.

"Oh fuck. Please don't. Today's already been enough of a nightmare. Okay, fine. We picked up massive amounts of chatter late yesterday. It originated somewhere in the Middle East—probably Saudi Arabia, but I can't confirm that. It had all the earmarks of an attack on US soil. It took all night to narrow it down to the general DC area. Most of it was heavily encrypted, but that one piece was in the clear: *Burn the fields.* My cyber people tell me that it has all the indicators of being accidental rather than intentional that it was unencrypted— whatever the hell that means."

Miranda and Andi exchanged a look that Clarissa couldn't interpret. Andi was the one who spoke first.

"I would have to check with Jeremy, but I expect that there was a follow-on pulse of communication after that message was in the clear, to remonstrate the sender."

Clarissa wouldn't know and didn't care. She'd learned not

to bother paying too much attention when Harry and Heidi started on one of their technical rambles. If she did, she'd lose the big picture, which was why the cyber twins worked for her and not the other way around.

Miranda pulled out a notebook and wrote, *Burn the fields.* Directly above that was the windspeed and temperature. Above that was: *Poison. Oxy. Generator. ...Dying(?)*

"Poison? What the hell is that?"

"The pilot's final transmission."

"Why the hell would someone poison Clark?" And why hadn't she known that herself?

"Why comes later," Miranda stated without so much as blinking.

"Do you suppose that's what they meant by *burn the fields?*" Clarissa couldn't make sense of it.

"Would that be a metaphor? I have a really hard time with metaphors."

Miranda turned to Andi before Clarissa could think how to answer such a simple question.

"Do you see the fire chief anywhere?"

Andi pulled out her phone and dialed. "Hello, Chief. Andi Wu of the NTSB here again. Would you happen to know if there was any sort of an agricultural or field fire in the area this morning?"

She went through a series of uh-huh noises, then thanked him and hung up.

"It was literal, not metaphorical. Just outside of Frederick, a few miles north of here, there was a large and unexplained fire. It spanned a number of fields in a box pattern roughly a mile square. His fire marshal found accelerants at the site."

"Accelerants?" Clarissa knew she should stop merely asking questions and regain power by issuing orders, but her thoughts were in a jumble worse than after a session with...Miranda.

"Like gasoline and such, they accelerate the growth of a fire.

It means that it was intentional arson. This was home heating fuel oil, which makes a particularly dense and black smoke."

Clarissa swallowed hard.

"That implies," Miranda spoke carefully, "—strictly on the conjectural sphere level—that *burn the fields* was a literal instruction to do so. Doing that in a large square pattern would make a Marine Corps pilot exercise caution by cutting off outside air flow and engaging the emergency internal air supply."

"But who?"

"That comes second-to-last, Clarissa, just before *why*. However, it is a useful hypothesis of *how* if not *who*."

Clarissa felt a chill that she could guess.

Last night's chatter had come out of either Egypt or Saudi Arabia, ordering a fire to be set in Maryland.

Rose Ramson had said that the senator had been terribly upset at reports of the President's agenda regarding the Saudis.

Had Senator Hunter Ramson done something that had gotten Clark killed?

45

"Any chance of getting out of here?"

Danziger just shook his head at the President's question. "I'm sorry, Mr. President. We're keeping you in the PEOC until we know how, who, and that we can block them. The others are welcome to leave."

"Not a chance," the President sighed. "If I'm stuck here, so are the two of you."

Drake had called Lizzy the moment he'd arrived safely. Though he'd asked if she wanted to join them, she'd gone to her office at the NRO to see if she could do anything to help.

Danziger returned to his security console, which left just himself, the President, and Sarah at the main conference table. This being the White House, someone had rustled up a surprisingly delicious meal. Slow-braised beef in a thick mushroom gravy, over baked potatoes with a side of roasted Brussels sprouts shouldn't be possible inside a bunker.

"You have a PEOC chef?"

The President grunted. "I have no idea. You'd have to ask Danziger how this got here. Not that I'm complaining."

Drake wasn't either and decided it was best not to interrupt him with such trivia.

There was a soft beep from the phone in the middle of the conference table. "We have a video call for General Drake Nason from General Elizabeth Gray," an invisible operator announced.

"On screen." He waited until he could see her face on the central display screen. "Hi, honey. Why are you coming in on the secure line instead of my phone? Oh, never mind. Sorry, I think I'm still on Kiwi time."

Lizzy barely smiled. "I also have Miranda Chase on the line." A small window opened beside Lizzy.

"Hi, Miranda. How is the investigation going?"

"Busy."

Sarah laughed briefly. The President didn't.

"Why the call?" He knew that Miranda always liked going straight to business.

"Miranda called me to see if we had any satellite imagery of the Vice President's final flight. Specifically four miles northwest of the crash site. I felt that you all needed to see the video that I found."

Drake watched the nondescript farmland long enough for the satellite's view angle to shift. Lizzy had once explained that low-earth orbit moved along at eight kilometers a second, so it didn't take very long for the view to change, but this time it felt as if it was taking forever.

"What are we looking for?"

Then he saw.

A line of black boiled up out of a field.

As the satellite's view continued to shift, he could see that it was a wall of smoke and fire.

Identical fires burst to life to the right and left.

"What's our scale here?"

"So far, a mile on a side."

He whistled. That meant the fires were throwing aloft fifty-to hundred-foot-thick smoke walls.

Then a bright red circle appeared in the upper left, northwest corner of the three-sided box.

"This is Marine Two," Lizzy announced.

The instant it entered the box, a fourth fire bloomed to life behind the aircraft.

"They were boxed in." Even as he said it, the helicopter flew a small circle as if looking for an escape. Then it once again aimed for the southeast corner and drove through the smoke wall.

Now Miranda spoke up. "None of the other aircraft had a problem. Mike has started interviewing their pilots. None of them engaged their emergency air systems. It is unknown why the pilot of Marine Two did so."

"That's easy, Miranda. The pilot didn't want to risk that the fire itself was a gas attack on the Vice President."

"I always forget about the people. Sorry."

"Or maybe..." Sarah looked puzzled, then shrugged. "Maybe the pilot just didn't want the smoky fire to stink up the cabin for the Vice President's ride."

Someone spoke off to Miranda's side. She nodded before explaining.

"Colonel McGrady said that either scenario would fit within standard HMX-1 practices. He said that for either reason, it was guaranteed that the pilot of the primary aircraft would switch to internal air."

"Good work, Miranda. Anything else?"

"No." And the picture disappeared from the screen as she hung up.

"What the..." Sarah gave a half laugh of surprise.

"You get used to her ways." Drake remembered just how strange and irritating he'd found her at first. Now he wouldn't change her.

"Do you have more for us, General Gray?"

His wife rolled her eyes at his sudden formality. "Yes, but I wanted to wait until Miranda was off the line as this doesn't relate directly to her investigation. You know the trouble she has with distractions."

"You're the best, Lizzy." Damn but Drake loved this woman. "No matter what Sarah says about you."

This time it was Lizzy who laughed in his face rather than Sarah. She continued before Sarah could get in her jab.

"We've tracked the entire flight path end-to-end—sheer chance that there were no gaps in our coverage over Maryland during the time window. There were no surprises along Marine Two's entire flight path other than the fire."

"I think one surprise of that scale was plenty."

"I agree. Each side of the box was laid down by fuel trucks for home heating oil. We were also able to track the fuel trucks backward. It was a coordinated strike. Each truck belonged to a different supplier. Three of the original drivers have been found, dead at the point of the carjacking...or truck-jacking. The police are still looking for the fourth one."

The President and Sarah looked as ill as he felt.

"A lot of planning went into this," Lizzy continued. "One more thing. After each truck spilled several thousand gallons of heating oil down those four lines to form the box, each was parked at the middle of the line. And," Lizzy herself swallowed hard, "the drivers were still sitting in the trucks when they burned."

"Brainwashed jihadis?" Drake wanted Lizzy to deny it.

But she didn't.

46

MIRANDA HAD BEEN INTERRUPTED SO MANY TIMES THAT SHE hardly knew what was happening anymore.

There were so many people and pieces, and every one of them seemed to be in motion like...like...the molecules in a superheated gas.

Another metaphor.

That made her feel enough better that she could open her eyes once more.

Andi was standing so closely in front of her that Miranda could barely see the wreckage.

"Is there anything I can do to help?"

"I wish."

Andi held her hand for a moment, then slipped away Miranda's phone. "I'll take care of any more calls, okay?"

Miranda could only nod in relief. A whole cluster of connections were snipped off with that simple act.

"I need..."

Andi didn't ask what, she just waited.

Miranda knew that she'd stretched herself nearly to the

limits of her autism. The only place she'd ever found to recharge after too much interaction was on her island.

"I need," she tried again at the cost of repeating herself, "you to stay close beside me."

Andi's eyes shot wide. "Me?"

"Remember, you're the calm one. I need," again a careful breath, "to be able to trust that right now."

"The calm one! I punched out Jon. I threatened to attack Colonel McGrady, a bird colonel."

Miranda nodded. "Exactly. You create a calm space around me. Holly tries, but she's so much harder for me to understand. All her...bravado. I constantly have to *think* around her."

"Whereas I don't make you think at all?" Andi had a half smile.

"Yes."

Andi laughed outright. "Perfect. Just perfect."

"No," Miranda rested a hand on Andi's arm and didn't mind making the contact. "Holly's...the safe one. I know I'm always safe around her. You're the calm one. I don't *have* to think around you. You're just...Andi. Like the earlier tautology that Jeremy is Jeremy. It's a good thing, Andi."

Andi rested her hand briefly over Miranda's. "When all this is done, Miranda, we're going to have a long talk."

"A good one or a bad one?"

"Not a bad one," but Andi's shrug suggested that it might not be a good one either. What other option was there?

"Okay." Miranda couldn't think of one more thing right now. Not even enough of it to make a note in her notebook.

She turned to face the wreckage.

They were at the leading edge of the debris field, mere feet inside the store's main entrance.

In the lead, sniffer dogs patrolled the edges seeking any signs of human remains. After creating a path across the parking lot and finding no survivors there, no hope remained for those inside. But she supposed they still had to look.

After the cranes lifted away sections of the steel roof and beams, Jeremy, Holly, and Taz forged as far ahead as they dared.

Next, the body removal teams worked among the rubble.

Then, finally, she and her debris team moved in to look through stacks of boxed sneakers, scattered high heels, and twisted mounds of t-shirts, women's dresses, and boy's undies.

It was quite difficult to follow the primary path at first. She could see a section of rotor blade protruding from Subway's sandwich bread oven. Another portion, that had flown in the opposite direction, had speared an ATM, scattering twenty-dollar bills like...like...twenty-dollar bills on the floor.

Metaphors *were* tricky.

Once they were inside the entrance, tracing the debris path became easier the farther they penetrated into the store. With only minor exceptions, the helo had remained intact as it raced deeper into the building. The path was also easy to trace—once the roof cladding and beams were lifted aside—by the long-running scars that had been scraped into the concrete floor.

There was also an overlay of soot that was wider than the damage path, but not by much.

She and Andi kept the lead of the debris team so that she could see everything as undisturbed as possible.

Terence might have retired from the field, but he'd personally created whole sections of crash-investigation methodology and he followed close behind. Clarissa, rather than being a distraction, had begun taking notes for Terence as they moved ahead. She also had an adept hand for diagraming.

General Macy led the AIB because he'd been an investigator for years and was working close beside Terence. Jon was helping him, under the sole condition that he was only allowed to speak to the general.

As Mike finished with interviewing each of the pilots, they

formed a muscle team along with Colonel McGrady and his crew chief. They did the heavy lifting that was too small for the big cranes but too heavy for the NTSB team.

Miranda allowed herself to act as guide and Andi as photographer. Every scrap of the helicopter was GPS located and imaged, then labeled and gathered by McGrady's team.

It took three long hours to forge a path through the wreckage until the trail led to the helicopter itself.

When they finally did reach it, there was the strangest sight. Several large sections of the roof had been lifted away to reveal the nose of the helicopter.

"That's crazy!" Andi exclaimed and the others stopped as well.

The big VH-92A Superhawk was mostly intact, parked among the melted frozen foods of the big walk-in freezer. Inside and out, the helicopter had been scorched black, but it looked intact except for a hard list to the right. And the missing rotors.

"The freezer's walls must have protected it from the brunt of the explosion that ripped apart the store." While it was conjecture, it was obvious enough that Miranda was tempted to move it directly to the "crash" sphere of information.

Jeremy, who must have slipped ahead of even the search team, stood up inside the cockpit and looked out at her through the missing windscreen. There was soot smeared across his face in a number of directions, but he was smiling.

"Hey, Miranda. Isn't this fascinating? As far as I can tell, there were multiple explosions. The first would have killed any survivors still inside the helicopter," he waved a hand to indicate the corpses of the pilots charred in either seat. "The doctors will have to do autopsies to see if anyone inhaled fire or if they'd already stopped breathing before it happened. Did you see that windshield over in garden hoses? The scorch marks on the inside but not the outside? First blast. Pow!" He slapped the palm of one hand against the other held at face height as if driving it out through the windshield.

Then he climbed out the window, slid down the nose to land on his feet, leaving a cleaner streak on the crumpled nose metal.

"The second blast looks like a conventional fire." He turned to face the helicopter and made as if he was throwing two fistfuls of fire at the nose. "Did you see the signs of the fuel leakage all of the way from the entrance? It must have been spilling fuel the whole way. I can't quite prove it yet, but I'm close, and I kinda think that the first explosion from inside the helicopter must have fired off the second fire. Then came the third one. Wow! Just wow! Come see. Come see."

He headed toward the still blocked side door into the helicopter.

As soon as they were out of the way, the corpse team moved in.

Miranda followed Jeremy.

47

"I've never seen anything like it," Sarah whispered as she watched the screen.

The incident commander had finally allowed one news team into the crash site, provided they shared the images with everyone present. CNN had the best gear and led the way—which had apparently so pissed off Fox News that they'd refused to broadcast any of it.

They'd kept the camera team at the very rear, well away from the NTSB team.

Drake simply looked over at the President.

They might not have seen this much carnage on American soil since 9/11, but they'd certainly seen more than their share during their military service.

"That woman is a little scary," Sarah apparently wasn't commenting on the wreckage. The camera had followed the cleared path into the center of the destruction and was filming the team.

"Which one?" Drake had watched Miranda as she forged in the lead of the group that included the camera, but it was Andi who'd been keeping them updated on findings.

"All of them!"

Drake laughed...then groaned.

Clarissa must have realized the power of the first view of the helicopter. She had drifted back from lead team and now stood front and center.

"Ms. Reese, we didn't expect to find the CIA's director here," the reporter greeted her.

Drake was actually impressed. Her red jacket was gone. There were several tears in her black blouse and red skirt. Who knew what kind of stains her black boots hid. She looked human—almost.

"I," Clarissa cleared her throat and wiped vainly at her hair, instead leaving a smear of soot across her cheek.

Or was that intentional?

"I'm not here as the Director of the CIA. I'm here for Clark. I hope that by assisting the team in discovering how this could possibly happen to my poor husband, I can appease some of my own personal grief. Perhaps I'm still in shock."

President Cole offered a thoughtful grunt on the last point.

"Altruism, my ass." Drake felt no need to restrain himself on the subject of the CIA director.

"She's there, Drake," Sarah pointed out.

"If it's selfless, it will be a historic first-time-ever event."

"If that isn't what's happening," the President spoke softly, "what does it tell us that she is there?"

"Other than bidding for the Vice Presidency?"

"Yes, other than that."

Drake watched as Clarissa apologized, saying she was needed, and returned to the older NTSB agent's side to resume taking notes.

What was Clarissa Reese up to?

Drake recalled the first time he'd met her. It was during the Caspar aerial drone debacle—a secret search-and-destroy project she'd developed. Secret, including from himself and the President.

She'd almost started a war with the damn thing.

So, why had she insinuated herself into the very front of the site investigation team?

"She either...suspects something or, even worse, knows something." Drake considered. "If it's the latter, she's there to keep it from being found. No, that can't be it. She's got to know that she could never hide anything with Miranda on site."

"Ms. Chase is that good?" Sarah asked.

"Yes," he and the President said in unison.

"Which means," Drake continued, "that Clarissa, in addition to wanting to be Roy Cole's new best friend, suspects something and is hoping that Miranda can prove or disprove it."

"Poison," Sarah stated flatly. "So we already know it's an act of terrorism. Domestic or foreign?"

"Assuming the latter, Ms. National Security Advisor, what are your thoughts on who might be behind it?" President Cole began tapping that giveaway left forefinger on the desk. He was thinking extremely hard, though Drake couldn't read quite what.

"Give me a minute," Sarah pulled over her tablet.

Drake made a show of looking at his watch.

If Sarah noticed, she ignored him.

48

Jeremy waved for Miranda to kneel beside him near the starboard sponson. The fuel tanks for the VH-92A Superhawk were outboard of the main passenger cabin. The streamlined extensions to either side were fifteen feet long, and both two feet wide and high. The landing gear folded up into the very rear of the sponson. The rest was fuel, four hundred gallons per side.

"The other side was gouged open by a cash register. I found nine dollars and thirty-seven cents in assorted change caught in the wheel well. That's what caused the spill all along the fire path that we followed in."

Miranda nodded. It made sense; the scarred and scorched line across the concrete was undeniable.

"But look at this side. I found it just before you arrived."

The helicopter leaned heavily above them and the floodlights didn't reach in here.

Jeremy aimed a flashlight at the front end of the sponson. The outer aluminum skin had been pierced by numerous holes, the largest nearly the size of her fist. She lay down on the floor to look at the underside. Equally large holes had been melted through the bottom of the tank.

"Whatever it was melted all of the way through, dropping right through the fuel in the tank without being extinguished."

Miranda looked, but all of the concrete in this area was so badly scarred that no obvious patterns showed. "The location of these holes implies that the fuel would have poured out... that way."

They both rose to their feet and looked to the south.

"But see," Jeremy led the way. "It would have deflected off these cases of soda and poured in that direction."

And sure enough, fifteen meters away was a massive crater punched down into the concrete. Rather than any of the roof collapsing into the crater, it had been blown up and outward in a circular spread.

"Have you determined—" Miranda started.

"There's a few garden supplies scattered around the crater's edges and a few melted riding lawnmowers over there. I think we got a jet fuel-fertilizer mixture. Under the right conditions..."

"...an ANFO."

"Exactly. Ammonium nitrate from the fertilizer and fuel oil, or in this case kerosene jet fuel. That actually makes it an ANKJF. Oh, that's awkward. ANFO is much easier to say."

Miranda nodded, it all fit. A shipload of ammonium nitrate had degraded and destroyed much of the harbor of Beirut, Lebanon. Mixed with nitromethane as a fuel, making it ANNM, it had been used in the 1995 Oklahoma City Federal Building bombing.

"How about ANJF? Then you can pronounce it *an-jeff*."

Jeremy nodded rapidly. "I like that. That's good. I'll use that in the report."

Miranda felt the stab in her gut. In the past he'd have said *We'll use that...* or *You can use that...* But he'd already moved on to think like a team leader, even if this was technically her investigation.

To distract herself from the painful line of thought, Miranda turned back to the helicopter, but couldn't see the full scenario yet.

The wall between the front and back of the store and the freezer wall, supported from behind by the thirteen-ton helicopter, had protected the Superhawk from the worst of the blast.

The teams were now swarming the wrecked helicopter. With a clear path, some were extracting the bodies. Others were struggling to clear the debris along either side.

It took everything she had to walk back into the crowd and return to the damaged sponson. It was still a quiet haven tucked into the debris, which let her think again.

"But what caused the initial holes?"

Jeremy shrugged. "I only had a moment to look at the materials in the tank, the hull material, and the crash-proofing lining inside the tanks. Nothing seems wrong other than the holes themselves."

A circle of light briefly strobed by them.

"Do that again."

Jeremy shook his head, "I didn't do anything."

Miranda just waited.

After half a minute, Jeremy whispered, "What are we waiting for?"

Fifteen seconds later, another light strobed by. This time she was able to trace the path.

"Who's inside the helo?" she called out.

"Just about the whole freaking population of Virginia," Taz called back.

"Somebody shone a light on the starboard side. Do it again."

"There," she cried out. "Go back a bit. Good. Hold it."

"Wow! How did I miss that?" Jeremy pushed to his feet to look at one of the passenger windows.

"You have to remember to look up, Jeremy." A good reminder to herself, as she hadn't either. Andi had even said that was how to find things back on the Opera House stage.

Above the sponson, there were several long holes that penetrated the hull. One of the bullet-proof windowpanes had a particularly large hole.

Miranda rose and inspected the tilted window carefully. Because of the clear material, she could see the line of the hole that had entered the glass high on the inside, bored through the center, and emerged several inches lower down the pane. From there, it was directly over the largest hole in the sponson.

She tapped it experimentally.

Someone knocked back. Then Taz waved through the window.

"Jeremy, do you have a silicon carbide tool handy?"

"Saw or angle grinder?"

"Grinder. I just need the wheel." In moments he handed her a four-and-a-half-inch grinder wheel. She scraped it down the window. It left a very light mark.

"Taz," she yelled through the hole. "Try scraping it with your knife."

She did, but Miranda couldn't see anything. By the way Taz rubbed at her side, she couldn't either. She went to try again.

"Don't! You'll just dull your knife."

Taz hesitated, put away her knife, and stepped out the nearby doorway that had finally been cleared enough to open.

"Not much will dull my knife."

"Jeremy?" Taz's presence reminded her that she was supposed to be training Jeremy. Or testing him or...something.

"I've never had a chance to play with ALON before." He practically pressed his nose against it.

"ALON?" Taz didn't know it.

"Al—" Miranda bit on her tongue to stop it. This was so hard. Thankfully, Jeremy didn't notice and began explaining.

"Aluminum oxynitride. Transparent aluminum, like in Star Trek IV, *The Voyage Home*, only now it's real. Strong, lightweight, eighty-percent transparent (window glass is only high eighties, so not bad), radiation resistant, and super tough. This looks to be three-centimeters thickness, just over an inch. That could stop even serious armor-piercing rounds like the .50 BMG."

Miranda waited, but Jeremy didn't make the next step.

And that was the problem. Jeremy saw what was right in front of him, but he didn't always think of the next question. It was the reason he would have trouble leading his own team. Unlike Jon who missed vital details, Jeremy didn't see past them.

Miranda tried to think of how to prompt him when Taz poked a finger at the hole.

"What's its melting point?"

Miranda could only look at her in surprise. That was *exactly* the right question.

Jeremy smacked his forehead as he often did after having the next step pointed out to him.

"Centigrade it's about twenty-one hundred degrees, thirty-nine hundred Fahrenheit. So what can melt a hole through that and pass through a tank of fuel without being extinguished by the liquid? The first thing that I can think of is thermite. Iron thermite burns at over five thousand degrees F. Where did the thermite come from?" Still talking to himself, he rushed into the helicopter, actually bouncing off the other workers like a pinball.

Yes! Another metaphor. Miranda was sure of it and gave herself a pat on the back.

Taz was gazing after Jeremy with a soft smile. "Gods! He's so cute when he gets like that."

"How did you know to ask that question?"

"Hello, not an idiot, Miranda. It's obvious that Jeremy gets too hyper-focused. Worse than you in some ways because you're aware of that aspect of your autism and always struggle against it. Jeremy? It's just the way he is. I used to point things out for him. But if I hit him with a question instead, he unsticks himself and figures out the next steps on his own from there. That's probably enough time. Let's go see what he's found."

Miranda stopped her. "You're really good for him, Vicki."

"Hmm... You're using my real name. Is that a good sign or a bad one?"

"Why wouldn't it be good?"

"Never can tell. As long as I'm just Taz, people see the dangerous bitch with the Taser. If I'm Vicki, then I'm suddenly the girl who's gone soft in her head for Jeremy. Personally, I wouldn't trust the wench, younger man and all. I prefer being Taz with her nine-year-younger boy toy. I understand her."

"Yes, but Vicki is the woman Jeremy loves, isn't it?"

And Taz seemed to crumple. "It is. From the first time we met, when I was being even less nice than I am now, if you can imagine that. I just don't understand him."

"Do you have to? He seems to understand you."

"Could you cut out the tough questions, Miranda?"

"Okay. I just thought it all made sense. Sorry."

Taz sighed again. "It *does* all make sense, that's the problem. Turn it around. If I think like Taz, I'm fine. If I think like Vicki, then I get all mushy. It's just...weird. Like an alien possessing my body." Taz shuddered, then ended the conversation by following Jeremy.

Miranda considered if that's what had always been her problem understanding Taz: she was two people inside.

It was an oddly comforting thought. Maybe she was both

Miranda Chase air-crash investigator, and a still easily spooked girl with ASD—at the same time.

Yes. Both were true, without diminishing the other. She liked that.

Miranda and "the girl" followed Taz inside the crashed VH-92A Superhawk helicopter.

49

"THERMITE?" COLONEL BLAKE MCGRADY REACHED OUT, BUT THE short Latina slapped his hand aside hard enough to sting. "Hey!"

"Unless you have a death wish, you don't want to be touching that without gloves."

He jammed his hands in his pockets as a reminder to not touch, then leaned in to inspect it. It looked like any normal oxygen generator, a steel tank six inches square and sixteen inches long. Except the end had been burned off.

"Thermite?" he repeated because he didn't know what else to say.

Jeremy was apparently all too happy to explain. "The ignition trigger for a standard oxygen generation system burns at five hundred degrees Fahrenheit once an airliner passenger pulls down sharply on the mask to trigger the chemical reaction, or in a cabin-sized unit like this one, the pilot ignites it. Thermite burns at ten times that, over five thousand degrees Fahrenheit."

"I know all that!" Blake cursed himself for snapping at the investigator. It was creepy as hell inside the VH-92A helo. The walls were all scorched black. The plastic elements of the aircraft had partially melted in the fire before cooling enough to congeal once more. It left the entire interior looking like one of those paintings of melting clocks and whatever.

Harsh splotches of light poured in from the floodlights beyond the missing windows. Everything else was dim and shrouded in comparison. Because of the bright floods, the flashlights were of only small help in the murky shadows.

He'd also been unnerved by leading the honor guard. He'd made sure that he, his pilots, and Sergeant Whalen had escorted the stretchers bearing the Vice President and each fallen Marine out through the rubble-bordered pathway they'd forged. He still held the scorched briefcase of the Vice President's backup nuclear football that he'd actually had to pry from the dead Air Force colonel's fingers. The Secret Service teams on the site were still overwhelmed with removing the other bodies and hadn't thought of it yet. Until they did, he was keeping it close.

"Sorry, go ahead."

"Well," Jeremy jumped back in, but the Latina was scowling at him hard enough that he reminded himself to watch his tone. "We can't pin this to the cause yet, but that someone changed the trigger material definitely makes the whole unit suspect. Maybe a chemical reaction that requires thousands of degrees to trigger rather than merely hundreds makes this a likely source of the poison mentioned by your pilot before the crash."

"What kind of reactions?"

"There are so many possibilities. They could—"

"Were their hands or feet blue?" Miranda Chase spoke up. "I'm sorry, Jeremy. I didn't mean to interrupt. You go ahead."

"Blue?" He looked at his fellow investigator with deep puzzlement.

The woman was biting both of her lips together hard.

"Spit it out if you know something, woman."

"Blue?" Jeremy looked at the Latina, who only shrugged.

"Would *someone* explain what's going on?"

The Miranda woman glanced toward the Latina.

"It's okay, Miranda. I wouldn't have known to ask that question. Why did you? What does it mean?"

Still she wrestled a bit longer before she finally gasped in a hard breath, then pointed at the Air Force colonel.

Seated at the very rear of the helicopter, his was the last body aboard, lost in the shadows farthest from the floodlights shining through the missing windshield.

The Secret Service team approached the body.

"Hey, where's his briefcase?"

All of the agents jolted in surprise, only breathing a sigh of relief when Blake handed it over.

"Thank you, Colonel McGrady."

"No problem. We need to inspect his hands and feet."

The Secret Service agent looked at him askance for a moment, then waved a hand as the med team lay him on a stretcher.

Before he could find the nerve to move closer, the Chase woman had knelt beside the corpse. She flicked on a high-power flashlight and inspected his hands. They did have a bluish tinge. Then she slid off one of his boots and his sock. Distinctly blue.

He knew he should kneel to inspect the foot more closely, but it was one of the scariest, most alien things he'd ever seen. It simply wasn't...right.

Blake's career before HMX-1 had been entirely stateside and Pacific Rim. He'd seen injuries, but he'd never seen mass death before. The closest he'd ever come to a war zone was boot camp in Parris Island.

"Thank you, gentlemen," she rose as composed as if she'd just been reading a supplies requisition.

They all stood in silence as the team spread the sheet over him and carried this last victim out. There was a strange silence. The cranes had moved to clear other areas of the building.

"What does it mean?" he whispered once there were only the investigators in the helicopter.

"I can't be sure until we get this unit into the lab," the Chase woman sighed as if she was sad that they weren't there already. "But I think I know what killed them. Roy isn't going to be happy."

50

"Hydrogen cyanide gas? How the hell did that get there, Miranda?" The President looked ill as he faced Miranda on the screen.

Drake felt as if he himself was choking on the stuff. He wished she hadn't started by describing how the people would have died in such detail.

"I don't like to conjecture. The other unfired oxygen canister remaining on this aircraft looks to be completely normal, though we'll take that in for testing as well. It might not have been tampered with. Therefore, it is difficult to be certain. However, it would most likely be a form of an ammonia-methane compound, wrapped in a platinum catalyst. Add the high temperature of the thermite trigger and hydrogen cyanide gas would be produced in quantity. In fact..."

She tipped her head sideways for a long moment.

"Jeremy," she looked to the side. "Could you look up the Degussa process?"

He answered from out of view. "Let's see, no oxygen required to react, high heat source and, for every HCN molecule, it would produce three pairs of bonded hydrogen atoms."

One of the National Security Council techs who manned the PEOC helpfully put a chemical equation on the side screen that Drake had no idea how to read except that it was labeled Degussa Process.

Jeremy continued, "If the gas permeated the cabin to lethal levels, that would also imply a three-times-higher concentration of hydrogen. Does that fit the initial explosion? It wouldn't take much of a spark to fire it off, and it would certainly have the force to blow out the forward windshields. I'd have to do a bit of computer modeling to figure out how much more, but it fits."

Miranda turned back to the screen. "That's how it probably got there, Roy."

Sarah pointed at the chemical formula and whispered, "Do you understand that?"

Drake just shook his head and Sarah offered a sigh of relief.

"If it makes sense to her, it's good enough for me."

"Is Colonel McGrady still with you?" The President asked.

"Right here, Mr. President," he stepped into the frame. "I was just about to call my team and the Air Force One commander. The Secret Service is already on to their technicians."

"Full security on this one."

"Yes sir. I already have my people watching each other in case it's internal."

"Well done. And truly exceptional, Miranda. It's midnight. Get some rest."

Clarissa hovered into view in the background as Miranda responded.

"Okay, Roy. We'll be at the NTSB lab here in DC tomorrow to confirm all of this. We're going to recover the flight recorders now." And again Miranda hung up just as Clarissa was opening her mouth.

"Bet that pissed off Clarissa," Drake would be amused if this wasn't so grim.

"Not my problem," President Cole turned to Sarah. "What's your best theory?"

"I have about six."

"Run them down. I want the full analysis, not the normal executive summary."

"I'm going to leave the most-likely scenario to last," she began.

By the end of the next hour, Drake was glad that his body was still in another time zone because if it was in Eastern Daylight he'd be beyond exhausted. The threat matrices that Sarah Feldman had on tap in her head matched several of the worst-case scenarios that his team had modeled for him over the last year. His own observations had offered a disheartening backup.

The three of them dissected each one, and determinedly discarded each possible explanation for this attack for one reason or another.

"That's five," President Cole noted.

"Good. So it only *felt* like fifty," Drake refilled everyone's coffee from the pot on the sideboard.

"Right. Now give us the sixth one, Sarah."

"I'm afraid that we're right back to where we started yesterday, Mr. President—Saudi Arabia." And she spent most of thirty minutes breaking down the supporting information.

Drake wished it was like Miranda's report on the poison and he wouldn't understand any of it. Regrettably, he understood every word.

President Cole was quiet for a long time afterward. Finally, he asked a question so softly that Drake barely heard it.

"Drake, did I get Clark killed? With my speech at the G-7?"

"No sir," Drake shook his head. "The logistics to get that equipment into place inside HMX-1 took months, possibly a year or more of work to infiltrate the personnel necessary. The fact that they succeeded is a different issue that I'm sure is keeping the entire Marine Corps awake tonight. Your talk at the G-7 was in the last thirty-six hours. The Marine Two bird was already in place at Camp David by then."

"Well, that's a relief at least. Okay, Sarah. Next thoroughly egotistical question: were they aiming for me and botched the play?"

"No sir. Nor was the Vice President merely a target of opportunity. His meeting at Camp David was intentionally very public. The party has already been working on his image for the next election."

"I have twenty more months in office, I still can't believe they're already campaigning Clark." Cole huffed out a hard sigh. "Okay, so his meeting was predictable—scheduled and announced publicly."

"As were his politics regarding Saudi Arabia. Remember," Sarah continued, "this is all conjecture. If it was them, they're probably shielded with near-bulletproof deniability—they learned a lot in managing to deny any involvement with 9/11. There's probably a cut-out for them to not be pinned with this either."

"It sounds as if tracking that would have been a better use of Clarissa's time," President Cole scowled toward the now dark television screen.

Drake held up his tablet. "I actually have several reports that she forwarded from her people. They're still working the data, but they're weighting it sixty-forty that it was actually sourced from Riyadh itself. They say they need a couple more days for the computers to chew on the codes before they can change those numbers."

"Make sure they get what they need."

"Clarissa already has."

Cole nodded for Sarah to continue.

"But if I were the Saudis, I wouldn't want Clark's negative attitude toward their leadership in the region to become a debate platform in the next US election at all. So..." she made a scissors motion with her fingers, "...snip it off before it begins."

"Shit!"

"What are we going to do about it, Mr. President?"

"Stop thinking so much like a soldier, Drake. There's a reason I'm in this seat and you aren't."

"Thank God for that, Mr. President. Please tell me that we aren't going to do nothing."

"No. Not nothing. This will take some thinking, which let's you out, Drake."

Drake considered giving him the finger, but even soldier to soldier that was too much, so he rose to his feet, snapped to full attention, and saluted.

When the President gave him the finger in return, he just laughed.

"The PEOC has bunks. Get some shut-eye. Since Danziger still has us trapped in here, let's use it. Next meeting starts at 0600 sharp."

Then the President pushed to his feet and was gone.

51

Her driver was pulling up to the house at One Observatory Circle when she noticed something strange.

"Where are all the agents?" Normally, the grand Queen Anne Victorian house that served as the Vice President's home had several agents and a dog team in clear view.

"The Vice President's detail has been dismissed, ma'am. For another week or so you will have a full Second Lady detail just in case there is an unanticipated collateral risk to your safety. After that, you will be granted the detail due to a former Second Lady and it will be the CIA detail taking over your primary security." His tone was so carefully neutral that she wondered if he was enjoying that slap in her face as well.

She wilted against the seat as the driver pulled up to the front entrance.

She had sold her fucking prime-location condo in Foggy Bottom because Clark's coattails into One Observatory Circle and then the White House were supposed to be reliable. She'd liked that condo and would be hard-pressed to replace it with the way the DC housing market had exploded over the last two years.

And she hated Clark's place out in Poolesville, Maryland. Why anyone would want to live where the number one-rated attraction was a farm stand was beyond her. She'd dump that the minute the will came through. Thank God they'd amended those, so it was one thing to not worry about. It was about the only thing not to worry about.

However, as soon as there was a new VP, she'd be homeless. Maybe before then, if Roy Cole was feeling stingy. Maybe tomorrow if that asshole in charge of Homeland Security was being his usual self.

A sole agent awaited her on the porch. Two more would be out on the grounds, but that was all.

"We're so sorry for your loss, ma'am." At least he sounded sincere.

About the loss of Clark probably; she knew there was no love lost on her account.

She was too numb to even address him as he held open the front door for her.

It clicked shut behind her.

Clarissa made it across the hardwood foyer floor, tripping over the white oriental rug that covered most of it, then navigated up the three-turn flight of stairs and into the master bedroom. She stripped off the remains of a fifteen-hundred-dollar power suit and her favorite ankle boots, which had cost another twelve.

She spent a long time just holding them as she stood naked in the bathroom before she actually looked at them.

Damaged beyond any repair.

All of it.

Only by clamping her teeth hard on the side of her tongue did she avert that judgment extending to all her plans. It was better to focus on the pain.

She dumped the whole mess in the garbage and stepped

into the shower. She turned it to scalding hot, the way Clark liked it.

Then, very slowly, she eased it down to a humane temperature.

It was one thing too many.

As the stink of a shattered, low-lifer Walmart washed down the drain, Clarissa could finally give vent to her emotions.

She screamed rage at losing her entire world today. She screamed until her throat was past functioning.

Clarissa curled up on the shower floor too exhausted to even notice the tears of sorrow spilling down the drain as well.

52

"YOU MUST BE EXHAUSTED," TERENCE HELD OPEN THE DOOR AND Miranda steadied herself on the door jamb as she crossed the threshold.

"I slept..." then she remembered that she'd managed just one hour last night, in a different time zone. Terence would not be pleased to know that she'd fallen asleep at her desk. He always talked about the importance of sufficient sleep during a crash investigation—which seemed to be the only time she couldn't manage any. "...some."

"This is far better than a hotel. Thank you, Mr. Graham," Jeremy looked around as if he was entering a palace, not Terence's home.

"Haven't you ever been here before?" Miranda typically stayed in the guest bedroom whenever she was in DC.

Terence chuckled as he ushered the others in. "I never bring students here, or other investigators. This is my home *away* from the NTSB. Just you, Miranda. You needed a quiet place to learn. Besides, when you came along, my kids had just left for school and I was glad of the company." She knew he rarely mentioned his wife, who had walked out on the family years before.

"I always liked it here, Terence. It feels like a second home to me." And it did, even more than the Tacoma team house. Miranda settled into the chair that had been hers on so many evenings, a wingback covered in a cheery sweet pea print. The wear marks where she'd sometimes have to rub her hands over and over on the arms to maintain her control were still there, now worn as smooth as silk across the heavy brocade.

Terence's armchair had been replaced by a luxurious cordovan red-leather recliner since her last visit. That bothered her, so she didn't look at it too closely.

"What was she like?" Mike settled on the sofa beside Holly, Andi dropping beside her. Jeremy was in the last chair, with Taz perched upon one arm.

Terence looked at her for a moment, and winked before turning to the others.

"She was a brilliant mess."

The others laughed, but Miranda was unsure how to interpret it. Terence's winks had always been an indicator that he was about to tell a story, and she was too tired for that tonight. But now that she'd sat down, her body buzzed with such exhaustion that she doubted she could stand.

"On the first day of class, she knew my accident reports better than I did. In fact, she knew everyone's better than they did. Much like you, Jeremy, in that respect. Except she had already analyzed the best and worst aspects of each of us inspectors' various...quirks and developed her own best-case report structure. You've never varied from that, have you, Miranda?"

"Was there a reason I should have?" She tried to find the motivation to pull out a notebook in case he had revision suggestions, but even her hands seemed to be asleep.

"Not a one."

That was a relief. She decided that if it was okay to let sleeping dogs lie, it was probably also okay to let sleeping hands do so as well.

"She knew more about reporting than any of you will ever learn—including you, young Jeremy, so don't get cocky when you get your own team."

And there it was.

Jeremy—leaving.

Someone new—joining.

She woke her sleeping hands and placed them over her eyes.

But she could still hear Terence.

"A pilot, materials and aerospace engineering degrees...all of that knowledge. But she had no order to it. It would all just jumble up in her head whenever she faced a new training scenario. At first, our time here at my house was working out that sphere system that she uses to approach a crash."

She tried shifting her hands to her ears. The sounds of their voices dropped closer to a genial murmur.

But now she could see again.

Mike's head tipped back in laughter.

Jeremy's hand clasped in Taz's with all of the excitement of heading his own team.

Miranda wasn't going to lose just one person—she was going to lose two!

And what if someone else left?

Everything changing.

Why did everything have to change?

Didn't people like them understand the cost of change on people like her?

If they would only—

Andi was squatting down in front of her chair.

Miranda cried out with relief.

"I think we need to get you into bed," Miranda half read her lips as her ears were still covered. "How long did you sleep last night?"

"An hour? Except I didn't mean to say that."

Andi took her wrists and tugged her to her feet. It was awkward as Miranda decided it was best not to let go of her ears, but they were soon standing.

"I'm so sorry, Miranda." Terence's voice was deep enough that there seemed no point in still covering her ears, it rumbled right through.

"You and Andi take your usual. You don't mind sharing, do you?"

Miranda shook her head. As long as she could get away, she was past caring.

Andi was looking at Terence with an expression that Miranda needed her notebook to interpret, so she let go of her own ears and looked it up as Andi guided her stumbling up the stairs.

"Horror?" she asked Andi.

Andi's mumble sounded like, "Close enough."

Then Miranda saw her familiar bed and didn't remember anything else. Not even getting into it.

53

"MIRANDA?" JEREMY'S VOICE WAS FUZZY WITH SLEEP.

"Shh. Don't wake Taz." Miranda kept her voice low. She'd been trying to sneak past them on the living room's sleeper couch.

"Too late," Taz whispered. "What's up?"

"Go back to sleep. I'm heading in to the NTSB office."

Taz's phone glowed for a moment in the darkness. "At five a.m.? You thought of something, didn't you?"

"No."

"But the idea of something is there anyway, isn't there? We're coming with you," Jeremy declared as they both climbed off the bed and dressed quickly. The couch was soon once more a couch, and they were out the door.

"What did you think of?" Jeremy asked as Taz drove them toward NTSB headquarters.

"I just said I didn't. I think we need to start with the recorders and the videos, then work our way through the whole thing."

"Mike and Andi worked on the videos and did the interviews last night. Should we wake them?" Taz had her phone out already.

"No," Jeremy stopped her before she could. "It could take a couple of hours to transfer the flight recorder data if there was any heat damage. The outer cases didn't look bad, so they should be okay, but there was a fire, so there could be melted solder connections or even cracked chips or a shattered board. That can all take a while."

Miranda was impressed. Jeremy had thought of the people, which was more than she'd done.

She'd simply had the impulse to go into the office and get to work.

Jeremy had leapt past her and thought about the fact that, in addition to being exhausted, the others might not be needed for perhaps several hours.

Maybe he really was ready for his own team.

Taz drove, stopping briefly at a just-opened coffee-and-muffin drive-up, then parked them under the NTSB headquarters building.

As they carried their to-go cups around to the front door, Miranda couldn't help smiling up at the back side of the International Spy Museum. The wall had been covered with seven story-tall rows of narrow light-and-dark panels that were in no obvious pattern. But it had just enough regularity to imply that it had been intentional.

A code.

Rather than being a highly publicized public relations challenge for the eventual opening of the museum when it was finished, the museum's designers made a crucial miscalculation —the code wall directly faced the NTSB headquarters across L'Enfant Plaza. Within a day of the contractors finishing the installation, the NTSB techs had solved the wall's code and tweeted their finding to the Spy Museum—and the public.

Once you thought to break it into eight-bit binary word groups, it was easy to read. The light and dark panels indicating zeroes and ones respectively. Except for two possible errors that may have been intentional as they still hadn't been changed—induced errors were a common enough cryptographic practice—it read: *All is not that it seems at the spy museum.*

Every time she saw it, it reminded her of all those years working codes with her father. Her first set of blocks were simple numeric substitution codes. If she arranged them as 13-9-18-1-14-4-1, then rotated them all a quarter turn, she got her name from their relative positions in the alphabet. She'd learned how to spell by the increasingly complex code groups he'd provided to her.

He hadn't started her on ASCII, hex, and binary until she was seven. Or working on the *Kryptos* sculpture until she was eight. She patted the tenth *Kryptos* notebook, tucked in with her others.

They were the first ones into the lab. Then she remembered it was a Sunday and they were likely to be the *only* ones in the lab all day. That was a relief.

Jeremy sighed happily.

"What?" Taz asked him.

"I've always loved this set of rooms. You can process anything here. I've only been able to assess the absolutely intact recorders at our Tacoma office. Here, everything from long-term saltwater exposure to medium-high fire damage can be addressed. It's just brilliant." He stroked the equipment lovingly.

"Is this where you'd want to work?" Taz's voice became even softer.

Miranda checked her emoticon notebook surreptitiously: *worry?* Taz's expression matched, but Miranda had no idea why.

Jeremy tipped his head to one side, then the other. Finally shaking it, though his expression matched *sad...*mostly.

Taz's now was unquestionably *relief,* though Jeremy didn't seem to notice.

"Yes but also no. I love the lab work. It's what I always figured I'd be doing once I joined. But in a weird way, you spoiled me for computer lab work, Miranda. The puzzle of the field is far too fascinating. Once Terence sent me out to you on that Groom Lake crash, I've never wanted to come back. Now I want both."

Unsure how to interpret any of that, she turned for Andi, but she wasn't there. She was probably still asleep in the big bed in Terence's guest room, curled so close to the other edge of the mattress that it was surprising she hadn't landed face-first on carpet. At a loss for what else to do, she turned to Taz.

"Should I be apologizing? Or…"

"What? *No!*" Jeremy spoke before Taz did. "You showed me such a bigger world than the lab. *So* much bigger," and he took Taz's hand.

She rolled her eyes, but didn't let go.

"Okay." Miranda didn't know what else to say. "Could you please pull out the recorders?" She'd woken trying to guess at the heat effects on the recorders and had been unable to go back to sleep.

Jeremy went to the safe where he'd locked them last night on their way back from the wreck. He pulled the two devices they'd recovered from wreckage last night and set them on the steel-topped workbench in the middle of the room: the combi —combined cockpit voice and flight data recorder—and the quick access recorder's drive.

They quickly removed the cover on the combi's electronics section that gathered the data and fed it into the hardened recorder module. No data was stored in this section, but the heat of the fire had cracked and melted several of the boards.

That meant that the chassis was cooked and unrecoverable without even needing to test.

They both donned gloves and static-dissipation grounding bracelets before disconnecting the recorder itself from the ruined chassis.

Four Allen screws freed the data module from the chassis. It was more soot char black from the fire than the usual alert orange. The connection cable protruding from the bottom was partially melted as well, which said the fire around the recorder was hotter than she would have expected.

They pulled off the baseplate and peeled off the thick foam insulation layers to expose the circuit board. Three by six inches and covered in memory chips, it looked okay visually.

Jeremy showed Taz how to use the visual and X-ray microscopes to check that none of the solder connections had reflowed with the heat and that none of the chips had fire cracked.

"Even with chips that were submerged for a long time in the ocean, we can get most of the data every time. Fire is a different problem. This container is rated at a minimum of thirty minutes in a two-thousand-degree-Fahrenheit fire, and sixty minutes at five-hundred degrees. But we didn't see the fire and have no clear measure of how long the recorder was exposed. That worried me. But see, the solder all looks clean. And no chip browning or cracking. It means we should be able to read the data without any delay."

Miranda had never been interested by this stage of recovery process, so she would simply trust Jeremy.

Once they'd crossed from the Chip Recovery Lab into the Data Recovery Lab, she felt much more at home.

She double-checked the model of the recorder, then pulled a pin cable and a brand-new chassis from the shelf. With the new cable installed, they were able to plug the chassis into the main rack.

"Um, we have problem." Jeremy had slid into the computer station's chair while she'd been hooking it up.

"What's that?"

"We don't have a configuration file for the HMX-1 helicopters."

Miranda could only blink in surprise. Every manufacturer was supposed to send the configuration files for each aircraft to the NTSB. A large airliner recorded over a thousand different parameters into the recorder. Without the data map, there was no way to know which binary words were, for example, air speed and which were the status of the starboard economy-class toilet's smoke detector.

54

COLONEL BLAKE McGRADY GLARED DOWN AT THE STEEL TABLE and could only rub his forehead.

The HMX-1 hangar was buzzing with the second shift change since he'd declared the lockdown.

Spread across the table was every single emergency air generator from all three models of the White Side aircraft: the retiring VH-3D Sea Kings and VH-60N White Hawks, and the new VH-92A Superhawks, including the ones he'd flown during the President's recent tour.

He waved everyone away except for his crew chief.

"Are you sure, Whalen?"

"Yes sir," his crew chief answered with no question in his tone. "We confirmed it with the manufacturer's rep. There's nothing nonstandard in any of these units. They're absolutely what they claim to be. We even fired one from each class of aircraft and they behaved exactly per spec. No overheating. No HCN. Absolutely stable for their entire thirty-minute life cycle. Nothing produced except oxygen and salt."

"Bloody hell!"

"Yes sir. We're tearing down the complete air system on each bird, but still nothing out of the ordinary."

Master Sergeant Whalen would know what that meant as well as he did. Someone had known precisely which bird to sabotage in order to target the attack on the Vice President. Which helo was the designated transport and which were the decoys was known to very few people.

And they were *all* inside HMX-1.

Whoever had killed the Vice President and everyone else aboard the Superhawk was a Marine.

The thought was intolerable.

He was pulling out his phone to call the Commandant of the Marine Corps when it rang sharply. He almost lost it to the concrete.

"McGrady here."

"We need the Black Box data mapping of the VH-92A Superhawk."

"Who the—" he pulled the phone away enough to see the name. Miranda Chase. It took him a moment to remember that she was the flight investigator from the NTSB.

He really needed some sleep, he was the one who'd insisted on having her contact info. He looked at his watch. He'd only gotten in from the crash site four hours ago. Well, he hadn't missed *much* sleep.

"Why?"

"So that we can interpret the data from the Cockpit Voice Recorder and the Flight Data Recorder," she said it like he was the dumbest man on the planet.

Whalen had stepped back to give him privacy. Blake waved him closer.

"The Black Box data map for the NTSB?"

"Yes, that's what I asked for," Miranda said in one ear as Whalen actually smacked his own forehead.

"I'll send it to them right away."

Blake shook his head. "Where are you, Ms. Chase?"

"NTSB Headquarters in the Data Recovery Lab at L'Enfant Plaza."

"I'll deliver it myself in twenty minutes," and he hung up. "Whalen, go get whatever it is she needs, then get that Viper spun up. We're airborne to Anacostia in three."

Whalen saluted and raced away.

Blake stopped himself before he called out Tamatha's name.

But his Number Two was dead. Poisoned, then burned to death in a fucking Walmart.

Sweet Christ, he'd shopped in that goddamn store—his dad had a weak spot for the place. They'd eaten lunch at the Subway counter any number of times because it was the only way Dad could wolf down a foot-long meatball sub without Mom going ballistic on his diet—as if she didn't know.

But last night had creeped the shit out of him. Even if they rebuilt it, he'd never be able to go in there again. Maybe not ever hit a Walmart again. He knew that every time he did, all he'd see was a corpse burned past recognition except by which seat she'd sat in.

He called over Captain Velasquez.

"I need you to get on with personnel. First, I want every single Marine in HMX-1 accounted for. If they're on assignment, just transferred out, hell, if they're in the hospital giving birth, I want eyes-on confirmation that they haven't tried to skip town or the country. Then start reviewing every single file, including yours and mine."

"Shit, Colonel! Internal?" Velasquez was as aghast as he felt.

"Just check it out for me."

Velasquez saluted and trotted off, signaling his copilot to join him because, for the foreseeable future, no Marine traveled alone.

The borrowed AH-1Z gunship began winding to life outside the hangar.

No one traveled alone, but he'd sent Whalen off on an errand by himself.

Shit! If he didn't trust his crew chief, the world was going to hell.

55

"THERE YOU ARE."

Senator Hunter Ramson leapt out of his chair before he recognized Rose's voice. For once, he wished she hadn't tracked him to his office in the Capitol Building. She came here so rarely.

He glanced at the clock. Six a.m. The sky outside his office window was already fading from black to palest blue.

"You're up early."

"You're up late," she countered as she slid into the chair across his desk. Thirty-one years together. Thirty-two if he counted from bedding her shortly before she won the Miss Utah pageant he'd been judging. And she still looked incredible. She wore a dress right out of the Kennedy era, but Jackie would never have looked so good in it. Rose had resurrected the sleeveless, knee-length summer dress as a fashion statement practically on her own.

Looking at her this morning, the main thing he felt was his age.

He wasn't quite sixty, but he felt as if he was a hundred.

Rather than speaking, Rose began tinkering with her

wedding gift to him. All those years ago, before he'd even thought of running for any office, she'd given him a beautifully engraved triangle name plaque, appropriately made of rosewood so that he'd think of her every time he saw it.

On the two facing sides, it read "Senator Hunter Ramson."

"You always knew and believed in me."

She tipped it over toward him. He now faced his name upside down, which was also far too appropriate.

She tipped it again, exposing her private message to him that was always there: *Keep asking.*

"I do that." Then he studied her eyes, but couldn't read her thoughts. "Don't I?"

"About certain things, dear."

Thirty years had taught him that his best strategy to avoid the uncomfortable was silence. Not that it worked often, but if he was the one who *started* speaking, then the conversation always seemed to go directly where he didn't want it to go.

And tonight...this morning, he definitely didn't want to talk about what was actually going on.

"You ask me to keep loving you," Rose spoke softly.

"And you do, don't you?"

"Of course, silly."

He relaxed at her smile.

"But in addition to love, you can ask for help."

Hunter could feel the pressure of the black tsunami he'd been contemplating all night. "I would if I needed any."

She tipped the name plaque right side up again. Then began tapping it with a perfectly manicured blood-red fingernail. Rose's silences were as powerful as her words.

"I truly don't think you can help with this one, honey."

"What did you do, Hunter?"

Christ! He'd never been able to hide a thing from her.

56

TRUE TO HIS WORD, COLONEL McGRADY AND HIS CREW CHIEF arrived in just twenty minutes.

Miranda appreciated the punctuality. So many people said twenty minutes and meant thirty...or forty. She considered asking if that was part of being a Marine, but decided against it. She *was* getting better at sorting distractions from the main line of focus. Per Mike's recommendation, she patted herself on the back for that.

Sergeant Whalen sat beside Jeremy and they began loading the profile into the conversion software.

They sat before an arc of four screens.

To the left were all of the zeroes and ones of the chip's binary readout.

The next screen rapidly populated with scores of graphed parameters. Neatly grouped into clusters of flight characteristics, engine, even voice curves of the four internal microphones.

There was a massive disjunction in the middle of all the lines.

"What's that?" McGrady pointed.

"Because the original chassis was damaged beyond recovery, we lost the final time marker on the chip's data set. Jeremy will fix it in a moment—there." The curves all smoothed out. "This is now a time-correct diagram of the Marine Two aircraft's flight. Jeremy let's—"

Except was this supposed to be her investigation or his? Terence and Andi had said it was hers, but Holly and Mike had indicated that it should be his. How should she factor that her most senior and most junior people said one thing and her two midlevel team members said the other? The averages balanced.

Yes, the field investigation had been hers, but Jeremy was more skilled in the lab than she was.

She nodded to Taz.

Taz in turn jabbed Jeremy sharply in the ribs.

"What?"

"Your chart." Taz's comment didn't mean anything to her, but Jeremy started nodding rapidly.

"Chart? Right! The list of steps we made of an investigation! Got it. Let me show you something seriously cool, Sergeant Whalen." In moments his fingers were running across the keyboard. The third screen of the console filled with an aerial map.

The sergeant and Jeremy were whispering questions back and forth as Jeremy kept entering commands.

"Let's start with the flight path," Jeremy finished another spate of keyboarding and a thin red line was overlaid on the image.

Miranda hoped that it wasn't being too forward when she reached between them to set the switch so that the large, wall-mounted screen now echoed the third console's flight-path image.

On the fourth screen, Jeremy loaded the vertical view, then slid it to appear side by side on the big screen.

She and Colonel McGrady stepped forward in unison for a closer look.

"Starting at the final takeoff from Camp David," Jeremy began narrating.

The colonel took over, "I'm seeing a normal takeoff and climb out. For the next three minutes, I see nothing unusual in the flight pattern. Here, north of Frederick, we see the Superhawk first turn sideways, then execute a circle. That must be the area of the fire that boxed it in."

Miranda held out her VH-92A notebook for Jeremy and pointed at the fire's geographic coordinates.

"You're so good, Miranda." Jeremy keyed it in and a neat red line formed a box around the area that the Superhawk had circled. "So that's confirmed."

Taz pointed at the graph, "What's that?" A vertical cursor line had been scrolling across the screen as it interpreted the data for display.

One of the lines had a distinct, notched change.

"That's the initiation of the emergency oxygen generator system." He placed a red dot on the flight path about halfway around the circle.

"Goddamn it!" McGrady cursed. "Tamatha was so damn good. At least five seconds ahead of when I'd have made the same decision."

The flight path then remained clean as it raced through the southern perimeter of the box.

"Look!" Taz pointed to the far-right screen on the console. The helo climbed abruptly, then dropped again.

"A brief lift due to the fire's heat," McGrady noted. "It doesn't match any control inputs." He was right, the controls-group on the second console remained stable.

Then the line on the cyclic revealed a slow roll to the right and the helicopter began to descend.

No, Miranda decided, it began to fall.

57

"You did...what?" It wasn't the first time in their thirty-odd years that she'd wanted to slap Hunter, but it was definitely the closest she'd come to doing so.

When she'd bedded him for the win at the Miss Utah competition, she'd known exactly what she was doing—even if he hadn't. He'd actually been sweet and surprised.

He also had the balance she'd been seeking of desire for power matched with a slightly directionless aim for it. It would have helped if he'd been a little smarter, but she'd worked with what she'd found. With her guidance, he'd finally become one of the most powerful senators in the entire Congress, and she'd become the "First Lady of DC."

In answer, Hunter toyed with that stupid Viet Cong knife his father had given him. The thing was creepier than even the judges she'd refused to bed. Thank God the girls were so much better protected now. She'd seen what several of her fellow contestants had been forced to do before being tossed aside. She hadn't just bedded Hunter for the win, she'd done it for the life.

"Why does that knife still intrigue you?"

"I like the rawness of it. The truth of it."

"The truth that your father was psycho enough to be a tunnel rat in Vietnam, willing to go down into those holes to kill. That he named you for that ugly Viet Cong blade soaked in American blood."

"Dad was—"

"A bastard!" Normally she didn't give voice to her real feelings about the man but she was so sick of his hold over Hunter that it slipped out.

Hunter merely grunted but kept toying with the blade. She knew he hated his father, too, but had never let him go.

Rose took a slow, deep breath and forced her voice to the calm tones that let her host even the greatest fool at one of her parties—if he was well connected.

She tapped a fingernail on the triangular name block and no longer felt the urge to beat him with it.

"You know why I never let you run for President, Hunter?"

"Because you said a life of power for term after term was better than eight years and done."

"Yes, and I still think that's true. But also, even by the time I met you, you were already making deals that would never survive the scrutiny of a Presidential campaign."

"But—"

"Finances. Corporate games. Your close ties to too many of the defense contractors. And you don't want me pointing out your barely hidden roles in breaking several careers."

Hunter frowned as he fooled with the Viet Cong blade.

"But do you know what you just cut off?"

"I didn't! I only—"

"I only... If I just... They can't trace it to me..." Rose bit back on the bile that threatened to choke her.

"I didn't kill Clark!" He leaned forward and thumped the butt of the blade hard enough on his desk to dent the cherrywood. It was his "fierce Senator" role. Did he forget that she'd trained him in how and when to use that?

"No, you just opened the door for someone else to."

"I didn't know that was going to—"

Rose held up her hand palm-out to stop him.

He dropped the blade and began rubbing a finger on the dent in his desk as if that would fix anything.

"I don't care that much about Clark."

"Neither did I. His position on the Middle East was intolerab—"

She held up her palm again. "However, you also cut off Clarissa's best chance."

"Her best chance for what?"

"To become the Vice President and then the President, you fool!"

And Rose felt the jab in her chest as clearly as if Hunter had just knifed her.

From the moment she'd met Clarissa, Rose knew that the woman had the abilities so few people—male or female —possessed.

Clarissa's play to install Clark as the Vice President had been flawless in its execution. She'd created a once-in-a-lifetime opportunity.

And yesterday—was it just yesterday?—Clarissa had confirmed her intention to take on the Presidency, *and* to offer her the title of Vice President Rose Ramson. It was a dream for *herself*—that had been murdered aborning. The wonders that she and Clarissa could have done together...

But her popinjay of a husband had "opened a door" that had killed the Vice President. With Clark gone, their chances of success at the Presidential horse race had gone from being a top finisher to betting on the extreme long shot—moments before he came up lame.

It took all of her years of self-control to not spit out the words she could never take back.

Instead, she rose carefully to her feet, smoothed the Oscar de la Renta summer dress, and stepped out of her husband's office.

He called after her once, but that was all.

He didn't even try to follow.

For once, she was glad that her lesson on the importance of that hadn't stuck.

58

"What the hell, Miranda?" Holly's outburst was so loud that it rang in the lab.

Andi punched her in the arm as hard as Holly usually tagged others.

Holly glared at her for a long moment, long enough for Andi to wonder if she was about to die. Then Holly muttered, "Dumb as a dingo," before smacking her own forehead.

"Sorry, Miranda. Why didn't you wake us when you came in?" Holly's tone was much more moderated, though far from calm.

"I was just trying to come to work. I accidentally woke Jeremy and he didn't see any reason to cut off everyone's sleep for the first technical stages of the process."

Personally, Andi felt as if she'd slept about five minutes. First in worry, because Miranda had been so near her breaking point. Then lying there next to Miranda, listening to her sleep as if they were a couple, was just too bizarre and had kept her awake for hours.

"Mike and Andi," Taz spoke up, "you two have all of the collected videos, right?"

They both nodded.

"Good. Do a quick trawl of social media to see if anyone posted anything new. Then start syncing them up to that profile." Taz pointed at the screens that showed the final flight of Marine Two. She wasn't even pretending that instructions were coming from Jeremy at the moment.

Andi moved closer to the screen. "What's that?"

"What's what?"

"Run that back to exiting the smoke screen and play it again, normal speed."

"It's—"

"Shh! Sorry, Colonel, just be quiet. Roll it, Jeremy."

She watched the flight path. It didn't last long—under sixty seconds.

Andi shuddered and called for Jeremy to roll it again.

"Freeze it! There."

"She lost control for a moment," Colonel McGrady stated.

"And there?" Andi pointed at a near identical control input twelve seconds later. "It's the wrong shape. Something slammed the controls, smacked them right out of her hands."

"An attacker in the cockpit?"

"No. Look at the voice recorder. Nothing going on. No shouts. Standard emergency-only pilot crosstalk. You don't even have to hear that to see it in the visual sound graph." Andi closed her eyes. "I know exactly what caused it." If ever there was an excuse to revisit a PTSD moment, this was it.

A steadying hand rested on her shoulder, keeping her in the present.

"Ken?" Miranda asked the crucial one-word question.

She could only nod.

"Colonel McGrady," Miranda spoke louder but didn't let go of her, which was good. "What you see is that one of the pilots lost physical control of their body. Spastic seizures are an element of hydrogen cyanide poisoning."

"Who's Ken?"

"Ken," Andi forced herself to answer because the yawning black chasm wasn't as far away for her as everyone seemed to think, "was my copilot. He was killed by a grenade when he and I were as close as Miranda and I are now. I was flying nap-of-earth in hostile territory. His..." she swallowed hard "...remains were thrown against the cyclic. By bracing with my grip and swinging in my left leg, I managed to retain flight. Otherwise, my final flight profile, from ten feet above the ground, would have looked just like those two moments."

"Mike, play the Beckstein video." Then she forced herself to open her eyes and stare at the screen.

He patched a tablet into the computer beside Jeremy and opened the video.

The Becksteins had posted a video of the five-helo Vice Presidential flight. Rather than capturing the crash, they'd been near the area of the fire.

Jeremy rolled the image back and forth, making small adjustments until he had it synced up with data and voice streams. Then he hit Play.

The helicopter burst through the wall of smoke, leaving a great swirling plume behind it.

Exactly on her mark there was a jink to the left.

At her second mark, there was another. Except the second recovery was much slower—and by then the helicopter was on its side and falling fast.

She jumped when a slurred voice spoke, "Poison. Oxy. Generator."

"Tamatha," the colonel groaned. She could hear the pain for his captain. "Sounds like she'd been on a three-week bender."

The Superhawk was still sideways when it fell out of view of the Beckstein's video.

"Nineteen seconds between the two moments with no

change in attitude but with enough control input to indicate that someone was holding the controls steady. Now run the prime video."

"Prime?"

"It's still the best video we have of the crash itself."

Again, she waited while Jeremy got it synced up.

It picked up in mid-fall, approximately a mile after the helicopter had emerged from the smoke wall.

"There. Captain Jones is still alive, see on the graph. Marine Two is rolling level due to control input, not chance."

"Hey!" Sergeant Whalen called out from beside Jeremy. "I have an initiation notice on the pilot-side emergency air bottle just before she drove through the smoke wall."

Miranda stepped over to confirm the observation. "Good. That explains why she was still functioning after the copilot's body was already in spastic shutdown."

"Good? That she lived through that?"

Andi turned to McGrady. As a fellow pilot, she knew just how clearly he was picturing the moment in his head. She also knew the only lifeline she could offer him to appease that image he'd never be able to erase.

"She was a pilot *in extremis,* Colonel, still trying to do her duty. Try to never forget that."

He spun away to face a double rack of computer equipment. She gave him a moment while she checked that Miranda was okay. Was she her normal calm...or *too* calm? Andi couldn't tell. Not that she had a lot of reserve in her own mental balance at the moment.

"Okay, Jeremy, let's finish it." Andi needed *something* other than her own past to focus on.

She watched the rest of the data play out, long after the helo had smashed and disappeared into the store. After the final leveling, there were no more control inputs. If Captain

Tamatha Jones lived through the crash, there was no sign that Andi could see in the data.

She forced herself to watch until the power loss had ended all of the helicopter's data feed. Just before the end, there was a sudden, extreme spike in the cabin pressure.

"The first explosion starts building right there," Jeremy noted.

After that, most of the instrumentation flatlined. But this was a new generation combi unit that had an integral battery and it had kept recording. With the helicopter losing power, no instruments were sending data, but there were two more large audio spikes over the cockpit microphones.

"See, I was right," Jeremy sounded pleased. "Three distinct explosions. I'm going to need time to filter it down and see what else is in there."

"Keep on that, Jeremy." Miranda sounded fine as she continued.

So it was just Andi who felt as if she was losing it.

"Andi can help you and Sergeant Whalen with interpreting the flight data and any special systems information. Shunt the audio over to the Listening Room. Colonel McGrady, Mike, and Holly, if you'd come with me, we'll see what we can recover from the audio tracks."

Miranda led the way out of the room without once turning to look at her.

Andi would pay a lot to know if there was another reason that Miranda had assigned her to stay in this lab with Jeremy as she moved to the other.

59

When Clarissa answered the door at One Observatory Circle, she looked like hell. So bad that even the lone Secret Service agent simply gawked in surprise.

Rose ushered her inside quickly and shut the door behind them.

Clarissa's long hair was in such disarray that it looked tattered. She wore a La Perla chemise and a man's thick bathrobe completely askew and missing its belt. Her eyes were heavy-lidded with lack of sleep.

"This won't do, Clarissa."

She looked around as if bewildered.

"I was...cleaning up. Upstairs. I have to..." Then she turned and simply walked toward the staircase.

Rose had been here for a few parties. Rather than following, she turned left through the dining room with its twelve-seat mahogany table, brass chandelier, and broad fireplace. Past that, the pantry kitchen had not been prepped with breakfast. The Navy staff who ran the main kitchen downstairs had probably been called off duty with the Vice President's demise.

There wasn't time for niceties.

She found a large mug, a teaspoon, and dumped in a double dose of instant coffee. Filling it from the instant hot water tap, she then added a heavy splash of cream to cover the taste. She stirred it as she followed Clarissa up the stairs.

In the main bedroom were two large piles of clothes: his and hers.

"What are you doing?" she pushed the mug into Clarissa's hands.

"They're going to throw me out, aren't they? Why in the world would I want to take any of Clark's clothes?"

"And those?" Rose pointed at the impressive display of designer lingerie. It had far more variety than she herself had ever collected. She put a finger on the bottom of the coffee mug and nudged it upward.

Clarissa, or at least her habits, took the hint and she drank.

"They were for…him. This is awful."

"Drink it," Rose ordered before Clarissa could set it aside.

It was definitely time for a dose of woman-to-woman therapy.

"Sit," Rose pushed her toward one of the Chippendale armchairs by the Federal Period walnut-and-brass dresser. "No, first give me that stupid robe."

Rose tossed it on Clark's discard pile, then flipped through the pile of Clarissa's clothes and came back with a lovely Carine Gilson hand-painted silk robe that Rose would snitch if Clarissa ever parted with it.

"I *wish* I still had your body. I miss that body," Rose handed over the robe, held the coffee while Clarissa slid into it, then pushed the mug back into her hands. She strode into the bathroom.

"I'm just praying that it's still as good as yours in twenty years," Clarissa raised her voice from mumble to audible. That was a good sign. She was starting to sound more alive.

"Less words, more coffee."

"It's hideous."

"It's caffeinated. Drink." She handed over a hairbrush. "Fix."

"Yes ma'am."

Rose began sorting through all of the designer silk. "This is a lifetime supply. You are hereby outlawed from buying anything new for at least a year." Most of them were keepers. Every now and then she'd find one that wasn't even bedroom sexy, but was just pure slut.

"I've sworn off men for life."

Rose laughed and picked up another horrid lace teddy. "Please tell me these were foolish experiments in your misguided youth."

Clarissa made noises that might be hair-snarls, or might be trying to avoid the question.

"Seriously, girl. Were you thinking your body was still twenty?"

Clarissa winced like she'd just been slapped, so Rose tried to find a softer way to put it.

"Men may act like they're permanently twelve. But any man worth having wants the sexy sophisticate more than the teen fantasy. Finding one who's actually interested in this—" she tapped her temple "—neither you nor I was so blessed."

"Clark did, sometimes. He always encouraged me."

"Well, that's a bonus." Hunter had just liked showing her off. She definitely needed a distraction from that line of thinking and began tossing more rather than less. "The slut pieces are going in a burn pile. I don't care what they cost. You can't be caught having ever even owned these."

Clarissa was done with her hair before Rose had finished sorting the clothes, so she sent Clarissa to do her face while Rose began on the business clothes. There were only a couple of business-slut pieces to be tossed and they were tucked well to the back. But there were several more tasteful pieces she might borrow at some future date. Clarissa had incredible taste in clothes, probably when she was thinking about herself instead of her men.

Clarissa returned with her hair hanked back in its trademark severe ponytail.

"No, down. You're in mourning, not in power mode. And put this on," Rose handed her an Alexander McQueen black pantsuit cut long and lean to match Clarissa's length but full to match her figure, and a navy-blue tie-neck blouse. "Traditional black, but powerful. Every woman is powerful in a McQueen. Low heel shoes. Remember, mourning. At five-ten, you're tall enough to already dominate anyone you can't intimidate."

Clarissa obeyed.

"I'm afraid we'll have to fend for ourselves for breakfast; the staff are gone."

"Maybe not. I never eat breakfast, so they'd know not to set out anything for me."

"Blood sugar, girl. That's probably half your problem. Give them a ring. I'll eat anything: omelet, bagels and lox, pancakes. We need fattening food this morning because we both deserve it. I want a chocolate chip muffin if they have one. And coffee."

Clarissa groaned. "You may have cured me of coffee for life with that sludge."

"Nonsense. Order it to the veranda, it's a lovely morning, then come over here."

Clarissa called downstairs, then joined her in front of the big mirror.

"Look at these two fine women. Together they can do anything!" Rose absolutely needed to remind herself of that after Hunter's revelation. A detail that Clarissa could never, ever know or she'd murder Hunter personally.

She watched Clarissa's reflection as she inspected herself.

The girl slowly shifted to match the suit. Spine stiffening, confidence rising. Rose didn't speak until Clarissa was once more nearly her usual self. Maybe even a little better.

"That touch of...not sad, but thoughtful. Don't lose that look. It's particularly good."

"You're the best, Rose. I...needed a friend."

"Hard to say that?"

Clarissa's reflection nodded. "I'm not good at relying on others." At the moment, Rose could use a friend as well.

"Well, look in the mirror. Are these two women who are ready for anything?"

"We are!" Then Clarissa lost a bit of her shine. "The White House is going to be a much harder task now, Rose."

"That's why we're going to start planning over breakfast."

Clarissa gave her a sideways hug. "I was right, you *are* the best."

"Damn straight." It was probably best not to break Clarissa's spirit this morning. By Rose's estimation, the Oval Office was now wholly out of reach. But Rose liked having the Director of the CIA as a protégé. They would think of something.

And if she had to throw one Senator Hunter Ramson under the bus to achieve it, she certainly wouldn't be losing any sleep about that. But for now, she needed him.

60

THE NTSB LISTENING ROOM WAS AS UNIQUE AS EACH OF THE prior rooms for processing the contents of a Cockpit Voice Recorder. McGrady had never been involved in a crash investigation before, but this was like some strange monkish cloister.

In twenty-four years of service, he'd lost a few friends to training accidents, but never been in the flight. He'd lost more friends to the wars he hadn't been assigned to, but Marines were needed everywhere in the world.

And this was definitely a first for HMX-1.

The room was as plain-white-and-fluorescent-lights as any military conference room, with black two-foot squares of—he rubbed his fingers over one—cloth panels on the walls that must be for sound absorption. The parquet floor probably came from Home Depot.

But that's where the similarities ended.

The room was dominated by a large U-shaped desk with eight seats. Each position had a narrow counter, a set of headphones, and a computer screen. No keyboards or mice. In the center of the U was a full multi-screen computer station. And on the wall, a big-screen monitor.

"Please have a seat. Where you sit will make no difference," the Chase woman, as unreadable as ever, moved to the central position. They would fill only three of the eight positions.

"Where the hell is everyone? Secret Service? General Macy? FBI?"

"This is the NTSB's part of the process. Within twenty-four hours of an incident, we issue a report to the other parties that is as complete as possible. That will then steer the on-going investigation. To achieve that short time frame, we keep the initial team very small, only bringing in experts and other specialists as needed."

The woman looked around the room, apparently focusing on everything except the people there with her.

"I will try to explain this in your terms."

"You go, girl," Holly muttered.

"When you fly Marine One, do you have the mechanics, traffic controllers, White House Military Liaisons, the Marines of the decoy birds and the soldiers of the overwatch birds aboard, or do they stay off your aircraft and let you do your job? Did I do that right?" She asked the last to Mike and Holly.

"Nailed its ass to the Outback!" Holly declared. Mike just offered a thumbs-up.

"Okay. Please have a seat. Where you sit will make no difference." She repeated her earlier phrase verbatim. It actually sounded as if she was speaking by rote. "On the overhead screen, we will have the complete audio package of the flight. No instrument readouts. No visuals. Only the words and sounds matter here. On your screens I will be creating a timeline of every word spoken, every noise change, whether or not we can identify it. Your task is to aid in that identification."

Mike and Holly took side-by-side stations.

Knowing he was the outsider in this circle, McGrady left an open spot between him and Holly.

"Sucks, doesn't it, mate?"

"What?" He turned to the blonde. He didn't recall her having such a strong Australian accent last night.

"Not knowing whether to shit or get off the pot. Just brace yourself in the bucket, this is the worst part."

"Nothing's worse than extracting their bodies knowing they were murdered."

Holly's look of sympathy cut off his protest.

He shifted his focus back to Miranda just as the screens flashed to life. On the one in front of him, there were three column headings and nothing else but white: Time, Source, and Content.

On the overhead screen were the wiggling sine waves of four audio tracks and a time clock. They were labeled as well.

"Hot-1," Chase explained before he could ask, "is the continuous feed from the right-hand pilot's headset microphone whether or not they have keyed transmit. Hot-2 is the copilot and CAM is the Cockpit Area Microphone at the center of the cockpit that will monitor all ambient noise. There is also a channel for all radio traffic."

It was like looking at an alien script. He'd never had to actually look at a sound waveform before.

"We will perform the initial listen," Chase continued her rote explanation. "Once we concur, then we will bring in additional experts as needed to help create an in-depth analysis of any doubtful anomalies. Colonel McGrady?"

"Yes?" He stumbled before answering because it was all in that exact same tone.

"We'll be depending on your familiarity with the crew's voices to help us with those. Did you also know the Vice President?"

"I flew him a number of times, but he, uh, didn't commonly interact with the crew."

In response, the woman pulled out her phone and dialed.

He glanced over at Mike and Holly, but they weren't surprised by any of the woman's behavior. In fact, she'd been like this much of last night as well: sometimes deer in the headlights, but otherwise intensely focused.

"She always like this?" he whispered to Holly and now wished he'd sat closer.

"You have no idea, mate. When she's on a crash investigation, nothing else exists. Hope you slept last night; you'll need it."

He hadn't.

On the phone, Miranda jumped right into the middle of the conversation. "We are at the NTSB headquarters, beginning the review of the flight recorder information. It is unlikely that we'll be picking up anything of significance from your husband's voice—"

"Miranda!" Holly snapped it out.

"—but in the initial listen I heard several sounds in the background that sounded like Clark. Hold, please. What is it, Holly?"

Blake hadn't heard anything except Tamatha's voice.

"You can't just ask her to come listen to her dead husband like that," now Holly's voice had less of an Australian accent than he himself did, coming from Maryland.

"Why not? She's the most likely person to be able to pick out any words." She listened for a moment. "Besides, she's on her way." Miranda set down her phone.

Holly opened her mouth again, but Mike stopped her by resting a hand on her arm.

Even from the back of her head, Blake could tell that she was glaring at Mike.

"Christ on a crutch. I was hoping we were done with the

bitch after last night." Holly slumped in her chair. "Fine, whatever. Do it up, Miranda. I'm listening."

And without any other comments, Miranda did. As if nothing had happened.

She must have started well before the crash. Other than a steady low rumble that was placed in the notes as "engines idling", there was nothing for five long minutes. He was so used to that sound in the cockpit that he'd never have thought to note it down.

Then, on the CAM track, a massive wiggle showed up and scrolled toward the center of the screen as the clock advanced. When it reached the line in the center, the President's voice boomed out over his headphones.

"Damn sharp helo you've got here."

"Brand-new just for you, Mr. President," Tamatha replied without hesitation.

His headphones tore at McGrady's ears as he kicked up out of his chair and stumbled backward. They came free and thunked down onto the floor.

"What the hell!" He could see that smile Tamatha wore as easily as most people wore a shirt. No slur in her voice. It felt as if she was sitting close beside him in a cockpit at this very instant.

Miranda looked at him in surprise. Then blinked once. "I didn't think to warn you that the voice recorder retains the last two hours of information as I assumed you would know that. So, precisely one hour, forty-six minutes, and nine seconds prior to the crash and final power off, the President was boarding Marine One."

Bloody hell!

"Sorry," he picked up the headphones and pulled his seat back forward. "She just sounded so...alive."

"She was." Again, Miranda stating the obvious as if to a child.

"Can't we just skip to the crash?"

"We don't know if there is any evidence of earlier problems, or sounds of tampering with the aircraft. It is best to listen to all of the available evidence."

He looked down at his screen as he tried to collect himself.

There were notes there now.

08:15:03 **CAM** *President Roy Cole (PRC): Damn sharp helo you've got here.*

08:15:07 **HOT-1** *.?: Brand-new just for you, Mr. President.*

"I recognize Roy's voice personally. Can you confirm that the second voice is Captain Tamatha Jones?"

He nodded.

On his screen the .? changed to *Capt. Tamatha Jones (CTJ).*

"Are you ready to continue?"

He absolutely wasn't, but these were the last two hours of his top officer's flights. He nodded again, unable to do much more.

Bracing himself to listen did nothing to help as they continued.

Holly was right, this was going to be much harder than escorting Tamatha's corpse out of the crash site.

61

"CAN SOMEONE TELL ME WHY WE HAVEN'T HEARD ANYTHING FROM them?"

Drake was surprised that the President hadn't bulldogged his way out of the PEOC yet. Instead, he was steaming under Agent Danziger's "stay safe" mandate and getting ready to take it out on him and Sarah. Oh joy.

There was no doubting the *who* they hadn't heard from.

They'd had reports from General William Macy's AIB site team. Because of the surprisingly intact nature of the helicopter, they were already reporting a better than ninety-nine percent material recovery. Apparently all they were missing was the rear rotor, a third of the main blades, and one of the windshields. Even now, CNN was showing the heavy-lift team, moving the battered and smoke-blackened helo onto a flat-bed truck.

Colonel McGrady of HMX-1 had called in during his brief flight into DC to report that all of the other HMX-1 aircraft tested clean. His conclusion that it was an inside job was *not* unreasonable. He'd also outlined the steps he'd ordered to begin that aspect of the investigation.

It was that report that had Agent Danziger keeping the President locked in the PEOC. An assassination that was an inside job was *the* worst case scenario.

The Secret Service had already supplied the FBI with a list of every authorized person on the Vice President's and the Governor's flights as well as everyone at Camp David.

Both groups reported hourly on their progress with file reviews and interviews.

The CIA's assistant director had done the morning's intelligence briefing, including a list of possible threat matrices from their computer team.

Riyadh, Saudi Arabia, had been high on the list.

And still there hadn't been a peep from Miranda.

"Maybe she's sleeping in?" Sarah suggested.

Drake managed to not laugh in her face. "You've never seen anything like when she's on a crash investigation."

"So call her."

"I tried twice," then he shrugged and hit redial on the conference room phone.

"This is Miranda Chase. This is actually her, not a recording of her." She answered on the first ring.

"Good morning, Miranda. I tried calling you a couple of times."

"Probably while we were in the Chip Recovery Lab and Data Recovery Lab. They're isolated with full Faraday cages to avoid interference with the electronic data recovery—hence the names of the labs. No cell signal can get in. If you'd called on the landline, you would have gotten through."

"But I got through now." He decided that mentioning he'd had no idea that the NTSB was where she'd gone wouldn't be constructive. Though perhaps he should have guessed.

"We have a split team now. Jeremy is leading the Data Group Recovery. I'm working with Mike, Holly, Colonel McGrady, and

Clarissa in the Listening Room to transcribe the audio from the recorders. This room does not have a Faraday cage as we are no longer dealing with isolating electronic signals."

"Clarissa is there?"

"Yes, Drake. She's assisting with picking out the Vice President's voice from the background clutter. Her familiarity with his voice is a great advantage."

Drake whistled in surprise.

When Roy looked up, Drake just held up a hand to hold off questions.

"How long did he survive?"

"We haven't gotten that far yet. We're only at the landing at Camp David four days ago. And even if we do find his final spoken words, we won't actually know how much longer he survived as he wasn't wearing a heart monitor. Though, if he survived until the fire, and happened to be breathing in at the moment of the explosion, an autopsy should reveal charring in the lungs commensurate with a five-hundred-degree fire—that is the burn temperature of hydrogen, though there were impurities in the air, such as the hydrogen cyanide, that could skew that. That's centigrade. It would be...nine-hundred-and-thirty-two-degrees Fahrenheit. Though I suppose the ultimate effect would be little changed even if there was an unlikely temperature swing of even a hundred degrees. Centigrade or Fahrenheit."

Sarah blanched white and the President looked grim.

"Keep us posted, Miranda."

"Could you be more precise about that?"

Drake couldn't help smiling. "If you find anything that... How about if you just give me an hourly report?"

"I'll call next at 11:17." And she hung up the phone.

Sarah gave a half laugh of surprise.

"Don't worry, you'll never get used to her ways. But they

always work." Then he turned to the President. "Whatever we think of her, Clarissa Reese is there."

"And why is that particularly significant? You were actively surprised, Drake."

Drake wished he didn't know. "I've done two of those, Mr. President. Listening to the tape of the dead's voices. Sitting in a safe, clean room, with a cold Coke on the desk, and debating if one particular sound is an anomaly, or a final grunt of extreme pain the moment before death. It's a brutal task. I have no idea how those people do it. It's one of the reasons that they rarely release the actual recording, only the transcript. Those tapes of the 9/11 crash of Flight 93 in Pennsylvania, that they had to release for the trial of one of the planning conspirators, took a horrendous toll on the families."

Drake noticed the President's continued interest.

"It's no secret that I don't trust Clarissa Reese. Yes, she's proving to be an exceptional CIA Director. But what she's doing right now, that's hard. Damned hard."

The President nodded, keeping his thoughts to himself as usual.

62

"WHO WAS THAT?" CLARISSA CIRCLED A FINGER FOR MIRANDA TO hit replay.

Over the last hour, their communication had actually become surprisingly easy. For each time she spun her forefinger in a circle, Miranda would back up five seconds.

A pinching motion, and Miranda sliced off sections of background noise, such as the engine.

Three circles this time. Fifteen seconds. And a pinch.

The sound replayed.

"Clark: *You wanted to meet with me?*" She echoed his words aloud.

They appeared on the screen almost as fast as she spoke them. Miranda, the only one here with ears as sharp as her own, must have concurred or she wouldn't have typed them.

"Unknown person:" she continued to echo what she could barely pick out of the background despite all of the noise cancelling. "*Perhaps later in private, Mr. Vice President. I will be at* —or maybe *on—your convenient disposal.*"

She watched as the ? of an unknown speaker proceeded the transcript words.

"Damn it, McGrady. Why didn't you people put in a cabin mike? It's fucking hard to pick them up on the open cockpit one."

"HMX-1 provides executive transport. We specifically do not eavesdrop on high-security conversations of our transportees."

Clarissa wanted to slice at him. To keep slicing. Clark had died in his squadron's care.

Something about that Marine-stiff facade, showing not one iota of outer emotion, made her want to poke and prod until she found the cracks.

But Rose had been emphatic about how Clarissa must behave during any aspect of this investigation. And that didn't include sparring with a Marine Corps colonel.

"Ruddy peculiar syntax," Holly spoke so softly that Clarissa wouldn't have heard it if she hadn't been sitting right next to her.

On her arrival, Clarissa had dropped into the chair between Holly and McGrady before she remembered how much she couldn't stand Bitch Holly Harper. At least she didn't have to hide any of her true feelings from Holly—the hatred was completely mutual.

She looked back at the words on her display: *Perhaps later in private, Mr. Vice President. I will be at/on(?) your convenient disposal.*

A chill far deeper than the excessive air conditioning cut into her.

No one else was reacting to the phrase.

Then again, only she and Holly had been in the Middle East War Zones. And—

"Oh fuck me dead," Holly's whisper was even softer this time.

Too bad it completely confirmed Clarissa's worst fear.

"We have to call the President."

Miranda looked puzzled. "It isn't 11:17 yet."

"Trust me. Call him."

63

"Go ahead."

"You're on speakerphone," Miranda had learned to always announce that. It still didn't make sense to her that the opposite wasn't also required, for politeness sake, to announce that a call was private. But she knew that was true.

"So are you," the President replied.

"I'm sorry to call before 11:17, Roy, but Clarissa insisted that you'd want to know. I do feel bad about that." Only after she said it did she realize her error.

Drake had initially asked her to call with any updates. For clarity...for her sake?...he'd amended that to hourly.

So perhaps it was okay.

If so, she should just proceed.

"While in flight from One Observatory Circle to Camp David, an unidentified person spoke with the Vice President about a private meeting. Clarissa feels that the unusual syntax of the reply is sufficiently pertinent to bring to your attention. It reads: *I will be at*—or perhaps *on*—*your convenient disposal*."

"Shit!" Drake's voice. Apparently he knew what it meant as well.

Clarissa nodded at the rightness of that even if neither she nor Holly had explained what had upset them.

That made Miranda feel better about calling. Not that she wanted to upset him, but now the importance was confirmed.

"Danziger!" Drake called out loudly enough to hurt her ears.

"I'm unfamiliar with that word, Drake." Too late she recalled that the head of the President's Protection Detail had threatened her in her own home just yesterday morning. She'd spent the last two hours straining so hard to pick out every word that she hadn't thought about connecting a word to a person.

"It's not a what, it's a who. Hold on." Drake didn't mute the phone as he continued speaking. "Danziger. You had someone on the Vice President's flight who speaks clear, even fluent English, but slipped into an inverted syntax, possibly Arabian."

"There's the Vice President's assistant. He's—"

"It wasn't Avi," Clarissa called out. "I know his voice. Besides, he's Indian, not Arabic. And he's from Cleveland. Get your— Sorry." She looked as if she was biting her tongue painfully hard.

"She's right, mate," Holly chimed in. "Which is a really nice surprise, Clarissa. Well done, you. Danziger, get your shit together. Arabic, not Ohioan or Indian."

"Was he still on the flight for the return?"

Miranda searched for a metaphor of what Danziger sounded like...but all she came up with was "an angry agent." Like an angry...dog?

"We haven't gotten that far yet. Do you always snarl like a dog?" Miranda decided that she was rather proud of her metaphor. No, she'd used the word *like* so it was a simile not a metaphor. Yet it accurately aligned with his attitude on three separate occasions in just twenty-four hours: at her home, aboard the E-4B Nightwatch, and now on the phone. It was rare to discover statistical significance when assessing human interactions.

There was a sputtering sound from the speaker that sounded like a...sputtering sound. Maybe she shouldn't push it.

Holly stood up out of her seat enough to reach over the intervening desk and held out her hand.

Miranda high-fived it, making her feel better about the secondary metaphor-attempt failure.

"What was that for?" Miranda could hear Clarissa whisper to Holly.

"She nailed a simile."

Clarissa turned from Holly to stare at her for a long moment. Miranda could feel it, even if she kept her attention on the computer screen.

Then Clarissa also rose to her feet and held out her hand.

Clarissa had never done that before, but Miranda high-fived her hand as well.

But she looked pleased when Miranda had, so she must have done it right.

Miranda hung up the phone and replaced her own headphones.

When the others were ready, she pressed play on the next segment.

64

DANZIGER HAD THE VIP GUEST LISTS UP ON THE SCREENS IN THE PEOC conference room. He hated to involve the President at this level, but the man was insisting and he *was* The Man.

The inbound and outbound trips rarely matched. Both the Main Man, as Danziger had always thought of him, and the VP were so heavily scheduled that it wasn't abnormal for someone to fly out to somewhere and catch a ride on Air Force One or Two for a thirty-minute meeting in a six-hour flight, then jaunt home from the next port of call.

Twelve passengers on the Superhawk. Minus four: VP, chief assistant, the colonel with the nuclear football, and the head of the VP's protection detail. He'd known the VPPD for ten years but reluctantly put him back on the possible list. In fact...might the VP have poisoned his own aircraft for some reason? Shit! He'd have to look at everybody.

He also cursed himself for the remark about Avi. He'd been Clark's right hand since the week after he'd ascended to the Vice Presidency. He knew damn near everything about the man, including having personally done the security clearance interview with his parents—at their home in Cleveland.

The prep for a global trip had been horrendous, and the trip itself beyond brutal. He'd spent seven years of his life keeping the President alive, but it had never been this hard.

He should release the President from the PEOC, but it *was* easier to control his security here. Given the chance, he'd lock the Main Man in here for the rest of his term. And then recommend they do the same to whoever succeeded him.

Not an option, no matter how stretched he was personally.

He'd already been over these lists several times, as well as lists of everyone else who'd been near the Vice President, his home at One Observatory Circle, and Camp David in the last month.

"Mr. President. I think it's time for you to…" He hadn't looked at the in- and out-bound guest list on Marine Two side-by-side before this.

"Time for what?" President Cole asked.

Danziger had been about to release him back into the White House at large.

But there *was* a difference between the two lists.

Only one name had been on the out-bound flight, but not on the return. Marine Two had flown to its doom with a single empty seat. And the missing passenger had taken a midnight drive back to DC rather than waiting until the morning.

"Danziger?"

He placed the two lists side by side on the screen.

The Man read down them.

Over the years, Danziger had learned to read the President's body language even through his ex-Green Beret shield.

He spotted the discrepancy immediately.

President Cole tipped his head slightly to the side as if to deny the possibility, but caught himself.

For ten seconds he didn't move.

Then he looked up.

"Here. Right here. Do it personally."

Danziger headed for the door.

"And do it nicely."

He nodded. And if he couldn't, whatever force was needed wouldn't bother him for a second.

65

THE MARINE TWO AIRCRAFT HAD BEEN PARKED AT CAMP DAVID for three full days and nights, departing the morning of the fourth day.

Miranda had done a quick review of the overall recording to bookmark the long gaps between activity when the recorder had switched off.

Each morning like clockwork, the three voices that Colonel McGrady had identified as the crew's boarded the helicopter.

Miranda never had their arrival on the recording because the systems were powered off. But she could set her watch by when they powered up the helo.

"It's their prime duty during a layover," Colonel McGrady had explained. "Every morning at seven a.m. they have to make sure that the helicopter is ready for immediate departure in case of an emergency. They perform a full preflight. At 0703, because Tamatha's crew is—was that good, they power up, start the engines, and spin the rotor for ten minutes. Shutdown at 0713 with checklist and report done by 0715. Textbook efficient."

The battery in the Voice Data Recorder allowed it to record another ten minutes of audio before shutting down itself.

On Day Two—their first full morning at Camp David—it had recorded the few words the crew exchanged as part of the power-down process.

Captain Vance Brown had then asked who was up for a run and received a pair of yeses.

The door closed.

And then there was an odd, rising-and-falling sound that took several minutes to identify. When they did, it had made them all laugh: beyond the helicopter's heavy sound insulation, someone at Camp David was mowing the grass.

They were now starting the detailed review of Day Three.

Through to 0715 and crew's subsequent departure, there was hardly a word of variation or timing, except this time it was Major Tamatha Jones who asked about the run.

"Marines run a lot," McGrady said with a shrug. "Get grouchy if we miss our run for more than a day or two."

"I get grouchy if Mike wakes me before noon," Holly groused.

"Says the woman who keeps dragging me out of a nice warm bed to go running in the rain with Taz."

"I can't believe someone a foot shorter than me can run me into the ground. It's simply not right."

"What? Someone who does something better than the supreme Miss Holly Harper?" Clarissa's voice had a sharp edge that Miranda might identify as...gleeful? A tease or a nasty jab? Despite several interactions, Miranda still lacked sufficient data to map Clarissa's vocal personality traits well enough to generate even a first-order approximation.

Holly, however, resolved the uncertainty by giving Clarissa the finger. A definite sign of teasing with an eighty-three percent accuracy across all individuals—one of her better correlations regarding humor. Though oddly, Holly's snarl said it might fall in the seventeen-percent category.

As they continued their banter, Miranda wound back the

recording to before McGrady had first spoken and began listening again.

People were always so distracting.

For seven more minutes after the crew's departure, she heard nothing and saw nothing. All four audio channels showed as a flat line on her screen.

Nothing. Not even a lawn mower.

Then, at nine minutes and forty-nine seconds, there was a very distinct sound, one she'd already heard twice: the opening of the helicopter's door.

At nine minutes and fifty-six seconds, there was a noise.

At ten minutes, the recording automatically stopped.

"What was that?"

They all stopped talking. "What was what?"

Because she couldn't figure out how to say it politely, she resisted pointing out that, if they'd been listening like they were supposed to, they would already know the answer to the question.

Miranda rewound to the door opening and keyed the time into the transcript.

She typed 7:24:49 **CAM** *Door opens.*

She then pre-keyed 7:24:56 **CAM** for the cockpit area microphone and kept listening.

It was soft. No more than a step.

Except it wasn't a step.

"Again," McGrady ordered. After three more listens, the others began guessing.

Miranda opened the spectrum view, which showed the sound as a pillar that was time wide and from low bass to the upper limits of hearing high. The pillar had a very distinct shape. Again, she should recognize it, but didn't.

She opened the library of comparison sounds that the NTSB had built and began eliminating.

It lacked the sharp percussive shape of an explosive or a

strike—even a bird strike. But neither did it have the unruly shape and slow build of a spoken tone. Sharp exclamations had slower build curves than the one on her screen. It also split high and low.

"Maybe it's in the main cabin."

Miranda twisted to look at Holly.

"Check the pilot's headsets to see if there's any time differential of when the sound arrived at the various microphones."

She zoomed in the display until they could see only the first arc of the first curve of the sound in each channel.

"Camp David rests at an elevation of seventeen hundred feet. I don't have the temperature there, but I have the temperature and elevation at the Frederick crash site." She opened her VH-92A notebook to look at her entry from yesterday. "We arrived six hours after the crash, therefore there are inaccuracies, but evening and morning temperatures are often similar. Adjusting for standard temperature drop for the increased altitude at Camp David's elevation, the speed of sound would be approximately two meters per second faster than the normal dry air value. Hence..."

Miranda happened to look up and see that Clarissa was frowning and Holly smiling.

She finished her calculations in silence.

There *were* variations of the noise's sound wave arriving at the three microphones, but as she didn't know their precise locations—and the variation was so minute, under three thousands of a second—it was hard to be sure.

"This...suggests," yes, that was a good word, "that the noise came from the right side, high in the cabin. I have to repeat, this is only a suggestion that I'm not yet able to accurately verify."

"The emergency air generators," Colonel McGrady said softly.

"Yes." It fit with the ceiling mounted units.

"I think it's two sounds, not one."

Miranda looked at the shape of the sound and decided that Clarissa was absolutely right.

The moment she isolated them, they each became familiar. Very familiar. She isolated each and played them separately. Familiar, but even then she couldn't lay her finger on it.

Before she could write anything into the transcript, the Listening Room door banged open.

Agent Danziger strode in, looking no nicer than he had when he'd been on her island. His eyes were bloodshot and dark with lack of sleep, or excessive drinking. She could look at them briefly because he wasn't looking at her.

She finally connected his snarl to the origin of the simile— he was worse than the Chow dog that had scared her so badly at seven. She'd never approached a dog since, and there had never been another allowed on the island. Besides, they always chased the sheep and deer, and she didn't like that.

Danziger came into the room that way, all snap and nerves.

Miranda looked to Holly, who wasn't reacting, which meant it must be all show.

Still, Miranda slumped lower in her seat, hoping that he wouldn't notice her.

66

"Ms. Reese. Could you come with me, please?"

Clarissa rolled her eyes at the President's Secret Service agent. "That's Director Reese. And I'm busy here."

But as she turned back toward Miranda, two more agents slid into the room, standing to either side of the door. Behind them, Jeremy, Andi, and the others moved to peer in from the Data Analysis Lab.

"*Director* Reese," Danziger's voice managed to drip with vitriol that belied his polite words. "Now. Please."

She felt a frisson of fear sliding up her spine.

What could the Secret Service want with her?

Had they been monitoring her and Rose's conversation this morning about how to reach the White House? Not a day went by in DC when someone wasn't planning how to get their own seat in the Oval Office. Of course, it wasn't usually the CIA Director doing so.

But Danziger was head of the President's Protection Detail. What could *he* want with her?

"Why do you need *me?*" She managed to say it as if she was an asset, not a target. Her gut said otherwise.

"I've been requested to escort you to a meeting in the Presidential Emergency Operations Center."

Clarissa wanted to burst out laughing. To call Rose and tell her they were on their way.

She'd been in the Situation Room for any number of briefings, but she'd never been in the PEOC where rumor said that the President was still locked down. Never one to waste time, President Cole was obviously thinking about the replacement for his dead Vice President.

She pushed to her feet and checked her clothes. Rose had selected well. The black pantsuit and the slightly frilly navy neck-tie blouse said nothing flashy, but pure professional. Her hair being down still bothered her, but Rose had insisted. *You must invite people* into *your sphere of influence. A bit of vulnerability on the outside goes a long way.*

Halfway to the door, Miranda called out behind her.

"But you can't go. We aren't finished yet."

Clarissa opened her mouth, then closed it again. Whatever issues she had with Miranda's people, Miranda herself was almost pleasant. Clarissa appreciated her dedication and focus. In fact, the ease with which they'd worked together over the last several hours was surprisingly pleasant—aside from the subject. Which gave her how to answer.

"It's okay, Miranda. You're doing fine."

Holly looked at her in surprise.

Eat that shit, Harper! I was just nice to your little Miranda. Bet you have no idea what to do with that in your squidgy brain, do you?

"I'm glad I could help," Clarissa let her tone go sad, "but I don't want to have to listen to my husband die."

Then she turned and followed Danziger out of the room.

Because if she listened to him die, it would just make her all the angrier that he wasn't alive for her to kill him herself.

67

Breezing through White House security had never been so easy before. And once she was Vice President, she could do this any time she damn well pleased.

Two miles from the NTSB lab to her future home. It passed in a single blink of the eye.

Vice President.

Now! It was a triumph.

She'd have a year and half of training by Roy Cole. Even if she didn't agree with all his policies, he was one of recent history's most savvy politicians. Then the Presidency would be hers.

Driving right onto the grounds as if she already belonged, they strolled through the security scanners at the West Wing Foyer—and took that critical right turn into the Situation Room. Past the briefing room and watch center manned by the National Security Council.

At the far end behind a nondescript door, they entered a small elevator she'd never seen before.

Danziger unlocked it with a thumbprint and, once inside, spoke simply, "Presidential Emergency Operations Center."

Accepting the voice recognition security, the elevator descended. No indicator lights, but she'd guess they descended at least four stories.

It opened on a corridor that could have been inside any office building. To the left, it extended back toward the Oval Office and probably included the rumored direct entrance for the President—she'd find out about that soon enough. To the right was a large pressure door worthy of a bank vault.

Danziger didn't approach it.

Instead, he just waited.

Inside, some security agent decided they were safe and the door swung silently open. It was a massive thing that just might survive a nuclear blast.

On the other side was a set of rooms not all that different from the Situation Room.

There was a hum of serious activity. A heavily armed officer double-checked their security at the entrance. Clerks were at desks and on phones. Military personnel were studying their screens. This was exactly what she expected the PEOC to be.

The main conference room, despite being deep under West Executive Avenue, felt light and airy. The long conference table was mostly empty, except for the three people seated there, who all looked as if they'd been underground far too long.

"Mr. President, Sarah, Drake. How can the CIA be of service this morning?"

Cole waved her to a seat at his left hand. That placed her between the President and Drake as Sarah sat at the President's right. She couldn't help thinking that Sarah was sitting in Clark's seat. His Chief of Staff, when he was included, habitually sat at the President's left, but she wasn't here today.

"How are you, Clarissa?" If Cole's tone hadn't been quite so solicitous, she might have brushed it off with an "I'm fine." But his manner reminded her to behave.

"I'm okay, I suppose. It's hard. But last night and this

morning I appreciated being of assistance in determining what happened to my husband. That has been some solace."

Cole nodded, but looked uncomfortable. Not the look of someone about to announce her as his choice for VP. Perhaps she was here for an interview first. Yes, that fit. President Cole was never one to act slowly when action was needed. Time for a new VP, get it moving fast, but he was also a careful man.

While she was still trying to calculate what the right words might be to help move that along, Cole slipped two pieces of paper in front of her.

"Passenger manifests of Marine Two's trips to and from Camp David."

She scanned the lists. "I know most, but not all of these people. The only ones I knew at all well were Jake, the head of his detail, and Avi, his right hand. Sometimes I wondered if the four of us, rather than two, lived at One Observatory Circle." She tried a smile, but the joke fell flat in the room.

This was *not* a receptive audience.

Which meant that the movers were probably already there packing the house. She pictured the pile of clothes that Rose had insisted she dispose of, still on the bed. Well, there was nothing she could do about that at this moment.

Drake to her left was unreadable, and Sarah across the table was no better.

"Anything else about the lists, Clarissa?" Cole's dark tone belied his calm expression.

She scanned them again. "Four names I don't know at all." She might not even recognize their faces; they'd been little people. "The only difference I see is that I'm not on the return flight."

Cole didn't even blink, instead studying her face.

That was *too* absurd! She actually laughed aloud.

His expression didn't change.

Perhaps laughing in the President's face had *not* been her

best choice. She'd write it off to not sleeping a wink in the last two nights.

"Do you think I'm stupid enough to kill off my best path to the Oval Office after all the trouble I went to putting him in line?"

And then she heard her own words.

They were going to be much harder to write off.

68

"Would you care to repeat that?"

"I'd rather not," her voice was small—and Clarissa Reese's voice was never small.

Drake came close to pitying the woman. Clarissa's eyes were bloodshot, though he couldn't imagine it was from weeping for Clark's death. Her constant blinking implied that it had been even longer since she'd last slept than he had. Her skin was paler than her white-blonde hair, attesting that she was probably out near her limits.

Her skin paled another shade, making it nearly bloodless. Maybe she was a secret vampire. Drake wouldn't put anything past her.

"Elaborate." President Cole didn't make it a suggestion.

She blinked hard again, but for once Clarissa Reese was struck speechless.

"Oh fuck," Danziger whispered it. Then snapped to attention, "Please excuse my language, Mr. President. I just put together a couple of stories I'd heard regarding former Vice President Mulroney. I'm sorry. I shouldn't have even said that much. The Secret Service does not discuss the personal matters of protectees."

Drake tried to connect together the pieces, but even with that hint, he didn't have them.

The President growled, "Danziger. The person with the lowest security clearance in this room is the National Security Advisor, the Director of the CIA, or the Joint Chiefs of Staff. My vote is you, Drake, just so you know. So tell me."

Clarissa had buried her face in her hands.

Danziger stood stiffly and kept his jaw clenched.

Clarissa finally snarled in frustration and uncovered her face. "Christ, the Secret Service is so fucking lame, Danziger. Keep the President safe," she said the last in a singsong voice that then descended into a snarl, "even protecting him from the knowledge of his asshole running mate's vile predilections in two elections."

Without the slightest hint of tears, she turned to the President.

"I will not deign to speak that fucker's name. Last year it came to my attention that your first VP had a real taste for underage girls during foreign travel. He was *not* gentle about it. He put several in the hospital. I—"

She aborted some thought with a shake of her head.

"You deserved better than that, Mr. President. Clark was perfect. He loved being your Vice President even more than being D/CIA. I may have set the final trap that hit the world's headlines, but your first VP didn't walk into it, he ran—with his pants around his ankles before he was through the door."

"You pushed Clark to give me weekly in-depth briefings for six months before that, making him a natural choice for me when you took out Mulroney."

"I sent Clark your direction because you were underutilizing your greatest asset, the CIA. That was long before I found out about that—" her voice strangled with fury.

"*He* took himself out. I just helped him with a dose of press coverage."

Drake had never thought about how every major news service just *happened* to be in the right place or who had called the police with the tip off.

"Which let Clark take you with him to the role of Second Lady, and eventually First," Cole said softly.

Clarissa shrugged, then nodded.

Except Drake had long since learned how to read her. First Lady had *never* been Clarissa's goal. "No, you as Vice President to Clark's President. A first-ever family ticket."

Cole and Sarah looked at him in surprise.

Clarissa started the shrug again, but gave it up halfway done. "It was a good plan—until some bastard murdered him. Trust me, Mr. President," she tapped the lists still on the table in front of her, "I want to find out who killed him far more than you ever possibly could. I want to destroy him inch by inch—personally! *Before* I gut him!"

She glared about the table defiantly.

In her current state, she looked as if she'd do the same to anyone who got in her way. Probably while wearing her crazy-expensive designer suit.

There was such a long silence that the room's tension had time to bleed away. Enough so that Danziger even sat down in the chair beside Sarah.

President Cole was tapping that damned finger of his.

Drake knew not to ask him for his thoughts, but he did know that the President rarely considered something for so long.

They all twitched when the phone rang.

69

"HELLO, DRAKE. IT'S 11:17."

Drake noticed Sarah's smile. She was learning about Miranda.

If the President was amused by Miranda's punctuality, he didn't show it, but he did stop tapping his finger.

"Hello, Miranda. Do you have anything new for us?"

"Yes. We were able to analyze the sound that Clarissa helped me identify."

Clarissa sat up straighter, with a definite I-told-you-so smile.

"What did you find?" He knew that Miranda would wait forever without a prompt.

"It occurred on the morning of the helicopter's last full day at Camp David. After a standard morning runup test lasting precisely fifteen minutes, the Cockpit Voice Recorder ran for an additional ten minutes. At nine minutes and forty-nine seconds, the door to the Marine Two aircraft was reopened."

"Colonel McGrady here, Mr. President. That alone is very unusual based on our normal protocols."

"Continue, Ms. Chase." The President was listening intently.

"If I'm supposed to call you Roy, shouldn't you be calling me Miranda? Or did you reverse your choice and I should be calling you something else? If so, what?"

"Jesus, Miranda," Clarissa muttered to herself.

"Roy will be just fine, Miranda. Please continue."

"That's good to know. The final recorded sound was a heavy object being dropped on the carpeted deck and the pop and release of a plastic piece. Some high-frequency vibrations were transmitted through the helicopter's skin to the pickup microphone, indicating that the piece was most probably part of the helicopter's trim work. Probably high and to the right, which would fit with the location of the emergency air supply system."

"What else?"

"Nothing, sir. The recording stopped four seconds later. It is only designed to run for ten minutes after the most recent power shutdown. We've only just started on the fourth and final day, but the early morning runup test is proceeding precisely on schedule."

Danziger's twitch drew Drake's attention. For the first time in hours, he looked very wide awake.

"Danziger here. Thank you, Ms. Chase. Everything that Drake and the President said about you is absolutely true." He scrabbled for the intercom.

"We'll get back to you, Miranda. Thank you." Drake hung up and turned to watch Danziger.

"Get me everything you have on any late additions to the flight's guest list," Danziger ordered. Then offered to those at the table as an aside, "I'd still rather it wasn't one of ours." He continued to the intercom. "On our screens, right now, whatever you have so far. And then find me any surveillance video at the Camp David helipad from..."

"Friday morning, 0715," Clarissa offered with only a slight smugness.

"Do it."

They all turned to the screens and waited.

Four faces came on screen.

Drake did his best to not do a racial profile, but one face stood out clearly. He was a top assistant to the Saudi Arabian ambassador. A member of the extensive royal family—by marriage.

Cole looked grim as the other three profiles filled in.

A professor who was a specialist in Southern US political history. An appropriate expert for Clark to have brought in to help recreate the Southern Governor's Association.

A political consultant recently hired by the party to help prepare Clark for his election campaign.

And...

"Oh no!" Clarissa groaned.

"What?"

She again covered her face for a long moment before looking back at the fourth image. A lovely Indian girl. Her bio said she was a new hire for White House Legal Counsel's office.

Nothing jumped out at Drake as he scanned her bio.

"Sorry, it's just..." Clarissa looked as if she was going to be sick.

The viper actually *did* have feelings.

"Avi, Clark's executive assistant, told us he had a new girlfriend over in legal counsel. He was so excited about her."

"So he begged a favor from Clark to bring his girlfriend along to Camp David."

Clarissa nodded. "He must have. The days were busy and she kept a low profile. I was supposed to have breakfast with them the final morning, but I had to come back to DC."

"Why *weren't* you on the return flight?" Cole dropped the

question deadpan, which Drake knew was a bad sign. Apparently Clarissa missed that and simply answered.

"My people called me. They were tracking a significant rise in encrypted chatter commensurate with a pending terrorist attack. We worked it all night. The NSA couldn't crack it. My people had traced it to the DC area by...too late." She waved a helpless hand toward the screen.

"And the source?"

Clarissa heaved out a sigh, then pointed at the assistant to the Saudi Arabian ambassador.

70

"I swear I didn't know anything," Hunter practically groveled the moment Rose walked back into the house.

"You knew Clark's policies," Rose set down her handbag and shed her jacket into the front closet.

"Yes. I did. But I swear to God that Ahmad said he simply wanted a chance to meet with Clark to persuade him to change his attitude toward the Saudis." Hunter trailed after her as she headed into the front parlor.

It was such a soothing room, decorated in pastels and soft florals. The bursts of color came from the tasteful vases of flowers made twice as brilliant by the muted décor.

This was her domain.

Here is where she held her tea socials until they were the must-get invitation for any woman seeking power in DC. Congresswomen, senators, two Supreme Court justices, and many more had swirled through this room.

She'd so looked forward to hosting the celebration tea for Clarissa's ascendency in this room.

But no matter what she'd said to Clarissa this morning to

bolster her confidence, Hunter had effectively guaranteed that the Oval Office would never happen now.

Rose closed her eyes for a moment. She could still see the quiet post-election night party when they were *the* two women of the White House. But the image, so clear before, was now tattered at the edges, faded with age as that potential future died a fast death.

It wasn't over yet—if anyone could manage it, Clarissa Reese was the woman—but something told her that dream was done.

She forced her attention back to Hunter's worried face.

Without the White House for herself, she still needed Hunter. Without him, the second most powerful senator in the Congress after the majority leader, her own star would fade very rapidly—overnight. She knew better than anyone how fickle Washington society could be.

"What's done is done, Hunter. But in the future..."

"Yes? Anything!"

"Don't do something without asking me first."

"Never again. Oh, Rose. You're the best woman there ever was." He wrapped his arms around her in a warm embrace.

She returned it.

Besides, she too had known Ahmad for a long time and knew how influential he could be. She'd have suggested adding him to the trip if she'd thought of it herself.

Not that she'd ever tell Hunter that.

71

"WHO THE HELL IS THAT?" CLARISSA LOOKED AROUND THE TABLE, but no one reacted.

Whoever it was had avoided the surveillance cameras, at least with their face. There were shots of a leg here, a back there, but never a clear view.

She tried to make it be the Saudi Ahmad.

Or not be.

But couldn't conclusively do either one.

As much as she hated to suggest it, she knew what they had to do.

"Send it to Miranda."

72

"But we're nearly to the crash." Miranda hated to be interrupted at this point. Marine Two had a variety of systems that she'd never had the opportunity to study. The readout and sound characteristics were utterly fascinating. This was data at its purest about an aircraft she'd never seen in such detail.

"Miranda." Drake was always patient, which she appreciated. "We have partial videos of the person who created those sounds you identified, but we can't see enough to identify him."

"But people come last, Drake." They were the innermost sphere of all. Besides, people were Mike's and Taz's area of specialty, not hers.

"Jesus, Miranda," Clarissa snapped out.

Andi leaned forward and tapped the mute button.

Miranda could feel the pressure in the room drop by half.

Everyone had gathered in the Listening Room.

"Miranda," Andi said softly, "think of it as video *data*. We're still in the Flight Data sphere."

She never thought of people that way. Perhaps if she thought of people's information as data first rather than people first, she wouldn't feel the need to push it out as far as possible. "That's incredibly good, Andi. I can work with that."

Andi unmuted the phone just as someone asked if they were still there.

"Yes," Miranda answered. "Please send the video *data*. We'll review it now."

In seconds, the images had arrived and she put them up on the screen.

It was a jumble of times and angles of view: two seconds at the back of the hangar, three more from a different angle at the front corner, and so on.

This Miranda could do. It fit her autism well. This was the way that the world seemed to her all the time—images and events that were often a jarring jumble as too much detail came in too fast.

She let it all play through once, less than sixty seconds total, including an equally careful departure by the reverse route.

"The case he's carrying is the right size for a cabin-sized emergency oxygen generator," Colonel McGrady noted.

"How much do they weigh fully charged?" Holly asked.

"Between twelve and thirteen kilos," Jeremy chimed in. "It's actually twelve-point-five kilos plus-or-minus a half kilo on the manufacturer's specification sheet. That of course doesn't account for the different chemical compounds that were packed to create the hydrogen cyanide gas. I don't know the exact composition of their chemical compound yet, so I can't be sure. But that's what a real one weighs. They—"

"Hush, Jeremy," Taz patted his arm.

"Twenty-seven pounds, a couple of bowling balls. That matches his uneven stride," Holly concluded.

Miranda noted that down. It was something she'd expect a former SASR operator to know.

"Stride is more off than that," Mike leaned forward. "Replay that last sequence."

Miranda reran the view from behind as the person strode purposefully across the pavement to the helicopter, leaning strongly to one side.

"Not a man. A woman."

"You would know," Holly smirked. "But I think he's right."

"Only one woman's ass I care about now," Mike kissed her on the temple.

"Stop selling lollies to dingoes and I'll buy in," but she kissed him back.

Miranda applied simple metrics to get the person's height against the helicopter. A stride length measurement corroborated the estimate.

If she had long hair, it was tucked up inside her hat.

Her hat.

Even now, their whole team wore their bright yellow Australian Matildas hats.

The woman's hat was medium brown.

Miranda ran through the entire sequence, found the best view of the hat was at the moment the suspect paused to open the helo's door, and zoomed in.

There were no relevant markings on the back of the hat. Though there was a curl of dark hair that indicated her hair was indeed tucked up.

"Go back two seconds," Andi whispered to her.

Miranda did, but didn't see why.

Andi rested a hand on her shoulder as she leaned in to tap a finger on a corner of the screen.

Of course, Miranda zoomed in.

There, reflected in the pilot's side window, was the front of the hat.

Disappointingly, it was blank.

Then she panned down slightly to put the whole reflection on the screen.

She was near the limits of enhancement she could apply to it when McGrady cursed.

Everyone turned to look at him.

He was rubbing his forehead.

"Manufacturer's rep for our air system. Our birds travel the world and downtime for service is sometimes hard to find. She'd have the clearance to enter the grounds and service the helo. It should never have happened without my crew present, but she'd certainly have the know-how. This visit never showed up on our schedule or in our logs. We'd have spotted that already."

Miranda dialed the phone.

73

AFTER MIRANDA EXPLAINED WHAT SHE'D FOUND, DANZIGER pulled up the visitor list.

There it was.

Sign in at 0652.

Sign out at 0737.

His people *had* done their job, they'd even noted the model and serial number of the units the rep had been delivering.

But it hadn't been enough. He'd have to think about that later.

He picked up the phone, called the Oklahoma City office, and gave them their targets. A defense contractor was going down today—every one of its employees and executives would be in custody and questioning by nightfall.

Sick to his stomach, he turned to the President.

"Mr. President, I can hereby clear you to leave the PEOC, and as soon as aircraft inspections are complete, you are recertified for travel."

"Thank God for small favors." Cole didn't push to his feet. "We'll be in the Oval until we get to your final report on this."

Danziger knew when he was dismissed.

As he hurried out of the room, he heard the President speak softly.

"There's one more thing before we shift upstairs. Drake, cut the monitor to the watch officers."

Like so often in his job, Danziger could only guess at what the rest of that conversation might be.

74

CLARISSA WATCHED AS THE PRESIDENT DID MORE OF THAT goddamn finger tapping routine. He finally stopped and stretched out all ten fingers as if they suddenly hurt. Then he looked her square in the eye with that famously frank soldier's look of his.

"I'm sorry, Clarissa, but I can't suggest you to the party for the Vice Presidency."

And there it was.

Clarissa felt the gut blow land. Her stomach roiled all the way back to the toxic-waste sludge coffee Rose had made her drink this morning. But she'd sooner burn in hell that show it to these people. She might not have the Vice Presidency but she had her pride.

"Not because I think you would be good or bad at it. I'd consider recommending you just because I think you could shake up many of the ingrained disasters that exist in our global status quo."

"Damn straight I could! Then why not?"

He began tapping his fucking finger again. If she took a

hammer and smashed it, would it stop? Or would it keep beating like Edgar Allan Poe's "Tell-Tale Heart"?

He noted the direction of her glance, half smiled, and stopped.

"But the ultimate reason I can't put your name forward is what you just told us. You have no idea—honestly, you can't—of the hideous vetting process that is a modern Presidential election. Even when it's a midterm replacement. That story would come out. How many people outside this room know of your involvement in Vice President Mulroney's getting caught with that pair of preteen hookers? Or have sufficient pieces to figure it out as Danziger just did?"

Clarissa felt a chill. "Eight, maybe ten." One of which was Senator Hunter Ramson who'd given her the idea, even flown to Brazil with the former Vice President as part of the setup. The man would sell her soul for a dollar the second that he slipped out of Rose's control.

And Hunter *had* just slipped out of Rose's control!

Over breakfast on the One Observatory Circle's veranda this morning, Rose had been furious about something. Though she wouldn't say what despite Clarissa pushing.

The pieces began connecting in her mind.

The Middle East chatter from two nights ago, the Arabic voice on the Marine Two flight, the attack on Clark...

Hunter Ramson was a dead man!

Except she couldn't. With Clark gone, Clarissa *needed* Rose's help.

Shit! Shit! Shit! Sh—

"I'm sorry," Cole dragged her attention back to the room. "For that reason alone, you wouldn't make it through the interim vetting and approval by Congress, never mind the general election. Unless you're planning a coup, you'll have to let that go."

Clarissa caught Drake's hard stare.

"Jesus, Drake. I'm not a certifiable idiot who wants to kill off democracy and become the next dictator of a global superpower. Nor am I some lame-ass Russian former KGB agent or Chinese megalomaniac. People like that shouldn't be kept out, they should be *taken* out with a fucking bazooka. It's just that we need a President who understands the true power of clandestine operations. We at the CIA *know* how to deliver results in this asymmetric world."

His head tip said that maybe he believed her and maybe he didn't.

"Go to hell, Drake."

"Already a given," the President answered before he could.

Drake shrugged that the President might be right.

Clarissa couldn't help the laugh that bubbled up. It was all so fucking absurd.

The others all looked at her as if she'd finally lost it—and maybe she had.

"If this is how government really runs, we're in so much trouble."

The President's smile said that he fully agreed with the joke.

"So who are you going to choose to run this nut-hatchery once you're done, Mr. President?"

"That's easy." Cole hooked a thumb toward Sarah.

"You what?" Sarah's voice squeaked.

Her protests were buried as first President Cole's laugh, then her own and Drake's overwhelmed Sarah.

Clarissa hated that Sarah Feldman was a good choice. But she was.

And if Cole could half-convince Clarissa herself that vying for the White House was untenable, he'd eventually convince his National Security Advisor to fill the vacant VP slot.

She kept it light with relief for one key reason: Cole hadn't said anything about taking away the CIA directorship. And the

CIA was an amazing weapon for punishing those who had killed Clark.

At least she still had that to look forward to.

Besides, she had the first inkling of an idea that she wanted to run by Rose.

75

Miranda had insisted that they complete the data and audio review, but there had been no more surprises. Now that they knew the source, everything had followed completely predictably, right down to the final explosion sequence.

"I knew it! I knew it!" Jeremy did a victory dance. "The three-explosion sequence was the only option that fit all of the facts: interior explosion, the ignition of the long fuel vapor trail from the front entrance, and finally the ANJF of fertilizer and jet fuel."

Taz leaned back against one of the wall audio panels with her arms crossed, smiling hugely as she watched Jeremy.

Miranda recognized the look.

It was the way Mike and Holly sometimes looked at each other, at least until they caught themselves.

"He's ready, isn't he?"

Andi sat beside her. "He is."

Miranda covered her eyes for a moment. "This is so hard."

"It won't happen today, Miranda. You can ease into it. But even you can see that for Jeremy to keep growing as an investigator, he's going to have to lead his own team."

"Like I do, by letting others do the actual leading," she nodded toward the happily oblivious Taz.

"Yes and no. You and Jeremy both lead. None of the rest of us can do what you two can. You lead by example, then the rest of us come along to help make it easier for you."

Miranda thought about that.

Her team hadn't exactly made it easy, but they'd certainly been essential in making it possible.

And without Jeremy?

She'd miss him, but their skills overlapped so much that his loss wouldn't be crippling, merely tragic and uncomfortable.

There was one more hard thing she had to do, especially now that she was in Washington, DC.

"Would you do me a favor, Andi?" If anyone could make this easier, it would be Andi.

"Sure, what?"

"Come with me."

Andi looked at her in surprise, then asked carefully, "Where?"

Miranda closed her eyes again.

Somewhere even harder than losing Jeremy and Taz.

76

"Strictly domestic?" Cole asked over lunch.

Clarissa set down her BLT. Here it came, shutting out the CIA...and her. The Presidential dining room off the Oval just fit the big walnut dining table. Lincoln stared down at her thoughtfully out of The Peacemakers portrait made two weeks before the end of the Civil War and three weeks before his death.

"No, Mr. President," Clarissa stated before anyone could support such a ridiculous idea, though it took her a moment to remember how to support it. "The chatter out of the Middle East. And it was definitely tied to the instruction to 'burn the fields' that we intercepted. This was clearly a conspiracy between a foreign state actor and the defense contractors. We need to track those links. They'll be very well hidden, both domestically and overseas. I'll be coordinating our investigation in cooperation with the FBI."

At least them she could tolerate.

"So you don't think Ahmad was an innocent? He died aboard that helo."

"Maybe he was an innocent and they sent him in to try

negotiating with Clark but that defense contractor jumped the gun. Even if he was an innocent, indications are that his country wasn't."

President Cole nodded. "Okay. Keep me posted on that. Drake, what's the latest on..."

Clarissa's attention drifted long enough to miss the rest of the next question.

She was still here.

She was still the D/CIA.

Her husband was dead. She was about to lose her home. The Presidency now lay out of reach.

But she was still here.

Finally able to once more pick up her sandwich, she began to listen as Drake and Cole discussed how to better control the defense contractors going forward.

Half a glass of iced tea later, she was able to make an addition to one of Sarah's suggestions.

By the end of the meal, she felt more normal, other than her hair constantly slipping forward over her shoulder.

77

"YOU'RE KIDDING." ANDI RUBBED HER EYES, BUT THE VIEW DIDN'T change.

Miranda shook her head.

"Wouldn't you prefer Holly or Mike to be here with you?"

Miranda shook her head again.

"Why me? And don't say it's because I'm the calm one."

Miranda look at her imploringly, but didn't manage a word.

"Okay. Okay. It doesn't matter. It's me. Let's do this." The last time Andi had been through these doors was leaving through them six months ago. She'd been hustled out on an emergency call to assist Miranda's team and had never come back.

The NTSB Training Center in Ashburn, Virginia, had been a thirty-mile drive from the headquarters building. She tried to remember who she even was back then.

"I was so angry. So...lost."

"You were?" It was the first words Miranda had spoken since she'd given Andi the address in the car.

"I was recovering from PTSD—barely. I'd lost my career as a pilot and I was sure I'd never find myself or any dreams ever again." And that was a *kind* description of the mess she'd been on the outside. On the inside she'd been much worse. The black fear of every passing moment had loomed like an apocalypse. Funny, she wasn't sure when that had faded away.

"This place and Terence's house were my second home." Miranda smiled at the building as if it was a puppy dog rather than a sprawling two-story brick edifice.

As if to prove her point, the moment they walked through the front doors, the matronly receptionist looked up and exclaimed in surprise.

"Miranda! I didn't know you were in town. Are you coming in to teach a class this week? I don't remember you on the schedule. I'm on vacation next week to go see my new granddaughter in Atlanta, just came in today to make sure everything was ready for my fill-in."

"Hello, Priscilla. No. I'm just here for a visit."

"I'll call the director for you, though I haven't seen him today. Does he know you were coming in?"

"No," Miranda managed, then looked a bit panicked.

Andi turned to Priscilla. "We saw the director last night. I expect that he's sleeping still."

"You saw... Oh dear." She press a hand to her heart. "In Frederick. I'm so sorry. Has there been any progress on the investigation?" Only inside the NTSB would that be more than an idle question.

Even though Miranda was moving deeper into the building, Andi lagged for a moment.

"With her on the job?"

Priscilla smiled as she glanced after Miranda. "She did another one, did she? Never seen anything like that girl. I remember the first day she came here twenty years ago. A spook of a little thing, you couldn't even say boo around her. Of course I still had my hair color and figure back then." She patted her curly white coif and winked that her figure had probably been all big curves even back then.

Andi tried to imagine Miranda, who called the President Roy and could walk into a Marine Two wreck yet keep her focus so absolute, could ever be described as spooky.

"I'd love to stay and hear more, but..." Andi nodded toward where Miranda was most of the way down the long hallway.

"Shoo, Andrea. Glad to see you doing so much better."

Andi didn't even know she'd made any impression. She tried to speak but had no idea what to say.

"If you want to keep up with that girl, you best run, sweetheart." Priscilla waved her away.

Andi nodded her thanks, then just turned and sprinted down the long corridor.

Miranda had come to a stop at the end of the corridor as if she didn't remember how doors worked.

"Are you okay?"

Miranda shook her head.

"Can you tell me why we're here when you're strung out from exhaustion and two back-to-back investigations? Are you trying to out-do some opera heroine? Some prince here that needs beheading?"

"I'm beheading dragons." Miranda didn't even react to using a metaphor. It had been barely a whisper.

"Like Xuanlong sitting on the opera stage?" Andi leaned in closer.

Miranda just kept staring at the door, then spoke even softer, "My personal dragon."

Andi looked at the door sign: *Practical Lab.*

She knew that the vast warehouse space was littered with wrecks—the remains of real ones used for training. Several were scattered remains to simulate a debris field. An intact Huey helicopter and the long fuselage of a twenty-nine-passenger BAe Jetstream 41 turboprop. And—

Oh gods! She was an idiot.

Now she knew why they were here.

"You need to do this?"

Miranda nodded tightly.

"Okay." Of all crazy things, she'd asked Andi to be here because she was *the calm one.* The one person Miranda could feel calm around.

She took Miranda's hand, which was ice cold, and wrapped it in the crook of her elbow, then left her hand covering Miranda's fingers.

"Let's do this."

She pushed a foot against the door and shoved it open.

78

Miranda hadn't been here in a year and nineteen days. A quick glance showed that nothing had changed. No new wrecks, no old ones removed.

She headed for the northeast corner where the largest wreck dominated the space.

The shattered middle hundred-foot section of the 747 that was once the most famous crash of them all.

"Can you believe that there are people who don't know about TWA 800?"

"Twenty-five years is a generation," Andi reminded her.

"I remember the day it exploded."

"Because your parents died aboard this flight."

"Yes." And somehow Andi's simple statement made her feel so much better.

"Your life changed that day."

It had...and it hadn't.

It was the day she'd discovered the one great passion of her life—aircraft crashes. She'd become obsessed, a natural enough tendency for an autistic anyway.

Aircraft were perhaps the most complex machines humans

had ever built, spaceships being but the latest extension of that trend. The puzzles were fascinating. And with each improvement, as the simple problems of flight were resolved, the generational changes became even more complex. It was a challenge that would never stop.

"Why was it so important to see it today?" Andi had stepped away to look at the rows of seat fabric draped over wooden frames outside the plane. Each had been matched to its original position inside the plane so that the investigators could map the shape of the explosive shock wave that had killed their occupants.

"Tomorrow we'll be headed back to Seattle. Or perhaps another incident. And this wreckage is being decommissioned."

"It's what?"

"They've decided that it's time to recover the warehouse space and put it to other uses than studying a fifty-year old plane that was destroyed twenty-five years ago. I probably won't ever get to visit it again."

"That's...huge."

Miranda appreciated that Andi didn't ask how she felt about it. She rarely knew how she felt about anything, least of all anything to do with her parents or this plane.

And it was huge. Both personally and in physical reality.

She decided against asking if that might be a metaphor. If it was, the tattered remains of the plane were so big and so...sad that she didn't want to know. Imagining her sorrow to be this big might crush her.

Miranda look at the ragged mass, the skin patched back together from a thousand pieces. "Trans Wo" of the "Trans World" logo was readable between the first deck and upper deck windows.

Ahead of that, the nose cone hadn't been attached. It wasn't relevant to the crash itself, so there was no reason to include it in the training center display.

Great rips of missing skin revealed glimpses of the interior structure.

"It looks like 'Trans Woe' the way the *R* is broken off."

Miranda had never noticed that. She'd spent hundreds of hours studying and later visiting this wreck, and Andi had found something new.

"Transcend Woe? Seems like a good message to me," Andi continued.

"It *is* a good message," Miranda agreed. "Have you done that, Andi?"

"Hey, what's with the hard question? Seriously, though. I miss Ken, he was a great copilot and a dear friend. I miss my old career. But doing what we do and working with you has been a huge gift." Andi went silent for a moment, took a deep breath, then turned to look directly at her. "I *really* like working with you."

"I feel the same," Miranda turned back to the plane and watched it sleeping there. Was it comfortable in sleep or would it be happier when it had been fully recycled and shredded?

"No, Miranda. I really like *being* with you."

"Is your voice strained? It sounds strained."

Andi gave one of her half laughs that told Miranda there was a joke somewhere that she'd never find.

"What am I missing?"

"Miranda, how do you...feel about women?"

"I like women."

"I mean as in a girlfriend."

"Doesn't friendship count as being girlfriends? You called me girlfriend at the wreck site in Frederick, Maryland."

Andi's look went dark, like a lightbulb that had gone out, "I guess so. Sure."

Miranda pulled out her notebook and flipped to the

emoticon page. Andi didn't look sad, exactly. Nor angry. Maybe frustrated. Or... "I can't find your emotion on the page."

Andi walked a couple paces away and scrubbed at her face. "Can we just forget I said anything?" She kept her back turned.

"You know how bad I am at that?"

"I do," Andi's shoulders sagged. Then she squared them up and walked back to face her directly. "Okay, I'm gonna be brave because, goddamn it, I was a Night Stalker pilot and we have a motto."

"Death waits in the dark."

"I was thinking of the other one." Andi's laugh lightened her face considerably, which was a relief.

"NSDQ. Night Stalkers Don't Quit."

"Yes. That one. Therefore, I'm going to ask you to believe me that if your answer is no, there are no hard feelings."

"The answer to what?" Miranda was sure she'd missed an important fact but couldn't imagine what.

"Miranda, I like women as partners, not men. And," she took a deep breath, "I find you very, very attractive. The more I get to know you, the better I like you."

"That's nice."

"I know you were with Jon. But I wondered if you ever thought about being with a woman as a partner?"

"No." At least now she knew what the question was. Solid footing.

"Okay." Then Andi spoke so quickly that it was hard to understand her. "I'm sorry I asked. Don't be upset. I just...had to. I had to know, you know, because—"

"Now you're sounding like Jeremy."

Andi slapped a hand over her mouth.

"No. I've never thought about being with a woman before. I don't know why; I just never did."

"For some people, it's not a choice."

"Like you."

"Like me. But some people *can* choose," Andi mumbled through her hand.

"You are aware that an autistic's difficulties in perceiving emotions includes difficulties perceiving emotional pressures to conform to societal norms. An autistic is many times more likely to explore a gender-diverse lifestyle because we don't understand society's need for conformance—we can't even perceive it, we just know we don't belong. Trust me, I often wish I could understand, so that I could fit in. But I don't."

"And would you ever choose to be with a woman?" Andi lowered her hand slowly.

"Why wouldn't I? See? That's the part I don't understand."

Andi swallowed hard. "Would you ever choose to be with me?"

"You're the calm one."

"Because I make you calm."

Miranda nodded. "Because I think I'm better at being me when I'm with you. Is that important?"

Andi offered one of those half laughs. "No, Miranda. That's not just important. That's *everything* that matters. It's the same for me."

This time Miranda got the good part of the half joke. "So how do we begin? Is it different when it's two women?"

"Just like that?"

"Yes."

Andi just shook her head. "You're amazing, Miranda. Okay. Here's how it begins." She held out her hand palm up.

When Miranda placed her own on it, Andi interlaced their fingers. Her hand was warm, her fingers were strong. She liked the feeling of Andi's fingers interlaced with hers.

"Okay. This is good. What's next?"

"I don't know. We have to make that up. Make it up together."

"I'm not very good at making things up."

Andi's smile was soft. "Don't worry, Miranda. We'll figure it out as we go."

"Like in a crash investigation. I can do that."

Andi laughed outright and gave her a quick hug, which also felt good.

Miranda hugged her back and liked the feeling of that as well.

Andi stepped back and smiled at her as she squeezed her hand. "Was there anything more you wanted to do here at the wreck before we go?"

"One thing," Miranda nodded. "It's why I asked for your help. I want to do it, but I don't know if I can."

She pulled out her *Kryptos* notebook.

"My father and I worked on cryptographic codes all the years we had together. I've kept doing it since he died on this plane, but..." She flapped the book, unsure of how to explain it.

Andi took it one-handed and began flipping the pages. "There's a lot of amazing work here, Miranda." Then Andi looked her directly in the eyes and squeezed her hand even harder. "Let me guess. It doesn't feel like it's quite a part of you anymore."

"That's it! How did you know?" Miranda gasped out a burst of held breath.

"Parts of being a Night Stalker will always be with me. But Ken? Flying at that level? Combat? If they offered to let me back in tomorrow? I'm not sure I'd go. Somehow that isn't me anymore. What do we do with it?" She held up the notebook and flipped it shut.

Miranda pointed to the wreck.

"Anywhere special?"

Miranda couldn't think of one. Her parents' seats weren't here. They had been in the long since destroyed nose cone that was irrelevant to the mid-frame explosion.

"How about if I set it into the cargo hold? Then, it can go on the plane's last flight."

"But this plane will never fly again. Look at it. No nose or tail. No wings or engines. It—"

Andi kissed her quickly, which stopped her words. "Now *you* sound like Jeremy!"

"Oh no!" Miranda half laughed.

Then she yelped with excitement.

"Wait! I get it now. Your laughs are because it's only half a joke. It's because it's...it's..."

"So sad that it's funny, too."

Miranda nodded fiercely. It was exactly like that. "Like comparing our learning about a relationship being like exploring a crash."

This time Andi laughed outright and they said in near unison, "Hope it won't *be* a crash."

Which left them both laughing again.

Then she spotted the book in Andi's hand.

Something *had* changed. She could put the book on the remains of TWA 800 herself now, but she knew she'd rather have Andi do it for her and waved her forward.

Andi stepped away, over the rope line, and slipped it through a gash in the hull and set it out of sight inside.

On her return, she took Miranda's hand once more.

"I won't ask if you're sure, because then you'd have to think about it all over again. So I'll just ask if you're ready to go?"

Miranda answered with a hand squeeze.

Andi leaned in to whisper in her ear, "Don't look back."

And she didn't as they walked hand in hand out of the NTSB warehouse.

She didn't need to.

From now on, Miranda was only going to look forward.

MIRANDA CHASE #9 (EXCERPT)

IF YOU ENJOYED THAT, HERE'S A TASTE OF WHAT'S COMING IN 2022

MIRANDA CHASE #9 (EXCERPT)

23 Days After the end of *White Top*
Washington, DC

"PULL TO THE CURB HERE!"

CIA Director Clarissa Reese's driver obeyed and slid out of the thick Friday night traffic on Columbus Circle. He eased over a block shy of the George Hotel. The US Capitol Building glowed orange in the sunset; the sun still touched the bronze Statue of Freedom atop the dome so that it shone brighter than anything else in Washington, DC, despite the dark finish.

It was just as well; she didn't want to face...anything.

"Pull yourself together, Clarissa." Her self-instruction wasn't helping. She'd been muttering some version of it over and over for the last month with minimal effect.

Her driver studiously ignored her. She'd long since made it clear that the last thing she needed was to interact with a security agent who'd never be more than a driver.

It was hard. In the last month she'd lost everything.

With her husband's death, her path to the White House had been blocked. Vice Presidents were *supposed* to be well protected. But not Clark. His Marine Two helicopter had gone down in flames, the bastard.

Instead, the goddamn President had elevated his National Security Adviser to Vice President Sarah Feldman.

That had put Clarissa on the street when the new VP had moved into One Observatory Circle. She never should have sold her goddamn condo, but Clark had been such an obvious shoo-in to the White House that she'd been assured of her future residence for years to come.

Their new MERP—Middle East Realignment Plan—had captured the imagination of everyone from the unwashed masses to all but the most jaundiced Washington elite. Even marginal allies were flocking to the call. President Cole had made sure that the bulk of the credit had gone to the VP.

If the woman didn't screw up, she had the next election in the bag a year out.

Of course, when Sarah ran, she *would* need a Vice President.

Except the scandals—thankfully, all classified top secret but littered with her name—had guaranteed her shut-out of any future chance at the Oval Office. It was clear that "certain parties" would release everything if she tried to run.

Bush's route of CIA Director to Vice President was lost to her.

Clarissa looked back at the George Hotel and did her best to discover some shred of composure. It had gotten harder and harder since Clark's death as she discovered more pieces of herself that she'd lost besides her home and her best path to the White House, like the surprising revelation that she missed Clark himself. Immensely.

Even in death he wouldn't leave her alone.

At the White House's request, she'd drawn up a master list

of every known terrorist action by any nation from Pakistan to Egypt against the US, and every CIA counterstroke.

It was supposed to be a strictly internal document, but it had predictably leaked. She'd learned from the disastrous 1974 leak of the dreaded "Family Jewels" memos—that had chronicled hundreds of times that the CIA had overstepped their charter.

This time, she'd made sure that all of the questionable activities were chronicled under Clark's tenure as the CIA Director before her. Sometimes having a dead Vice President for a predecessor and a husband came in handy.

It was always better that they blamed a dead man.

Except, instead of the leak wreaking domestic havoc on release, it had become a key document in the President's proposed MERP. It had justified massive realignments and the disavowal of several long-term Middle East allies with their fingers deep in terrorism.

Rather than shaking the nation, it had inspired it.

It had also elevated Clark's posthumous popularity far past anything it deserved. It was impossible to take back the credit, even for her own operations, that she had so publicly given away.

Clarissa sighed. She was late for her monthly dinner meeting with Hunter and Rose Ramson in The George's penthouse suite.

She didn't need the influence of the Chairman of the Senate Armed Service Committee. Hunter had lost much of his power in his efforts to block the President's Middle East Realignment Plan because it had voided billions of dollars of foreign arms sales for his no-longer-so-friendly defense contractors.

To say that the contractors and Saudi Arabia, among others, were livid about his inability to quash MERP was a significant understatement.

No, she hadn't needed anything from Hunter since his fall.

There was even some question of his holding on to his seat for a fifth six-year term at the next election.

Tonight she needed the sharp mind of Washington's top socialite, Rose Ramson, "The First Lady of DC." Clarissa had a new idea, and while it didn't lead to the Oval Office, it would lead to great power.

She had once promised Rose the future Vice Presidency but, as hard as it was to accept, that was gone. The question was, would Rose still support her if that was off the table? Clarissa would leave it up to Rose to name her price.

Sadly, Clarissa suspected that she herself wasn't going to get any more collected together than she was now.

"Let's get this done already."

A gap opened in front of the car, but the driver didn't pull ahead. He wasn't even watching the traffic. Instead, he stared at his side mirror—ducking low to look upward.

He was so intent that Clarissa finally turned to look out the rear window. Instead of a big truck blocking the lane, she spotted a jet. It raced toward them—where no planes were ever supposed to be.

Downtown DC was the most protected no-fly zone in the country.

An idiot, hoping to be in tomorrow's headlines for buzzing DC, had swooped between the Capitol and the Supreme Court Building, and was now carving a hard turn at Columbus Circle.

A sleek C-21A Learjet painted US Air Force blah.

"Damn, they're low," her driver spoke for the first time since Georgetown.

They were. And fast.

In fact, they were so low that—

The plane raced into the narrow slot of E Street Northwest barely wider than its wingspan.

Below the tops of the buildings.

The roar of its jet engines reverberating along the brick-

and-glass canyon shook the car, moments before the wind of its passage slammed into them.

A block down, it veered to the right and flew into the side of a building.

It looked just like a Hollywood film.

The plane disappeared through the wall.

For a moment...nothing.

Just a dark hole where the outer windows and red brick no longer reflected the sunset sky.

Then a fireball roiled out in a massive plume.

A second later, most of the glass on that floor blew outward as the plane exploded.

A cloud of debris rained down on the heavy traffic. Her car rattled as if it was caught in a massive hailstorm when debris peppered the body. A brick embedded itself into the hood, making both her and the driver jump.

Screams of injured pedestrians added to the mayhem of car alarms and blasting horns of fender benders as drivers lost control.

Fifteen seconds later—while the last of the debris still pattered down upon them—a pair of "alert" fighter jets raced low over the city. Not a sonic boom, but so loud that Clarissa ducked despite knowing they were far above her and in better control than the first jet had been. Too little, too late.

When she looked up again, she finally recognized the building that had been struck.

It was The George.

The top floor.

The southeast corner suite—

Clarissa barely flinched as a car slammed into her passenger door. Numb with shock, she couldn't move a single muscle.

She was used to looking *out* that window, not locating it from the outside.

The Learjet hadn't been out of control.

It had impacted the hotel *precisely* where, at this very moment, she was supposed to be having her monthly dinner with Senator Hunter Ramson and his wife Rose. They stayed there on the first Friday of every month to enjoy the penthouse's luxury—after a fine dinner and secret meeting with Clarissa.

Either the defense contractors or the Saudis had just gotten even with Senator Ramson for failing them.

Or both.

Were they after her as well?

———

JEREMY HATED MOVING DAYS.

He lay on the carpet in the middle of a sea of boxes and wondered who had invented the idea of moving. If he found out, maybe Taz could do something about never letting it happen again.

She was, of course, being her usual whirlwind. The three-day cross-country drive in a U-Haul truck hadn't fazed her in the slightest. She was one of those unpack-right-away sorts; he was more of an I'd-rather-die-first sort. It was the fifth move of his entire life: college, grad school, the NTSB Academy in Virginia (all three of which he'd lived in the dorm rooms), Miranda's NTSB team in Washington State, and now the "other" Washington—DC.

How had this happened to him?

Four weeks ago, he'd been investigating the horrific crash of the Marine Two helicopter that had killed the Vice President and hundreds of Walmart shoppers. Happily a member of Miranda's team. Never wanting more.

Now he was head of a brand-new team.

What had he been thinking?

He now served two bosses. He was now a member of the National Transportation Safety Board's headquarters lab team. And, with Taz re-enlisting into the Air Force, he had seconded to—

His phone rang. Please let it be the cable guy. He needed to get online, for even an hour, just to clear his head.

"Are you going to answer that?" Taz swept by, making something perfect along the way.

Really, really done with her rootless life to date, she'd picked out the townhouse condo and was busy making it into a home...for them.

Which was too weird for words.

Jeremy had always assumed that he'd find someone someday. But he'd never thought about being a "them" until a four-foot-eleven Latina had slammed into his life. Someday had become very real and very now.

"No," he hoped he was referring to the phone call and not the future. Then answered it to prove that he was completely onboard, even if he could barely move from lying prostrate on the floor. "Jeremy here."

"Good evening, Jeremy."

"Hi, General Macy." He didn't need a call from their new boss at this moment.

"Did you make it to DC yet?"

"We're fully out of the truck and living in a cardboard forest. Maybe it's a mountain range."

"I know that you aren't technically starting until Monday, but are you available for a launch?"

It might be only a temporary reprieve, but it *would* save him from drowning in a cardboard sea. "Where?"

"E Street NW just off Columbus Circle."

Jeremy jolted upright. "In downtown?"

Taz stopped in mid-zip through the living room, which was a relief to his guilt about not helping.

"Yes. We even have the crash on camera from the Air Force alert fighters that were chasing the jet. It impacted the top story of a downtown hotel."

"We're on our way."

"Good man." When General Jack Macy said that in his "command" voice, it was very motivating.

Jeremy pushed to his feet.

"And Jeremy?"

"Yes sir."

"I don't want to bias the investigation, but it looks like it was one of ours."

"Ours? Oh, the Air Force's." He'd only ever been a member of the unaligned NTSB. Now he worked for both the NTSB lab and the US Air Force Accident Investigation Board as a consultant. "Really?"

"Really." General Macy hung up without another word.

"Holy afterburners, Batman."

"What's up, Wonder Boy?"

"We've got a launch. Here in DC." He began pushing around the boxes, desperately scanning each label. How did they have so much stuff?

"What are you looking for?"

"My field pack!"

Taking a single step, Taz tapped a finger on a big box that had bright red tape instead of the standard brown. It was the only one like that. He vaguely remembered that she'd said something about why it was red, but couldn't recall what.

She flipped out her fighting knife, slit the tape, then slid it back out of sight in that smooth move he'd never been able to follow. She folded back the flaps. Inside were their vests and crash-site investigation packs.

He scooped her against him, rested his cheek atop her hair, and held her tight.

Taz snuggled in close. "This had better work, Jeremy, or I'm going to be super pissed."

"The crash investigation? Why wouldn't it?"

"No, you doofus. Us."

"As long as I get to hold you tight, nothing else matters. No way could I do this without you."

Taz sniffled. "Aw shit, Jeremy. You know you shouldn't say stuff like that to me."

"Why?"

"Because if you keep doing it, I might start believing it."

"Good." He smiled as he kissed the top of her head.

She held him just a moment longer, then poked him hard enough in his ticklish spot to hurt. She broke free and grabbed her pack.

He fished out his own.

"Come on, lazybones. There's a crash, get a move on." And his personal whirlwind was out the door before he had even taken a breath.

———

FOR THE TWENTY-THIRD TIME TODAY, MIRANDA TURNED AND discovered that Jeremy wasn't there.

In utter dismay, she inspected the sprawl of the shattered KC-46 Pegasus air tanker spread down the main runway at Elmendorf Air Force Base. It was a Boeing 767 modified into a flying fuel truck—except this one had become a fuel bomb.

"How am I supposed to do this?"

"Come on, Miranda, you're the best there is. You've done more crash investigations than anyone in the entire history of the NTSB." Andi Wu held a fistful of small orange flags on wires for staking out the perimeter of the debris field.

"No, Terence has done more than—"

"Not according to him."

Miranda sat on the airplane tire that had rolled nine hundred and fourteen meters past the next nearest piece of debris. Andi had laughed that cheery laugh of hers when Miranda had insisted that it be properly staked. Usually her laugh made Miranda feel better, but not today. Andi had done the staking, Jeremy's usual task, without complaint but her laugh reminded Miranda of his excitement about every aspect of a new crash.

Only they weren't here. Jeremy and Taz had climbed into their truck, headed east, and were gone.

For two years she could just turn and there he'd be for whatever she needed.

Andi slipped a hand around her waist. "You know it was time for him to fly on his own."

"Knowing that and liking that are proving to be quite disparate thoughts in my head."

"You still have Mike, Holly, and me."

"I do." That cheered her up some.

"And the new guy should be here in an hour or so."

Miranda shuddered. *New.* Such an awful word. In these last months, her autism seemed to be becoming more reactive, squeezing in harder and harder like a cherry tomato that was going to burst and spray out everywhere with no warning. She *hated* cherry tomatoes for that reason—didn't even like removing them from her salad when a restaurant included them against her instructions.

Even finding a good metaphor wasn't cheering her up. Everything that was supposed to be getting easier seemed to be getting harder.

Although, perhaps Andi was right as usual.

"Last year *you* were new."

"Last year I was a goddamn train wreck," Andi groaned in that way of hers that said she was half joking. Miranda still didn't always get why, but it was a good measure of Andi's generally positive mood.

"But now you're a good thing."

In answer, Andi kissed her on the ear, then whispered so close that it tickled, "Let's go solve a plane wreck."

"Good idea."

They headed back along the runway to where Mike and Holly were already photographing the debris field itself.

Miranda turned to see if Jeremy was following...and sighed.

Twenty-*four* times today.

Coming in 2022

ABOUT THE AUTHOR

USA Today and Amazon #1 Bestseller M. L. "Matt" Buchman started writing on a flight from Japan to ride his bicycle across the Australian Outback. Just part of a solo around-the-world trip that ultimately launched his writing career.

From the very beginning, his powerful female heroines insisted on putting character first, *then* a great adventure. He's since written over 70 action-adventure thrillers and military romantic suspense novels. And just for the fun of it: 100 short stories, and a fast-growing pile of read-by-author audiobooks.

Booklist says: "3X Top 10 of the Year." PW says: "Tom Clancy fans open to a strong female lead will clamor for more." His fans say: "I want more now...of everything." That his characters are even more insistent than his fans is a hoot.

As a 30-year project manager with a geophysics degree who has designed and built houses, flown and jumped out of planes, and solo-sailed a 50' ketch, he is awed by what is possible. More at: www.mlbuchman.com.

Other works by M. L. Buchman: *(* - also in audio)*

Other works by M. L. Buchman:

Contemporary Romance (cont)

Love Abroad
Heart of the Cotswolds: England
Path of Love: Cinque Terre, Italy

Where Dreams
Where Dreams are Born
Where Dreams Reside
Where Dreams Are of Christmas*
Where Dreams Unfold
Where Dreams Are Written

Science Fiction / Fantasy

Deities Anonymous
Cookbook from Hell: Reheated
Saviors 101

Single Titles
The Nara Reaction
Monk's Maze
the Me and Elsie Chronicles

Non-Fiction

Strategies for Success
Managing Your Inner Artist/Writer
Estate Planning for Authors*
Character Voice
Narrate and Record Your Own Audiobook*

Short Story Series by M. L. Buchman:

Romantic Suspense

Delta Force
Th Delta Force Shooters
The Delta Force Warriors

Firehawks
The Firehawks Lookouts
The Firehawks Hotshots
The Firebirds

The Night Stalkers
The Night Stalkers 5D Stories
The Night Stalkers 5E Stories
The Night Stalkers CSAR
The Night Stalkers Wedding Stories

US Coast Guard

White House Protection Force

Contemporary Romance

Eagle Cove

Henderson's Ranch*

Where Dreams

Action-Adventure Thrillers

Dead Chef

Miranda Chase Origin Stories

Science Fiction / Fantasy

Deities Anonymous

Other
The Future Night Stalkers
Single Titles

SIGN UP FOR M. L. BUCHMAN'S NEWSLETTER TODAY

and receive:
Release News
Free Short Stories
a Free Book

Get your free book today. Do it now.
free-book.mlbuchman.com

Made in the USA
Monee, IL
26 June 2021